A Man of His Own

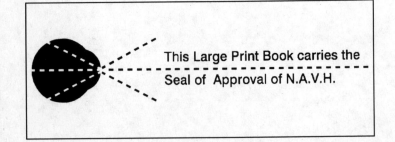

This Large Print Book carries the
Seal of Approval of N.A.V.H.

A Man of His Own

Susan Wilson

THORNDIKE PRESS

A part of Gale, Cengage Learning

GALE
CENGAGE Learning·

Detroit • New York • San Francisco • New Haven, Conn • Waterville, Maine • London

Copyright © 2013 by Susan Wilson.
Thorndike Press, a part of Gale, Cengage Learning.

Thorndike Press® Large Print Basic.
The text of this Large Print edition is unabridged.
Other aspects of the book may vary from the original edition.
Set in 16 pt. Plantin.

LIBRARY OF CONGRESS CATALOGING-IN-PUBLICATION DATA

Wilson, Susan, 1951–
   A man of his own / by Susan Wilson. — Large print edition.
     pages ; cm. — (Thorndike Press large print basic)
   ISBN 978-1-4104-6394-4 (hardcover) — ISBN 1-4104-6394-X (hardcover)
1. Disabled veterans—Fiction. 2. Service dogs—Fiction. 3. Dogs—War use—Fiction. 4. Life change events—Fiction. 5. Human-animal relationships—Fiction. 6. Domestic fiction. 7. Large type books. I. Title.
PS3573.I47533O67 2013b
813'.54—dc23   2013032557

Published in 2013 by arrangement with St. Martin's Press, LLC

Printed in Mexico
1 2 3 4 5 6 7 17 16 15 14 13

Dedicated to the men and women
of the United States armed forces
and to their brave military dogs
past and present.

And to my grandchildren,
Claire and Will

Every dog should have a man of his own.
There is nothing like a well-behaved
person around the house to spread the
dog's blanket for him, or bring him his
supper when he comes home man-tired
at night.

— Corey Ford

■ ■ ■ ■

PART ONE:
1938–1945

■ ■ ■ ■

PROLOGUE

His mother had sheltered him in the nest she'd made in a crawl space under the sagging weight of an old tavern tucked just off the main street of the city, which hadn't yet begun to recover from the Depression. She'd fed him first from her teats, all eight his alone as the only survivor of her brood of five, then from her mouth as she left him for short periods and scavenged for scraps, which she would share with him even as she withered from a decent-size purebred German shepherd to a scabbed scarecrow.

The puppy would never know her history, only that his mother had managed to survive long enough as a stray by falling upon instincts hard-coded in her blood — find shelter, find food, and trust no one — so that when she failed to return to their alleyway nest, he was almost capable of surviving on his own. Almost. What he didn't know about her was that at an earlier time in her life she'd been a show dog. Somewhere miles away, blue ribbons and a silver cup graced a dusty shelf. Not a runaway, but a throwaway when the neighbor's mongrel jumped the backyard breeder's fence.

He stayed in the nest, venturing out only to do his business, lap a little at a puddle of yesterday's rainwater. But his belly began to grumble. Sometimes it had taken her a very long time to return to the nest, so he made do with sucking on the end of his tail, comforting himself, one ear cocked toward the entrance to the blind alley. She'd be back. She always came back. He had no way to know how much time had elapsed except by the extraordinary hunger that refused to be satisfied with tail sucking, and his thirst, which was no longer satisfied because the puddle had dried up during the warmth of the day. Hours passed into days and the puppy knew only that his mother was still absent, and without her, he had no strength. What he longed for was to feel her body wrapped around his, to awaken to find her licking him ears to tail, to snuggle up against her warm body and let himself drift into deep sleep.

A noise. The puppy lifted his head, sniffed. A man had come into the narrow alley. His mother had always shied away from people, so he kept himself very still. When the human boldly urinated not three feet from where the pup hid, the odor of it filled the youngster with information. This person was male; this human being had eaten meat and wasn't thirsty. He couldn't help himself — the odor of food wafting out of the skin of this overwarm being drew him to his legs. He didn't consider revealing himself to the human; he just wanted to breathe in the tempting odor, as if by inhaling the scent of pastrami or ham, he'd be filled.

The rain came down and splashed into the hollows gouged out of the worn bricks. The sound of the soft late-summer rain and the earthy scent of refreshed soil confused the puppy. He ran his tongue against the rough brick, where a thin layer of moisture trickled toward him. There was no relief in it, only the torment of dissatisfaction. From the splintered access to his mother's carefully chosen nest site, he could see where the puddle he'd licked dry was re-forming. Nearly crazed with thirst, the puppy forgot his mother's rules and dashed out from beneath the building to lap at the new-formed puddle in an ecstasy of relief. And that's when his future was revised.

The sudden insult of big feet against his

washboard ribs made him yelp, but something kept him from running back to the shelter of the crawl space. As a dog, a youngster just newly weaned, he didn't have the experience to nip or protest, and being swept up in strong human hands had a calming effect on him. Here was contact. Here was touch. Soft vocalizations unlike his mother's voice, but with her intent. *Hey there, little guy.* As soothing as her heartbeat.

The puppy made a token protest, and with a wisdom far beyond his mere eight weeks of life, he chose to accept this human's touch; this man's bond.

CHAPTER ONE

The men's room stinks so badly that Rick walks past it and out the open back door of the tavern. He's in an alley, a brick wall conveniently placed, so that he conducts his business in privacy. Today was the last day of play for the Waterbury Comets, and Frederick "Rick" Stanton has just spilled his good news to his teammates. Despite the C-league Comets' losing season, he's pitched well, and in the spring he'll report to the minor-league AA team, the Hartford Bees. It was surprisingly hard to say, and he was a little embarrassed to have gotten choked up, especially when they all raised their beer mugs and toasted his good luck.

He's finally going to be able to say goodbye to cobbled-together amateur teams, and all his years of hard work, from sand lot to high school to playing in college, have paid off. Sacrificing steady employment in a respectable profession like his father's, banking or accounting, in favor of menial jobs he has no compunction about leaving when practice starts up has been worth it.

Still, he'll miss these guys, the oldest among them the catcher, "Foggy" Phil Dexter; the youngest, a kid of sixteen who cheerfully takes all their good-natured abuse, lugging most of the equipment, always riding stuck between two bigger players, fetching for the rest of them, and enduring persistent razzing about the state of his virginity.

Finishing up, Rick feels the first drops of rain on his bare head. Those few drops are quickly followed by a complete cloudburst, but he stays where he is. It's hot inside, and the cool rain feels good. Rick raises his face to the sky and opens his mouth, taking in the taste of fresh rain. "I'm the luckiest man on earth," he says to the sky, and in that moment, he's pretty certain that he is. Well, he should get back in. Eat another couple sandwiches, toss back one more beer; laugh at a few more tired jokes. The season is over and no curfew tonight.

Thoroughly soaked now, Rick turns around and trips over something, nearly pitching headlong onto the brick pavers. That something yelps.

It's a puppy, and rather than running away

after being tripped over, it stays put, and for a hard moment, Rick thinks he may have accidentally killed it with his big feet. In the weak light of the open back door, Rick sees the glint of life in its eyes. "Whoa, fella. Where'd you come from?" Rick squats down and the wet and trembling puppy inserts itself between his knees as if seeking shelter. It sits and rests its muzzle on Rick's leg. As quickly as the cloudburst started, it fades away, the rivulets trickling down the side of the wall, pooling in the interstices between the bricks. "Where're your people, little guy?"

The puppy shakes, spraying Rick with a thousand droplets. Rick scoops it up and heads back into the tavern. In the light, he can see it's a boy, silvery in color, with a darker saddle across narrow shoulders and along ribs that poke out like the bones of a chicken. His ears flop over at entirely different angles, as if they belong to two different puppies. Probably a German shepherd, or at least mostly shepherd. The bartender doesn't say anything when Rick comes in carrying a puppy, so Rick holds him up. "He yours?" The barkeep shakes his head no.

The barkeep's wife swings a new pitcher onto the table and considers the dog on Rick's lap. "Probably got dumped out back.

You found him, you keep him. Don't leave him here."

The puppy has settled neatly on Rick's lap, gently taking the bits of meat Rick offers without nipping those important fingers with his sharp teeth. He can't keep a dog; he's living in a boardinghouse. In nine months, he'll be at training camp. In a year, with luck, he'll be pitching for the majors.

"Got to name him if you're keeping him." Dan Lister, their manager, spreads a gob of mustard on his third corned beef sandwich. "How 'bout Spot?"

"Too common. Besides, he doesn't seem to have any spots, and who said anything about me keeping him?" Rick fingers another tiny bite of sandwich into the puppy's mouth.

"Lucky." Foggy has slumped in his chair, so that his chin is barely above the edge of the table.

"Well, he is a lucky dog if one of you bums keeps him." Rick holds the wriggling fur ball up as if offering the puppy for auction.

"Darby?" This from the kid.

"Darby?"

"I had a dog named Darby. My dad's Irish. It's how they say Derby over there. Darby was a real good dog, never left my father's side all the time he was sick with tuberculosis. We even let him come to the funeral."

The group grows silent. No one had known that the kid was a half orphan.

"Maybe I'll call him Rin Tin Tin. He looks like he might be shepherd." Rick scratches the puppy under the chin. "What do you think? You gonna grow up to be some kind of movie star hero dog?" The puppy yawns, drops his head, and is instantly asleep. Rick realizes what he's just said. If he names this puppy, how will he ever drop him back in the alley? It's not even fair to keep the dog on his lap, to allow the little thing to accept a few minutes of comfort, let him think that humans are trustworthy. The party will break up soon, and what then? Abandon the tyke to the elements? His first trust in humans to do right by him destroyed, and maybe he'll never trust another human being again. Rick can feel the puppy's beating heart in the palm of his pitching hand. The fluff of baby fur feels like the softest mink of his mother's fur stole as Rick strokes him, lifting the spatula-shaped paws and feeling the thick bones of a puppy with the potential to become a large dog. If he's not hit by a car or starved to death.

Dan Lister pushes away from the table. "I'm done in. Go to bed, gentlemen. I bid you farewell. Keep healthy and see you" — he looks at Rick — "most of you, in the spring." The manager presses both hands on the table, suggesting that he's more sober than he is.

The bartender hands Rick a length of string for a leash, but Rick carries the ten pounds of soft fur in his arms. Foggy is bumbling into chairs and tables while trying to find the front door. "Come on, Phil, throw an arm over my shoulder."

Foggy Phil Dexter gladly slings his arm over Rick's neck and leans into him. "You'll be great. Bees need a good curveball pitcher." His breath is rank with beer and pastrami, but Rick doesn't mind. Phil's been a good friend and taught him a lot about the game. "By God, you'll be in the majors in a year."

"Your mouth to God's ear." Rick bears the weight of the man and the small burden of the puppy as they walk the few blocks to their boardinghouse.

Everything that he's done has been fed by his lifelong ambition to play for the majors. Rick has never wanted anything else in his life. As a kid, he asked Santa for gloves and balls and bats; as a teen, he paid his own way to baseball camp, using the money he earned from a paper route. He never learned to sail, letting his father practically adopt the next-door neighbor's kid to crew for him. Tomorrow, he'll head down to his parents' Greenwich home. He wonders if, when he gives them his good news, his extraordinary and long-awaited news, they'll finally respond with some pride and enthusiasm.

The puppy in his hand wriggles himself up and under Rick's chin. Well, so what if they don't. He's a grown man, he's stuck to his plan, and now, at very nearly the last minute, at age twenty-seven, he's finally there. Almost. He doesn't want to be the world's oldest rookie when he finally gets the call to major-league baseball.

Maybe this will be the last winter keeping fit by any means possible while substitute teaching or doing temporary work at a busy accounting firm. In eight months, he'll be back in training, a hardball in his hand, sensitive fingers feeling for the seams, the magic of that perfect throw. The future spools out in front of him: a winning season with the minor-league Bees, then getting the call to the majors. His first appearance in the National League. Rick sees himself doffing his ball cap and waving at cheering fans. He's paid his dues, by God. Forfeited job security and Mary Ann Koble, who didn't want to be a ballplayer's wife.

The puppy yawns, burrows his tail end deeper into the crook of Rick's arm. Why not keep him? He could be a mascot. A lucky charm. A companion on all those miles of roadwork.

There is a church along the way, more beautiful than any other building on this defeated main street; its all-white marble facade glows softly in the newly rain-freshened air. Picked out in gold leaf on the pediment are Latin words: *Gloriam Deo Pax In Terra.*

"Pax. Peace." Rick looks at the puppy in his arms, now sleeping with utter trust in the man carrying him. It's started raining again, a warm drizzle that makes the wet pavement shimmer beneath the sparse streetlamps. "I'm the luckiest man on earth."

Pax. The puppy in Rick's arms suddenly wakes. He reaches up with his baby muzzle and his long pink tongue comes out to lick Rick's nose. Pax.

CHAPTER TWO

I just didn't see myself a farmer's wife. No insult intended to all my friends who found satisfaction in it, but I just couldn't. I was, at heart, a town girl, even if the town was little Mount Joy, Iowa, population insignificant, city limits something like six blocks firmly built on the banks of the Mississippi River. It wasn't that I didn't want marriage; of course I did. And kids. But I wanted something else for them besides the grinding work of feeding America. I wanted something more for myself than being sentenced to cooking three meals a day seven days a week for insatiable farmhands. Pickling and canning and putting up. Putting up green beans and tomatoes. Putting up with bad harvests and droughts and too much rain and corn borers. I was a town girl, but the domestic realities of my farm-bred girlfriends made an impression on me.

Thus I was flirting with old maidhood, a

ripe nineteen years old, my only significant accomplishment the high school diploma my mother had framed and hanging in the den. My high school chums were getting married one after the other, but I was determined that my knight in shining armor wasn't going to be one of the local boys, most of whom had already adopted the high seat of the combine as their throne and were deep in the family cornfields. Their chief currency was the half acre set aside for a new house, or the addition Daddy would put on the old one to accommodate the anticipated bounty of babies. More fodder, I thought, for the machine of agriculture. That's not what I wanted for my kids. I wanted for them what I wanted for myself, an indefinable *more*.

When I try to unravel the skein of circumstance that led me to meet Rick Stanton, I have to look to my cousin Sid. Cousins through our mothers, we were playmates, and then he grew into a boy, and I wasn't much interested in playing army or being forced into the damsel in distress role for Sid and his buddies to rescue on their imaginary chargers, wielding not so imaginary sticks as lances and swords. One unfortunate kid got his eye poked real good, as his imaginary knight's visor was a little porous, and the neighborhood mothers put a stop to stick play for a time.

The one thing Sid and I continued to enjoy together was baseball. We'd sit in our parlor, or his family's, the big cathedral radio on, our dads in their undershirts, sneaking Pabst Blue Ribbon beers past our mothers. We listened to the games of the St. Louis Cardinals, as close to a home team as those of us in Mount Joy, Iowa, had. We might have rooted for the Cubs, but my family had turned its back on the Chicago team a generation ago.

Sid sided with me even when I refused perfectly nice Buster Novack. Buster's family were good people, good farmers, but sown into the earth like the corn they raised. Life with Buster would mean respectability and church suppers, raising a nice family to farm the same acres as his grandfather farmed. The biggest excitement the daily corn futures. One day the same as the next. The truth was, I burned for something else. Something beyond watching a slender and good-looking Buster Novak take on a farmer's bulk. Maybe someday I'd regret a missed chance at an ordinary life, but right then it seemed more like a death sentence. So I told Buster no, thank you, and mystified my parents.

But Sid sided with me, and then told me I needed to get the heck out of Mount Joy, that the pickins were too poor for a girl of my standards. "You won't find a prince in this pack of paupers, Francesca. You've got to go farther afield." Sid, having reversed our pioneer heritage, was living in what we simply called the East, Boston to be exact, a graduate of Bryant College, in Rhode Island, and making a good living as an accountant for a shipping firm. He had become exotic. And when he invited me to visit him there — the East — I did. I packed enough so that, unbeknownst to my parents, should an opportunity arise, I could stay. I don't know exactly what I thought might comprise an opportunity, but I knew that should one arise, I'd recognize it. And I did.

So there it is, a friendly cousin, a girl on her first big trip, and a mutual love of baseball. Sid took me to Nickerson Field, traveling the whole way from his digs in Dorchester by subway, which for this country girl was almost as exciting as the train ride east had been, the shopgirls and the businessmen straphanging, looking bored, not the least bit uncomfortable as bodies bumped up against those of perfect strangers, as if this was all so ordinary.

Sid bought me a hot dog and a Coca-

Cola, even though I'd asked for a beer. The Braves were playing the Cardinals and Sid and I were in hog heaven. Our seats were perfect, just a few rows back from the bull pen, where the relief pitchers played catch with catchers, legs extended in a balletic arc, the hardballs whizzing into the mitts with satisfying smacks. It would be so romantic to say that our eyes met, or that one look and I knew he was the one, but the truth is, I didn't notice Rick Stanton in the bull pen because he wasn't one of the pitchers warming up. He was acting as one of the catchers. So it wasn't until the game began and the relief pitchers all settled down to watch the action, rumps in white trousers lined up side by side on the wooden bench like pigeons on a wire, that this catcher unfolded himself into a tall, thin man, unburdened himself of the chest protector and mask, and, for reasons neither he nor I ever understood, looked up at me. And I waved.

It still goes back to Sid. Consulting his program, he identified this dark blond, tousle-haired ballplayer with the strong jaw and Roman nose as Rick Stanton, recently brought up from the Eastern League's Hartford Bees. A curveball pitcher with a decent win-loss history in the minors. He wasn't scheduled to play today, unless the game went south and the three other pitchers on staff that day were tossed out. I was rooting for the Cardinals, so I hoped that maybe I'd get to see Stanton play for that reason alone.

He didn't and the Braves won, but I admit that I hadn't paid much attention to the game itself. Every few minutes, I glanced back down to where Rick was fence hanging, a study of concentration on the game. Every now and then, he'd lift his cap, run a hand through his hair, and glance back at me. I couldn't tell then, from that distance, that his eyes were the richest hue of blue I'd ever seen. The kind of blue that seems to have a light behind it, like an Iowa sky on certain fall days. By the ninth inning, we were smiling at each other, and when the game was over, he jumped the fence and made his way up the steps to where I was trapped beside Sid in our row. Rick stood in the emptied-out seats just below me, which put us almost eye-to-eye.

"My name is Rick Stanton and thank you for coming to the ball game." Wisely, he put his hand out to Sid first. Later on, I asked him how he knew that Sid wasn't my beau; after all, he might have looked like a piker horning in on someone's girl like that, maybe even gotten himself decked. It was simple, he said; Sid was a good-looking guy, but you were smiling at me, not him.

Sid stepped aside and let me out of the row. "Sid Crawford, and this is my cousin, Francesca Bell. Good game, but I have to tell you she's a Cardinals fan." With that, my cousin excused himself to go to the men's room and left me with the man who would become my husband.

The moment is crystallized in my mind, but I remember it as if I'm looking down on these two young people. I see the girl, dressed in a summer skirt that lifts slightly in the breeze. I see this ballplayer, all long legs and arms outfitted in his baggy white uniform, the number 65 on his back. He has his hat in his left hand, gripping the curved bill. He reaches out with his right and takes the girl's hand in his. There is a frisson, a jolt, as if they are both charged with positive and negative ions, two forces meant to join up. It was the first time in my life I'd felt physical attraction, and the longer he kept my hand in his, the stronger the sensation. I leaned forward slightly, breathing in the scent of his skin, my eyes closed. I don't know what possessed me. Or, maybe it's more reasonable to say, I didn't know then. I just knew that Rick

Stanton was what I'd been waiting for.

Our courtship seemed so fraught with complication: I lived in Iowa; he traveled all summer. The only thing to do seemed to be to get married right away, set up a home in the Boston area, based on his optimistic hope that he wouldn't be traded for a few years. But the thing I had the most trepidation about wasn't Rick, or leaving home, or setting up what might prove to be temporary housekeeping in a strange city. It was Pax.

"I want you to meet someone." What girl ever hears those words with enthusiasm? Usually, it's a doting mother who will assume you're not good enough for her boy, or a bad-boy pal who will resent you taking his drinking buddy away. In this case, it was Rick's eighty-five-pound spoiled-rotten German shepherd cross. And I knew right away that although I could certainly work my way into a mother's good graces, or charm a drinking buddy into brotherly devotion, with Pax, I had to earn his permission to be important to his man. We were rivals for Rick's heart.

CHAPTER THREE

Pax didn't like to share Rick with anyone, but he especially disliked it when Rick would bring home females. On the one hand, as a male, he certainly understood Rick doing so, but women made Pax nervous. Mostly because he made them nervous. However, usually this was only a very short interruption in the life that they enjoyed. Being a lucky dog, Pax went everywhere with Rick, and he especially loved going to the ballpark, where the other men would slip him treats and act as if he were one of the team. Recently, Rick had started leaving Pax home alone for days at a time, a teenage boy coming to walk and feed him. "Got to hit the road, pal. This organization won't let you come." Pax liked the boy well enough, but he sulked and refused to engage with the kid. No amount of stick throwing or walks around the block would soften the dog's attitude. Rick was his person, and only

31

for Rick was he going to act the puppy.

When the suitcase came out of the closet, it meant that Rick was going to disappear for a while, and then return happy or grouchy. Pax would greet him like a long-lost hero no matter what mood Rick came home in, and he had the knack of moving Rick out of the doldrums by simply reminding his man that he was there and ready for some playtime. For Rick, he'd flop onto his back, four legs waving in the air, all dignity abandoned.

In the winter, it was much better; then he and Rick spent most of the day together, working out at the gym and doing roadwork. They ran; they visited Shanahan's Bar and Grill, where the proprietor, a guy Pax thought of as Meatman but Rick called Dickie, would dole out chunks of raw beef as if he thought Rick didn't see him do it. Pax liked their first-floor apartment, where he had taught himself to open the back door; he loved that, especially when the neighbor's cat got cocky and walked along the perimeter. Rick liked it because then Pax could let himself out into the fenced-in yard. As Rick liked to say, win-win.

In the year that Pax had lived with Rick, Pax had only ever shared Rick with the stray teammates he'd invite back after games for a sandwich and beer, or the pals that would crash here at odd times when passing through town. That was fine; no one expected anything more of him than a polite deference. Once in a while, Rick would bring a female around, but they never stayed long.

Everything changed when Rick brought Francesca home. "I want you to meet someone." The dog didn't understand the words, but he understood the vocabulary of love. This woman wasn't going to disappear like all the rest. The pheromones spurted off them like fireworks, filling the dog's highly analytical nose with the truth long before the people themselves got it. These two were destined to be mates.

The woman reached to pat him on the head, as if he was some ordinary affection-starved cur. The indignity of her invading his space made him duck away, as if her touch would hurt. But he didn't growl. The tension in Rick was enough to put Pax in a state of readiness, but Pax didn't stiffen into his guard posture. Slowly, he sniffed the woman's still-outstretched hand and then took an olfactory tour of her whole person, ending with her knees. She let him sniff the most interesting part of her without shrieking as many females did when he arrived at that oh-so-revealing human spot, usually with a quick defensive shove against his skull. This one remained as aloof as he was, and that was fine. This one didn't try to force friendship on Pax, and that was one thing in her favor. So many of the females made that simpering cooing sound when introduced to him; this one spoke to him in a friendly, meeting-of-equals tone. Instead of keeping his wolf eyes on her as she and Rick sat side by side on the couch, Pax lay down on the rug at their feet and heaved a sigh. Instinct suggested that this new woman was about to be made a part of their pack.

CHAPTER FOUR

Besotted wasn't the right word. Or *bedazzled* or *smitten* or *bewitched*. Well, maybe *smitten* came close. Struck as if by lightning. Rick put his hand in Francesca's and knew that if she ever let go, he'd die. She was so young, almost ten years his junior, but they were equals in all else. Her sense of humor, her way of charming even the great Mr. Stengel. The smile that meant she was purely happy. The way she brushed back her blond curls just before she kissed him. She barely came up to his shoulder, but he felt as if she lifted him.

It was like being in a play or a movie; everything felt accelerated by the fact of her impending departure back to Mount Joy. They skipped the testing ground of going to the picture show, followed by a late-night snack at a diner, where they could talk about the movie if other conversation failed them. Instead, Rick moved ahead in the usual dating schedule. He didn't have the luxury of time to wait for what was typically his third or fourth date treat, so he took Francesca to dinner at the Ritz for their first outing. They held hands, fingers entwined. They had everything to say and nothing. The harpist lent an ethereal air to the moment, her gentle music speaking out loud what was going on in his heart. How could this be? Rick had certainly dated, even loved once — his impatient fiancée Mary Ann — but this was different. For so long his plans had been formulated around his career, every decision weighed against its effect on that single-minded goal. Sitting across from this girl with her midwestern, matter-of-fact, down-to-earth, speak-her-mind confidence, Rick found himself fitting Francesca neatly into his life. He saw his future so clearly: Francesca, the house, the dog, the blond curly-haired kids.

"She's swell, isn't she, Paxy?" Rick and Pax have just put Francesca on the train back to Sid's place so that she can get ready for their date tonight. She's been to the ballpark every day, meeting him at the players' entrance after he's showered following a game or practice. He counts his lucky stars that this is a home week, no travel. He won't let himself imagine if he'd had to climb on the team bus and maybe never seen her again. Or lost the momentum that they have been building to all week. They've jumped the T and gone all over the city, to the Museum of Fine Arts and to the Isabella Stewart Gardner Museum, shopping at Downtown Crossing, but mostly strolling through the Public Garden and the Common, Pax between them and happy to be included in their adventures. After dinner, they go to clubs and dance until Rick knows his manager is going to be mightily distressed with him, out so late on a game night, but it hasn't affected his game. If anything, this new-love euphoria has made him indomitable. Called in for the last inning this afternoon, Rick struck out all three batters facing him in thirteen pitches.

They have accelerated from hand holding to kissing. He made himself go slow, not meaning to test her willingness, nor frighten her away, but she nearly frightened him with her response. It was as if she'd been waiting for him all her life. He won't let himself take advantage of that enthusiasm; he's a gentleman and he respects the proprieties. He forces himself to remember that she's a small-town girl, and a young one at that, and he won't send her home in any way less perfect than she arrived in Boston.

Rick can't let himself think about what the end of the week will mean. Francesca will go back to Iowa. His travel schedule doesn't include Mount Joy. He's not a free man until after the season ends, and that seems like an eternity. For the first time in his life, baseball seems secondary.

"How long does it take, do you think, for a man to be certain about what he should do about a woman?"

Pax cocks his head, opens his mouth slightly, and makes that little *humpf humpf* noise that Rick interprets as conversation.

"What's that you say? Marry her, right?"

Woof.

"I think you're onto something." Rick thumps Pax's ribs, ruffles his fur, and kisses him on the nose. "Sounds crazy, but that's the answer."

Pax leans against the leash, his nose plowing the way to a new scent laid in against a telephone pole. He lifts his leg. Obviously, there's nothing more to say.

Rick has never felt so sure about anything — except baseball — in his life. Francesca isn't the first girl he's met at the ballpark, but he is certain that she will be the last.

CHAPTER FIVE

My last night in Boston, our last night together, Rick took me to Norumbega Park on the Charles River in Aburndale to dance at the Totem Pole Ballroom. One of the area's premier night spots, "the most beautiful ballroom in America," the Totem Pole featured the best big bands and popular singers in the world. That night, we danced to the music of Benny Goodman. For a small-town Iowa girl, this was a magical evening. Made more magical by the feel of Rick's arms around me, the grace with which this long, tall ballplayer danced. Even in Mount Joy, we knew the new dances, and before long Rick and I were the center of attention as he flung me up into the air, my full skirt belling around my legs. We laughed and gasped for breath, and when the photographer came to us to take our picture, I was certain that he wasn't going to need a flashbulb, we were so lit from within. He captured us so perfectly, that anonymous on-staff photog. A lovely couple, starry-eyed with fresh love. Our future written in our smiles.

Exhausted, we finally flopped down on one of the settees arranged around the dance floor. When I rested my cheek against him, I came up against something hard in his jacket pocket. "What's that?"

"Oh, this?" Rick reached in, and I expected him to pull out a pack of cigarettes, because that's what it felt like. "A little something I'm hoping that you'll like." Then he dropped the kidding tone and slipped his arm out from under my head. Rick got down on one knee, and I thought that my heart would explode. "I know this is really rushing things, but I have never been so certain of anything — or anyone — in my life. Will you do me the honor of becoming my wife?"

One week to the day since we had met. And I had no reservations about saying yes.

And then I was on the train, heading home to Iowa. Sid, God bless him, hadn't said a word as I slipped into his second-floor flat at five in the morning, only yawned and started the coffee.

"Is he downstairs?"

"Yes. Asleep in the car."

"Go get him."

I ran downstairs as quietly as I could, so as to not disturb the neighbors, but Rick was gone. Of course, he had to get home to Pax. He'd be back in a couple of hours to take me to South Station, when we would have what we hoped was the only separation we would endure in our lives together. A few days on the road for the team wasn't going to have the same weight.

Pax and Rick picked me up, the dog relegated to the backseat but leaning his big head over the front seat, so that I could feel his whiskers against my cheek. Impulsively, I kissed that muzzle. Pax sniffed my cheek in return. "I'll miss Pax, too, you know. It isn't just you." I think saying that made Rick almost as happy as my wearing his ring.

I was such a baby, quietly weeping most of the way to New York, where I changed trains for the Chicago leg of my journey, dabbing my eyes with a sodden handkerchief, as if I had the least concept of what true absence was. I wallowed in the sweet agony of separation from my beloved. As I wearily climbed aboard the final connection home, I tortured myself with wondering if absence would make his heart fonder, or would he wake up in a week and wonder what the heck he'd gotten himself into? Rick promised a letter a day, a telegram a week, a phone call every other. Would his letters begin to thin out; would the telegrams seem more ominous than loving? Would he forget to call?

A telegram was waiting for me when I finally arrived back in Mount Joy. "MISS YOU MORE THAN WORDS CAN SAY STOP CAN'T WAIT TO HEAR YOUR VOICE STOP WILL CALL THIS EVENING AT 8 STOP ALL MY LOVE RS"

The dark tunnel of doubt opened to a bright new day.

Rick and I tied the knot in mid-October, not four months after that day in the ballpark. As soon as the season was over, Braves foundering in seventh place, Rick took the train for Mount Joy and I introduced my fiancé to my astounded parents. He knew Casey Stengel. That was enough to win over my father. He was well-bred, and that was enough for Mother. It might have looked a bit like a shotgun wedding, but it wasn't. "Marry in haste, repent at leisure" might be a well-founded adage, but we laughed at the thought that if we hadn't married, we might have ended up with my father's shotgun pointed at Rick's back. After all, Saint Paul did suggest that it was better to

42

marry than to burn, and we burned for each other. That's the best way I can describe it. But I was an Iowa girl and he was a gentleman, and marriage was the only acceptable route.

My two best girlfriends, Gertie Fenster and Patty Olafson, stood up for me, and my older brother Arnie acted as best man, with Sid as his groomsman. At Rick's insistence, Pax performed ring bearer duties, wearing a black bow tie around his neck, the rings tied to it with blue ribbon. I was just glad he hadn't wanted the dog as best man. The guests threw rice for luck and I wept for joy.

We stayed in the Elyria Hotel in downtown Mount Joy. Our window overlooked the mighty Mississippi, but I'm not sure either one of us ever looked out at the view.

As much as I liked the big dog, to Rick, Pax was his baby. Pax was Rick's blind spot. He didn't see anything wrong with the dog following him around from room to room, so that anywhere Rick was, there was Pax. Even in our bedroom. Basking in afterglow, I'd look over and there would be Pax, the patient voyeur. At least Pax didn't get up *on* the bed, but I couldn't ignore the weight of his muzzle as he studied Rick's face for any damage I might have caused. Eventually, he'd humpf and flop down into his basket, clearly dissatisfied with my remaining in Rick's (in Pax's view) bed.

I began to feel like I hadn't passed some test, that I wasn't worthy of Rick. Those amber eyes would fix on me as I rubbed Rick's shoulders, sore from his day of hard practice, or sat in his lap as we canoodled while listening to the radio. Pax would lay with his head between his paws and sigh, exactly like my mother might do when one of us disappointed her. A hand-to-God sort of sigh. Rick thought I was nuts.

"He loves you."

"Does not."

"What makes you say that? Look, he's sitting right beside you."

"The better to keep me separate from you. He's between us, Rick." I wasn't sure if I was speaking metaphorically or literally at that moment, although Pax did always keep himself in the middle. We sat on the couch and the dog sat on the floor, his big head resting in between us.

"That's just so we can both pet him."

"What happens when we have a baby? How will he be?" As much as we knew that we wanted children, we were giving ourselves at least a year of marriage. The only advice my mother gave me on the eve of my wedding night was that if I relaxed, it wouldn't be so bad. The best advice I got was from the short-stop's wife, who knew a female doctor with a modern outlook on birth control and an admiration for Margaret Sanger.

"He'll devote himself to our babies. He has a massive capacity to love."

The very first thing I learned about being married to a professional ballplayer, was that I had to keep his state of mind in perfect equilibrium. Numbers were everything. In those days, there was no designated hitter, so Rick batted and pitched. He was a better pitcher, and no one expected him to be a great batter, but he still believed in his earned run average like it was tea leaves forecasting our future. Which, I suppose, it was. Those numbers dictated our lives. Good ones, and we got to stay put. Sinking ones, and who knew where we might end up. Bad ones, and his career might be over. Rick loved being a ballplayer; it was his first love, and I understood its importance in his concept of himself. Being a ballplayer *defined* Rick. So I swallowed my annoyance with having a big, shedding, slightly sloppy, all-boy dog in our one-bedroom apartment and molded myself into the best ballplayer's wife in the league. Supportive, pennant-waving, consoling, and laudatory.

Right after spring training, Rick started traveling two or three days a week; our honeymoon winter was over. Pax and I were left alone together.

It was rocky at first. The big dog didn't want to take orders from me, so I found myself cajoling rather than ordering: "Come on, Pax, let's go outside." "Come on, Pax, there's a good boy, don't get on my couch." Even though Rick expected me to, I certainly didn't walk Pax as much as he did. Just like the dog, I loved those evening walks with Rick, when we'd go hand in hand, talking about our days, or our future. But when Rick was on the road, I'd take Pax once around the block, me towing him along or being towed by the dog, depending on where his nose took him, and then head home to listen to the game on the radio, or wait for Rick's late-night phone call from a pay phone somewhere far away.

Rick was in Baltimore, and the heat in Brighton certainly rivaled that of Maryland. Hot, sticky, the only relief coming in those early hours before dawn, when the wind might shift a little and drag some of the cooler ocean air off Boston Harbor and inland enough to reach our stifling first-floor bedroom with its single window and no cross ventilation. Now, as a midwesterner, I knew heat. Our corn-raising community was unbowed by routinely high temperatures in summer; every woman carried a fan and a capsule of smelling salts in her purse to church. But this sticky, wet, humid heat was intolerable to me. The only cool place at night was on the front porch, so in the middle of the night, desperate and wide awake, I placed a thick collection of wedding-present blankets down on the deck of our first-floor porch and hoped that no one passing by in the predawn — the milkman, for instance — would notice a grown woman stretched out on the porch in a mysteriously glowing white nightie. Because of the arrangement of our front door and that of our neighbors', who, in their second- and third-floor flats, were more likely to be catching the thin breeze, I worried a little that Pax might dash down the steps. I gave him the first command I'd ever tried: "Stay." He looked at me with a dog's version of "Make me" but stayed, lying flat on his side against the short end of the porch railing. His soft panting put me to sleep.

I shivered, smiled at the sensation, then woke fully, to see the dog standing over me, head lowered, teeth bared. I fought the urge to push him away, freezing in place like a rabbit hoping the fox doesn't see it. Then I realized that Pax wasn't baring his teeth at me, but at the man who was urinating loudly into the hydrangea bushes planted against the porch. Pax's dewlaps twitched over his bared teeth. A growl percolated deep in his throat. I touched him, trying to tell him that it was all right, not particularly pleasant, but harmless. The growl went from barely audible to ferocious, and the man literally ran off half-cocked. Pax leaped over the railing, and the frightened drunk ran for his life.

"Pax! Come!" I had no real hope that he would, and I pictured this poor unfortunate guy with the seat of his pants torn out. Perhaps worse. Pax was fast; Pax was in high dudgeon. But he surprised me and returned to my side in three strides. If a dog's face can express "Wasn't that fun?" Pax's did. His long muzzle split wide and his long tongue lolling, he rolled his eyes up to me, and in them I saw that a sea change in our relationship had occurred. He'd protected me; ergo, I was now part of his responsibility. I hugged him then, and he took it as if it meant something to him, tail sweeping the porch floor. After all, it was possible that the drunk, seeing a woman in such a vulnerable position, had had more ominous plans post-urination and Pax had known that. Who knows? All I knew was that Pax had protected me whether or not it was really necessary. He'd done his duty by me.

We sat there a long time after that, Pax leaning his big body against mine as we sat on the porch steps. I kept an arm around him. The first bird sent out notice that the sun would make its appearance soon. Slowly, the night paled, and I heard the clop of the milkman's horse from down the narrow side street. I needed to get into the house before anyone saw me like that, dressed in my honeymoon negligee. "Come on, Pax. Let's put the coffee on." Before I could push myself up off the step, Pax did something that stopped me. He gently pressed his muzzle under my chin, just like Rick sometimes did to raise my face to his. Then he licked my cheek. Even though I didn't assign any human qualities to animals like, well, like Rick, I understood completely that I had been accepted. We'd always be rivals for Rick's attention, but at least now we could be friends.

CHAPTER SIX

The frightening rumblings coming from Europe were only mildly concerning until the mandate came down in September 1940 that every man between the ages of twenty-one and thirty-six needed to get himself registered for the draft. If the invasion of Poland hadn't prompted this belated Selective Service Act, the bombing of London had. Every day, the news worsened and the newsreels portrayed a sickening disaster seemingly without end.

Rick and Francesca went together, hand in hand, Pax tagging along, as if registering for a peacetime draft was a lark, an excuse to get out in the fresh air and stroll the city streets. The worst, and Francesca agreed, was that his number would come up in the Selective Service's lottery and he might have to spend twelve months in the service. It would take a year out of his professional life, but maybe he could still play ball or coach on whatever base he might find himself. Francesca teased that maybe he could plead conscientious objector status, as playing for the Braves was, after all, his religion. Rick wasn't about to let Francesca know how terrified he was that he'd be drafted. Not because he didn't want to serve, but the fact was that a missed season was much more than just not playing. He was twenty-nine now, and it wasn't getting any easier to keep up with the younger guys. His arm was still good, but he was soaking it longer and longer. Not to play, even if doing some playground-level pitching, meant that he might never make it as starting pitcher. He was so close. Rick really loathed the idea of a setback.

Besides, this was the year when they were going to have a baby. Maybe Francesca was already pregnant. With a renewed contract with the Braves in hand, life was certain enough that they'd commenced trying. Trying. That sounded so, well, selfless. What they'd been getting up to could hardly have been called anything but self-indulgent. Francesca had been knitting up a storm, booties and caps, buntings and crib blankets, all given away to the other team wives and to their neighbor, who was in her seventh pregnancy. Yesterday, Francesca had shyly handed him a little capelet in the palest green, nearly white, satin ribbon threaded through the eyelets. "This one's for ours."

He took her heart-shaped face in his big hands and studied her amber-flecked green eyes and the way that her eyebrows arched over them, sooty lashes oddly dark against the fairness of her skin and hair. This was the face he held most dear. The look of hope, anticipation, and love all given away to him. How could he imagine leaving her for longer than a road trip?

By April, Rick's number still hadn't been called, and he'd packed up for spring training. By July, he was promoted to relief pitcher. By September, the season was over, and if the Braves had finished a lowly seventh in the standings, Rick had gone home nonetheless confident that the upcoming baseball season of 1942 would be his year as a starting pitcher for the Boston Braves.

"What if Roosevelt changes his mind. What if he decides we should go to war?" Francesca took the newspaper out of Rick's hands and crumpled it up, throwing it to the floor, as if she wasn't the one who would have to retrieve it. It seemed like the headlines only ever spoke of the increasing possibility the president would succumb to the pleas of Churchill to throw the weight and power of the United States at Hitler's rapacious drive toward world domination. The political cartoons, the editorials, the talk on the street all pointed in one direction: the inevitable involvement of the United States in this global disaster.

"Sweetheart, we can't worry about it. We can only worry about the things we have control over."

"Like what?"

"Mmm, my batting average perhaps?" Rick pulled Francesca down onto his lap and smooched her, one eye on the big dog, who would very quickly come up with some distraction, like asking to go out, or for new water in his already half-full bowl, or dropping his rubber ball on their combined laps, begging them to stop and play with him.

"You get to worry about that, not me."

Pax had suddenly found some latent retriever in his heritage and scooped up the crumpled ball of newspaper, gently placing it in Francesca's hands.

"It'll never happen" was the consensus of opinion in the clubhouse and the street corner and at the Totem Pole Ballroom, where they went to dance on gameless nights, always claiming the same settee where Rick had proposed. "Roosevelt will keep us out. If your number hasn't been called by now, it probably won't be." Whistling in the dark.

By the end of November, Rick finally got word that the coming spring he'd be in the starting rotation. He'd finally be a starting pitcher.

"Maybe a move is in order. You know, to a place of our own, where Pax can run around and the kids —"

"Kids? Plural already?" They were lying in bed, fingers linked, still vibrating from their exertions.

"Yes. The kids can have a swing set and you'll never have to worry about men urinating in your hydrangeas. Some neighborhood with a good school, a house with a big yard. The neighbors will say, 'A ballplayer lives in that house, the one with the lily beds and rosebushes. The one with the beautiful wife and handsome dog.' It'll be the house where all the neighborhood kids congregate."

"Three bedrooms and a den?"

"Four bedrooms. And a two-car garage."

"Two cars?"

"Don't worry, I'll teach you to drive."

It all sounded perfect, even if the gods of conception had been stingy with success. The doctor they'd consulted could find no reason they shouldn't conceive. "Relax and give it time," he'd said.

On December 7, the Japanese bombed Pearl Harbor and all the best hopes for staying out of the war were blasted away, along with Rick's dream of starting for the Boston Braves and their more private dream of a baby.

CHAPTER SEVEN

It isn't that Keller isn't grateful — in a way — to his great-uncle for having taken him in when he did. If the old man hadn't shown up that snowy winter day two years ago, Keller would have spent the rest of his youth behind the wrought-iron fence of the Meadowbrook School for Boys. Orphaned, passed around from relation to relation, none of whom during those dark days of the Depression could afford another mouth to feed. A scuffle with the truant officer had landed Keller in reform school. He'd been living with Aunt Martha and Uncle Bud and their four kids, and they were visibly relieved to hand Keller over to the state, the burden of his presence in their overcrowded Revere flat nullifying any shame in doing so. Without a willing guardian, he went in, at age nine, without hope of release before age eighteen.

At Meadowbrook, Keller was fed, clothed,

educated in reading and ciphering; taught the rudiments of the carpentry and print trades and some of the more useful talents of lock picking and theft from his fellow inmates. There were friendlier boys, and there were enemies and bullies. Boys from whom it was all right to bum a cigarette and boys you'd never turn your back on. There were clear rules, clear punishments meted out by teachers and staff and by the concrete hierarchy within the community of the boys themselves.

No praise, but then, he didn't expect praise, so he never minded its absence. There was no affection, but then, he was unused to affection. As close as Keller got to tenderness was when he'd slip away and visit the groundskeeper's dog, Laddy. The dog, purportedly meant to guard the groundskeeper's cottage, would wriggle with pleasure at Keller's appearance, gobble down the crusts or bits of half-chewed gristle, and then flop himself across Keller's lap to soak up a belly rub. The touch of the mongrel's soft pink tongue against his cheek was as close to love as Keller had known since the last time his mother kissed his cheek. A time so long out of mind, he could barely conjure up her face in his memory.

■ ■ ■ ■

Clayton Britt drove Keller home from Meadowbrook in his ancient Ford truck, the bed filled with fishing nets and lobster pots. Every sideways glance at the boy sitting beside him on the rump-sprung seat bore the avid look of a man getting himself some free labor. Clayton was his dead father's uncle, Keller's great-uncle, and before he showed up in the superintendant's office, not someone Keller had ever heard of. Keller didn't like the greedy look in his uncle's eye. Clayton looked at him not like a long-lost and welcome relative, but as a potential slave, his ice blue eyes apprising Keller's man-size height and the size of his biceps. As they left the grounds of the reform school, Keller had bluntly asked, "How come I've never heard of you?"

"Don't know. Your mother's people never got on with mine."

"Then how did you know about me?"

"You're kin, boy. I'm the only kin you have that'll take you. Be happy I'm giving you a home."

Home is Hawke's Cove, a Jimmy Durante schnoz-shaped peninsula jutting out from the New England coast. Crossing the short causeway that attaches the village to the mainland, Keller gets his first sight of the eponymous cove, a deep natural harbor along which the village clings. The winter sun strikes blinding sparkles off the water and two fishing boats are iced in and coated with a frill of frozen spray.

Clayton doesn't stop, but passes through the village and deep into the center of the peninsula, eventually turning onto a washboard dirt road that leads to Keller's new home on French's Cove Road. The house is a four-square shingled fisherman's shack, two rooms down and two rooms up, with only the heat from the parlor woodstove to warm the place subjected to the relentless draft pushing through the uninsulated beadboard walls. Meadowbrook may have been a prison, and his sleeping arrangement a dormitory filled with forty-nine other sleeping, farting, stinking boys, but at least he was warm. Behind the house, a yard littered with the detritus of a coastal fisherman's life: nets, lines, mushroom anchors, a skiff belly-up on sawhorses. Below the bluff, the scallop curve of French's Cove, with two moorings and a short pier proclaiming Clayton's ownership of this slice of beach. On the moorings are a squared-off lobster boat also used for scalloping, and a small dragger. Neither vessel has a name.

Living with Clayton means lobstering in all weathers, standing hip-deep in the cove in leaky waders while a seven-knot wind blows in his face as he rakes for quahogs; or trawling for bottom fish and slicing himself on scales, hooks, and the sharp, savage teeth of menhaden-crazed bluefish. Life with Clayton means never being able to completely wash off the odor of marine life.

The only thing that makes this life bearable is the fact that Keller has been able to attend the local high school. He's had enough English classes to understand the term *ironic*. Being truant from school was what landed him in Meadowbrook; but being allowed to get his diploma is what will free him from Clayton. Once that piece of paper is in hand, he's out of here, and for that he can thank Miss Jacobs.

It was almost the end of March that first winter with Clayton when an official-looking envelope came in the mail. Clayton held it up to the kitchen light as if he could read through the envelope and discard it without opening it. "What in the heck is this?"

Keller had already become used to his uncle's rhetorical questions and kept his attention on a pot on the stove, giving the chowder in it a gentle stir. Clayton slit the envelope with his filleting knife, extracting a single sheet of paper, which he held aloft as he patted his pockets for his reading glasses. Glasses settled, he read the letter, then dropped it on the table. He folded his glasses and replaced them in his shirt pocket. Keller could feel the air being sucked out of the room as Clayton slowly turned to him. "You finish eighth grade, boy?"

"Yes."

"Get a certificate?"

"No. But that's as far as anyone goes at Meadowbrook."

"You sixteen yet?"

"Yes."

"Says here you need to go to school, but you don't." Subject closed, Clayton crumpled the letter and tossed it in the firebox of the range. "I didn't take you in just to send you off la-di-da. You can read and cipher, that's enough."

Clayton was right: An eighth-grade education was enough, and Keller shrugged off the idea as wishful thinking. Until Miss Jacobs showed up at their back door, tiny and trim in a shirtwaist dress, white hair permed into submission and the look of eagles in her eye.

"Clayton Britt, this boy needs to attend

school."

"He's of age to quit."

"Does he want to?"

"I have the say in this house." Clayton stood in the doorway, his bulk keeping the high school English teacher standing outside.

Keller was behind Clayton, looking over his shoulder, and she looked right at him past the old man. "Step out here, son."

"No. You come in." Clayton doesn't hold the door open for Miss Jacobs, merely moves aside to let her in.

She didn't come up to either of their shoulders, but her bearing was pure authority. "Keller, what do you want to do?"

In all his memory, no one had ever asked Keller what *he* wanted, and as much as he knew Clayton would make his life miserable for it, he answered with his heart. "I want to finish school. I do."

"Clayton, this boy is entitled to an education. You cannot deprive him of that. I won't let you."

"What's it to you?"

Miss Jacobs lifted her chin, as if Clayton were one of her unruly boys and she was about to bring the switch down on him. "Don't be rude to me. I won't have it from you. Not you, Clayton Britt."

The pair stared at each other, and Keller realized that they were long-term adversaries, that between them there smoldered a history.

"See that this boy is in class on Monday. Keller, please dress appropriately. Bring your own pencil."

Before Miss Jacobs had stepped off the porch, Clayton slammed the front door, spun around, and slapped Keller. "Why'd you say that? For what you're doing, you don't need no education and you know it. Just looking for ways to dodge work. Lazy bastard."

But Clayton never attempted to prevent Keller from going to school.

There is no love between them, no affection, nothing more than any two men working together might share, an occasional laugh, a curse at the weather, griping about the lousy price the fish market pays for the fluke they spend four days offshore trawling for. If Clayton is taciturn, Keller is quiet. Clayton reads the evening paper spread over the kitchen table while Keller reads a schoolbook. They do not converse. They coexist. Most of the time.

It's Saturday night and Clayton has cracked open his Prohibition-era bootleg bottle of Canadian Club. They lost a lobster trap today when Keller lost his grip on the chain and it slid out of the pulley and into twenty feet of dark December water. A tire on the old truck is too thin to hold air and the spare is shot. Clayton sits at the kitchen table and tosses back a third shot. Keller sits opposite, keeping his eyes on his plate of cod.

Not for the first time, Keller wishes that the old man would let him get a dog. It seems to him that Hawke's Cove is filled with dogs. Dogs that sit patiently in cars as their masters conduct the business of the day; the fish market dog, called Flounder, which Stan Long claims is so smart, he could spell if he wanted to, but chooses not to. The big Newfoundland that goes out to sea on the fishing boat *Jane Anne*. The newspaper boy's dog, which follows him around from porch to doorstep on his route.

A dog would give him an excuse to walk out of the house; a dog would side with him against the old man's rants. A dog would listen as Keller whispered out his loneliness. A dog might fill that hollowed-out space.

But Clayton has said no. He doesn't need any other mouths to feed.

"You're a piece of work, you are. Losin' that

pot. What kind of fool are you?" Clayton's indulgence in the whiskey most often follows days like this, when too much has gone wrong. Then Keller becomes an easy target for blame. "Kindness of my heart. I took you in. What's my thanks? Cost me a trap. Can't remember to put air in the tire. Like you was trying to make me mad." He goes from gruff to just plain mean. "You got plans to inherit this place? You just forget it, boy. I'd rather see this place go to the devil than to you."

"I don't want it. What gives you that idea? You keep me here like slave labor. Why would I want it?" Keller shoves the plate aside. He stinks of fish; he can't get the taste out of his mouth.

"I see you coveting it. Just like your mother. You come from nothing, boy. Your mother was a cheap whore."

"Don't."

"Tricked my nephew into marriage. Know how? Got herself in the family way. With you."

"You don't know that."

"Got her clutches on him, white trash."

"And just what do you think you are? A fisherman. High-and-mighty? Think your shit don't stink?"

Clayton pushes himself out of his chair,

stands waiting for balance, as if he's at the helm of his workboat. Keller watches his hands. Sometimes when Clayton gets into the Canadian Club, he likes to take a swing at him. Keller has no difficulty deflecting the wild swings, and some latent decency always prevents him from decking the old man, as much as the feel of that jaw against his own hard fist would go a long way in righting some of the indignities he's suffered out of the old man's mouth.

Clayton wobbles and Keller grapples with him, waltzing him into the parlor and down into his chair, where the old man falls asleep. Sometimes the sight of that mean old man, drunken sleeper's drool drizzling into his two-day-old scruff, his outrageous slanders about a mother Keller has little memory of, is enough to burn his eyes with unspent tears.

Sunday has always been the only day that Clayton Britt doesn't go out on the water, adhering to some vestigial notion of a Sabbath, despite never having entered the precincts of a church. In the same fashion, Clayton calls lunch on Sunday "dinner," and he usually cooks the only beef the two will eat in a week, the rest of their meals consisting of salted, boiled, fried, or raw seafood culled from their catches. Short lobsters, a dozen little-necks. And, always, boiled potatoes.

Nothing is said about last night. Clayton got himself up out of his chair long after Keller had gone upstairs to his lumpy and cold bed. Keller wants to finish high school, but sometimes he thinks that he should just up and go. Stuff a laundry bag with his few possessions and light out. He'll be eighteen soon, the age when the state would have set him free from Meadowbrook if Clayton hadn't intervened. But if he can hold on, that diploma will be worth it.

This December Sunday, there's a football game on the radio and the two settle in after lunch to listen to it, Clayton in the one easy chair in the room, Keller on the braided rug on the floor, rather than in the spindle-back chair, which is the only other chair in the sparse room, its skirted chintz cushion oddly feminine in this intensely masculine house. The woodstove smokes a little and Keller gets up to rearrange the logs. Outside, the midafternoon winter sun is already weakening into an early dark.

Seconds before the game is to start, the broadcast is interrupted. Keller and Clayton lean toward the radio, trying to make sense of the rushed and repeated bulletin: "President Roosevelt has announced that the Japanese have attacked Pearl Harbor from the air."

Regular programming resumes, but Clayton shuts it off, his gnarled hand lingering on the peak of the radio. He coughs, then scratches at the stubble on his cheek. He looks at Keller. "Guess that you'll be leaving."

"Yes, sir." Keller looks away; he doesn't want the old man to see the happiness on his face, the relief and the hope. His life sentence has been commuted. The attack on the naval station at Pearl Harbor was surely horrific, but by it, Keller is set free.

As Keller Nicholson figures it, Pearl Harbor is about the best thing that could have happened to him, although he'll never say that out loud. The national outrage at the loss of life and the subsequent call to arms certainly is greater than his private joy at having a rock solid reason to leave his great-uncle Clayton's house. Patriotism and duty to God and country. Even Clayton can't argue with that.

Keller doesn't wait to be called up. He isn't going to take a chance that the lottery will deal him a losing number, and there is no way he to going to miss out on this chance to extricate himself from Clayton Britt's life; no way, as a strapping young man, is he going to miss the excitement of going to war. As dire as the world situation is, he and many of his peers worry that they may miss it, that the war will be over before they can get into it. Four of the boys from last year's winning high school basketball team have joined up already and three boys, seniors this year and already eighteen, have talked their way out of finishing school and into boot camp.

The day after his eighteenth birthday, Keller strips out of his overalls and pulls on his only nondungaree trousers. He brushes the dirt off his shoes with a bucket brush and digs the dirt out from under his nails with the ice pick. If Clayton won't let him take the truck, he plans to walk the five miles to Great Harbor, or he'll hitchhike to the recruitment center that has been set up in the empty storefront beside the A&P. Someone heading from Hawke's Cove into Great Harbor will stop and give him a ride. No shame in sticking out a thumb.

Keller strops his straight razor and lathers his face with the bar of Ivory soap, shaving for the second time that day.

"You going somewhere?" Clayton leans against the bathroom doorjamb. Keller can see him reflected in the mirror, the old man's expression inscrutable. There is no way to see past the weathered skin into the man's thoughts. His eyes, ice blue and framed by crow's-feet earned by a lifetime on the water, study Keller with detachment. As if Keller means nothing to him, and his departure doesn't mean a season of hard solo work.

Keller rinses his razor, wiping it carefully on the towel hanging around his neck. "Recruitment center. I'm joining up." Keller sets the straight razor down on the edge of the sink and reaches for his shirt. "I'd like to take the truck. I'll be back in an hour." He buttons his shirt and jams the tail of it into his waistband. "Two at most."

Clayton doesn't move, doesn't answer. Standing in thick wool socks, his rubber boots left standing by the back door, Clayton is just a little bit shorter than Keller, or maybe it's just that Keller feels bigger, taller; his resolve to join up has pushed him from boy to man. He has nothing more to fear from this old man.

Clayton moves away from the bathroom door to let Keller pass. "I'll take you myself."

Is it his imagination, or is there a little pride in the old man's voice?

■ ■ ■ ■

Miss Jacobs came to see Keller before he left for boot camp. She looked so small and vulnerable, standing there in Clayton's sitting room; feminine in a way that he'd never noticed before. The raptor eyes and the hands that gripped a pointer like a lance were softened with a weary resignation. Even before he'd enlisted, she'd tried hard to get him to wait, to finish his last few months in high school, get that diploma, then sign up. But Keller no longer saw that bit of paper as his only method of emancipation. Now he had the army.

Keller asked Miss Jacobs to sit down, and she perched on the edge of the spindle-back chair, feet aligned, hands clasped together as if she was about to recite poetry. Sitting there in that unadorned parlor, looking every inch the schoolmistress she was, Miss Jacobs looked up from her clasped hands and directly at him, and Keller could see that she believed that she had saved him from ignorance, only to have him die a soldier. She reached into her handbag and extracted a book. "I'd like you to have this. It belonged to my father."

Keller took the copy of Malory's *Morte*

d'Arthur from her, opened it, and read the inscription. "To Alfred Jacobs upon his successful matriculation. 1892." Beneath those words was another inscription: "To Keller Nicholson as he begins the journey of a lifetime. Best wishes and good fortune, Miss (Ruth) Jacobs. 1942."

"Thank you, Miss Jacobs. I'll always treasure this." Urged on by an unaccustomed grace, Keller kissed her cheek, and was surprised to find it wet. "You've been so kind to me. I don't know why. But I'll never forget you."

Clayton drives Keller to the train depot in Great Harbor, where he is to catch the early-morning Portland to Boston run. Leaving the truck running, Clayton gets out with Keller, hands him the small valise Keller bought himself with the little money Clayton has given him over the years. In it just some clean underwear and his shaving kit. The book from Miss Jacobs. He has nothing else.

"That's it, then." Almost as an afterthought, Clayton offers him a hand, and Keller accepts it. Two work-hardened palms meet for the first and last time.

"I guess it would be right to say thank you. For taking me in."

"Yeah. Well, good luck." Clayton turns quickly and walks away, as if Keller isn't leaving him and his hardscrabble life behind forever. As if this journey is of no consequence, that his only blood relation isn't going to war.

"You, too." Keller is rooted to the sidewalk, watching the old man's back. It isn't affection or gratitude that he feels, but relief. Excitement. This is a ticking off of a phase in his life — like living with his mother's siblings until that became living in the reform school and that became living with Clayton. It's over and done with and now a whole new and completely self-chosen phase is about to commence. Keller feels like yelling: Yahoo!

Then, with a little hitch of reluctance, Clayton pauses, turns. "You know that you can come back."

"I do." But I won't, he thinks. This door is closing and a brave new one is opening up.

The Portland to Boston train puts Keller Nicholson into South Station half a day early for his connection to New York. After that, another eighteen hours to Fort Bragg. This is his first train trip, and Keller soaks it in, the novelty not yet worn off by the time he gets to South Station, and he's looking forward to the next leg of his journey. He has a few hours to explore what he can of Boston, and he roams happily up to the Common, window-shopping at Jordan Marsh along the way and eating a hot dog from a street vendor. The stiff breeze coming off Boston Harbor barely gets Keller's attention. He isn't far enough from home to sense a difference in the air. It's all too familiar, sea air chilled by a constant breeze. North Carolina is going to be a lot different. And from there, well, who knows what exotic places he may be in. Keller is back at South Station in plenty of time for his train. The crowd has grown, lots of uniforms, but many more, like him, still nominal civilians but wearing that excited, terrified look of new recruits. Keller feels like he's part of a club, and he is amazed at how there is no mistaking the other members. Maybe it's the families surrounding them, or the wives and girlfriends all "bearing up" under the circumstances. A guy just heading to New York on business wouldn't have a mother clinging to his sleeve and dabbing her eyes with a hankie. He wonders then if *he's* readily identifiable as a recruit. He has no one frightened for him, or proud of him. No one making him promise to write. He stands alone, his back against the wall. Keller thumbs through the first pages of the Malory, his attention on the bustle around him, but grateful for the shield of the book, giving him the appearance of a man calmly making the journey of a lifetime.

Keller jockeys for position in the line queuing up to board the Boston to Penn Station train. Ahead of him is an odd trio, a man and woman and a big handsome dog. Nice-looking dog. Shepherd maybe? A tarnished silver with black points. Keller has never had a dog, but he likes them. When the fellow hugs the dog and then his wife, Keller smiles, thinking that the guy has his priorities straight, but then he sees the anguish on the human faces and regrets his impish thought. A moment later, the dog is pushing people aside as the young woman gripping his leash follows like a blind person. Later, on the train, Keller keeps thinking about that image: the man and woman and dog and how separate and devoted the couple were to each other. In the midst of this crush, they had carved out a niche of privacy, guarded by the dog. In another moment, he's sound asleep and the image and the thought fade away.

CHAPTER EIGHT

It wasn't like Pearl Harbor happened and then Rick left. We had a couple of months of what I thought of as a grace period while the military got around to calling him up, and then he had a date for his induction, which gave us four more weeks before he'd depart for Fort Dix. We had time, but we wasted a lot of it anticipating the final moments. We played out the scene in our minds so often that when it finally happened, it was with an extraordinary sense of déjà vu. We should have spent the grace period walking Pax along the Charles, eating in restaurants we couldn't afford, laughing at mindless radio programs, and dancing at the Totem Pole. But instead, we clung to each other and made promises we couldn't hope to live up to. He promised to come back and pick up where we'd left off. I promised not to worry about him. We debated the wisdom of trying now for a baby. Rick even suggested that we sit down with a pad of paper with a line drawn down the center, heading the left column "Pro" and the right one "Con." As if he thought we were analyzing the concept of moving to a new house or buying a new car. I knew already what the biggest pro was — giving Rick something to hope for — and the biggest con — my becoming a widow with a small child.

"Maybe the fact that we haven't conceived is God's way of —"

"Oh, Rick, please don't say that it's God's plan."

"Okay. Maybe fate has intervened."

I blushed with the secret I had been holding so close to my heart, waiting until I was absolutely certain before getting Rick's hopes up. I was late. For the first time ever. We were inveterate calendar watchers now, and I counted four days. Four days of growing significance. And in six, he would leave.

In my mind, the real question was whether to get his hopes up and dash them in a letter, or surprise him in a letter by saying that our hopes had finally been fulfilled. One more day, I thought. I'll tell him in one more day. And then another just to be sure. A whisper in his ear the morning he leaves. I couldn't wait to see the beaming grin on his face.

Without jealousy, I let Rick go out alone with Pax on their evening constitutionals. Where I had always enjoyed the walk, now I understood on some level that these two buddies, man and dog, needed a little female-free time. Rick somehow had to explain to Pax that this wasn't a road trip, that this was something entirely different. This time, there might be months or even, God forbid, years before they'd be together again. I wept a little thinking how impossible it was to explain to a dog that you weren't abandoning him, that you hadn't forgotten him, that you were just the unwilling pawn in circumstances out of your control.

South Station. There was an icy breeze slicing across the tracks, so we went inside to wait. No one looking at the stiff-jawed man and the puffy-eyed woman said anything about the presence of the dog. In our obsessive playing out of this scene, we'd forgotten that the place would be crowded with other servicemen and their families. Somehow I think that we both saw this farewell taking place in a cocoon of privacy. Instead, the defiant smiles and unattended children running around shrieking so that the place echoed with their voices, didn't fade into the background like in some movie, but stood out as proof that what Rick was doing, and what I was enduring, was universal and unavoidable. We were not alone.

As if he understood that this wasn't an ordinary departure, Pax pressed himself up close to Rick, leaving silver dog hairs on his charcoal gray dress pants. We laughed, that awful strained laughter of people on the verge of tears. I brushed the hairs off Rick's leg, but they slipped off my glove and drifted back.

"Leave them." Rick held my hand, and I realized that he would spend the train ride picking those hairs off. I knew that he superstitiously put a few of Pax's hairs in his baseball cap for luck; maybe he'd do the same with these loose hairs clinging to his pant leg, collecting them, maybe even dropping a few in his wallet to remind him of this other family member he was leaving behind.

Waiting was interminable and, conversely, the departure was all too soon. When you have said all that you can say, the silence enfolds you and you cast about, searching for that last important reminder or anecdote, until there is only empty space in your head and your heart is screaming for relief.

And then the whistle blows and suddenly all these men scurry away, last kisses and hugs, last admonitions to be careful. Last I love yous.

Rick knelt on the platform and put his arms around Pax. I don't know what he said to him, but the dog licked his face, something he rarely did, and watched intently as Rick handed me the leash, as if the dog knew that there was a changing of the guard, that I was now the person in charge.

Then Rick took me in his arms in a way that he would never do again in quite the same way. He kissed me with a passion that I would never quite know again.

We didn't say anything else. No unnecessary reminders to write, no useless pleas to stay safe. The last thing Rick said to me was, "Don't stay. Don't stand out here in the cold and wave when I won't be able to see you. Take Pax for a walk. I want to think of you and him playing on the Common as if it's an ordinary day. Not here."

By now, the mass of enlisted men was funneling itself into the train; faces appeared at the windows as men jockeyed for position. Windows opened; heads and arms stuck out. I was nearly knocked down by the seemingly unending number of families that rushed the platform. Wives and children, mothers and sisters, little brothers looking jealous, fathers discretely touching eyes with handkerchiefs and maybe remembering their own departures twenty-some years before, leaving for another war. Everyone wanting a last look, a last word.

In the end, I didn't say anything. That morning, I had awakened with the thick rumblings of an impending period. Maybe it was for the best. Maybe this meant that Rick would come home to me, and our children would come easily after that. But it still felt like I'd said two good-byes — one to my husband and the other to the last chance we'd have to have a baby.

Pax rumbled in his throat, not a growl, but a warning to anyone pushing too close. I had to get him out of there. Rick was right. There was no way he'd catch sight of me surrounded as I was by taller, wider people all vying for that last look. I tried to fight my way out, but my "Excuse me" and "Pardon me" went unheard by a crowd aware only of its own farewells.

Suddenly, Pax barked, loud and full of warning. The masses parted, startled by the deep voice of the dog. Like Moses parting the Red Sea. I couldn't wait to tell Rick how his dog had taken charge of the situation. And with that random thought, the magnitude of what was happening washed over me. Rick was being sucked into the vortex of this new American reality of war. I wouldn't tell him this anecdote, but write it in the first of the thousand letters that I would pen for the duration. I shook back the wash of dread and told myself that I would write to him that night and tell him about how Pax had moved aside the crowd. I would tell him that we'd played on the Common and that we'd had leftover meat loaf for dinner. I wouldn't write down on that scrap of paper that Pax had had to guide me out of South Station because I was blinded by tears, doubly grieving Rick's departure and the thickly flowing evidence of our failure, once again, to conceive.

CHAPTER NINE

It felt wrong, this departure. The tension emanating from his people had put Pax on the alert. Pax understood that Rick was going away; it happened with enough regularity that he no longer worried about it. Rick always came back. And Francesca was good company while they waited for his return. But this time, for a long while before the actual moment of departure, this human pair had been exuding an indefinable vibration. Not grief, or hope, or happiness, or tension, or despair, but some amalgam of all of those. It was hard on his sensitive nerves, trying to sort out what exactly was wrong. Then the three of them went to that noisy, crowded place, and Francesca shuddered all night afterward, despite Pax keeping his eyes on her and his head on her waist, standing all night beside the bed without sleeping while she trembled. She was afraid, and he couldn't find out what the source of that fear was. He'd left her side only long enough to patrol the apartment, corner to corner, door to door, and nothing, absolutely nothing, seemed threatening.

There was always a rhythm to Rick's absences, and Pax could sense which day would be the day he'd be home. Sometimes it was what Francesca cooked. A roast with its meat juices sizzling in the oven meant that Rick would be home. Sometimes it was that she whistled softly as she changed their bed, stripping off the more interesting-smelling sheets and putting on crisp ironed ones that would take a night to acquire the comforting scent of his people's bodies. A third indicator that their little pack was about to be returned to normal was the scent that Francesca spritzed on herself. Pax couldn't understand this need to disguise her willingness to mate, but humans did a lot of things that puzzled the dog.

Even for an animal with no sense of the passing of time, Pax knew that Rick had been gone a long while. No roast in the oven; sheets changed, but no whistling. No perfume clouding Francesca's proper scent. The slowness with which Francesca moved around the apartment. Drifting. Settling the new black curtains more exactly against the sills. Wandering into the kitchen but making no move to feed herself. More and more, Pax kept to her side, something he never did when Rick was there.

As she drifts from room to room, Pax follows, his cold black nose an inch from her hand, so that when she sighs and reaches back, she knows that he's there, ready to take on her worry. Sometimes she presses her cheek against his skull and whispers, but of all the words she says, there is only one word he knows, *Rick*, spoken over and over. When she does that, Pax closes his eyes, vaguely recalling the feel of his mother's body covering his and trembling with fear.

CHAPTER TEN

I think that many of us went into this war thinking that it would be over fairly quickly. Or that's what we told ourselves, because it was inconceivable that our men would be gone for so long. It had been half a year since Rick shipped out, bound for the battlefields of Europe.

We had a brief reunion when Rick got leave just before shipping out. He couldn't get back to Boston, so Pax and I piled into our 1936 Plymouth and drove all the way to New Jersey. As we started out, my hands gripped the steering wheel like vises, and I was more than convinced that my inexperience behind the wheel was going to be the death of us. Rick had taught me how to drive in those last few weeks before he left for boot camp, but I rarely took the car out. By the time I reached Fort Dix, I drove with one hand casually on the wheel and the other elbow resting on the open window.

I'd become a driver.

I don't remember much of that reunion, just that it was a worse good-bye than that at South Station. Then he'd still been in civilian dress; now he stood there, crisp and stiff and unbearably handsome in his khaki uniform, his very scent unfamiliar. We had two days, and I don't think we saw the outside of our hotel except for taking Pax out. Rick made me leave him instead of him leaving me. I drove off in that Plymouth, Pax with his head hanging out the passenger window, me in danger of a wreck because of the tears. Rick briskly walked away from us in the opposite direction so that I wouldn't remember him with any other expression but a smile.

With so many of the men gone, the Fore River Shipyard had begun hiring women to fill in the holes in the line. My pal Connie Mills tried to chivy me into going in to see if I could be of use. Connie was married to one of the catchers, a player who hadn't waited for the Selective Service Act, but joined up the day after Pearl Harbor. "Do it with me. We can wear overalls and not worry about our hair. We can't keep sitting around; we need to do our bit."

"Doing our bit" was the constant refrain.

A serviceman was doing his bit; civilians who collected scrap metal and saved bacon grease were doing theirs. We were inculcated with the idea that we were all responsible for the outcome of this conflict and we all felt a personal responsibility. Beyond victory gardens and blackout curtains, the American way was to make every personal decision based on the war. We learned to do without, a lesson learned from our parents, who had survived the Depression and handed down to us their experience to serve a new purpose. We took great pride in drinking our tea without sugar and learning to like margarine. We debated every use of the car and saved our gas-ration coupons like misers. Self was secondary to winning the war and sacrifice was honor.

"I'll give it some thought."

"Francesca, you're just moping around here. It isn't healthy. I know you're still a honeymooner, but, honey, you need to get out."

"I'm not a honeymooner, not anymore."

"You're a honeymooner until you have kids."

I know that Connie couldn't have meant to hurt me, but her words were like little slaps. I had to forgive her, though, because she could have no idea how hard we'd been

88

trying to become parents, and that we weren't deliberately prolonging our honeymoon.

We were sitting at my kitchen table, Pax beneath it in what I called "his cave." Even as I swallowed Connie's words, I felt the weight of his paw on my foot, reminding me he was there.

"I have Pax. We have Pax."

Connie patted my hand. "Sweetheart, Pax is not a child."

But he was to me. He needed me. How could I leave him all day? Fore River was in Quincy, a long train ride from our little apartment in Brighton. Green Line to the Red. It would be highly irresponsible to leave the dog alone for what could be ten hours a day. He'd go mad. "No, I can't go that far every day."

"Then find something closer. Francesca, we all have to do something. Think of it as helping our boys over there with what we're doing here."

She made a good case. Connie was fired up, and I knew that she wouldn't let me be until I found some war work to do. And, truthfully, I was ready to do something. My little bit of volunteering with the other wives for the local children's hospital was good, but Connie was right: I needed to be a part of the war effort. Everyone I knew was doing something. Back in Mount Joy, my pal Gertie was taking a nursing course, and Patty was in charge of the blood drives for the whole county. And both of them were now wives and mothers, as Connie suggested; it wasn't like I had kids at home to take care of to fill my time. Only Pax.

The wire factory had geared up for the war, along with so many other peacetime businesses, and was running three shifts to bend wire into the war machine. Second and third shifts paid best, but I was content with first. After all, we had savings and I had Rick's army pay, which wasn't nearly as much as his baseball salary, but enough to support me, so I left the better-paying jobs for those who really needed them. Best of all was that it was within walking distance from home. I could be home in minutes and often went home at lunchtime to let Pax out.

We were a noisy crew, the bane of the one male floor supervisor, who had to put up with our jokes and gossip and insistence on popular music in the break room. The puke green walls of the break room were plastered in what in another country might have been called "propaganda posters," but we looked on them as patriotic reminders of our importance in the war effort: BUY WAR BONDS; LOOSE LIPS SINK SHIPS; DON'T TELL SECRETS ON THE PHONE; DO THE JOB HE LEFT BEHIND; and other variations on the perpetual theme of winning the war and the continued responsibility of every citizen to remain alert and focused on the effort. I found myself studying the images of European peasants huddled against ominous threats and, my favorite, the one of the sinister-looking man sniffing around for secrets.

The morning *Globe* was filled mostly with news of the war and the noble work being done on the home front. It cheered me in some way to read of the galvanized spirit of my adopted community and my country in the communal effort to defeat the Axis powers and return the world to sanity.

Rick had been overseas for almost six months. His letters had begun to thin out, not as if the effort of writing was too much, but because the relentless bounce between periods of insufferable boredom and hours, days, or even weeks of adrenaline-charged action was telling on him. How could he continue to write jolly, flirtatious V-mail letters when all around him the world was coming apart at the seams? It's pretty difficult to keep up a facade of optimism when you are mired in the mud of the battlefield. I'd get them in bundles, six or seven letters herded together from the various places where he'd had the opportunity to post them, and their sameness was blatant as I read them one after another. Eventually, I didn't even need to sort them in date order; the messages were the same: He missed me. He missed Pax. He was all right. They were hunkered down in fairly comfortable circumstances, or they were on the move. He got to be so careful, there were almost no censor's marks on his single sheet of V-mail. If he'd gotten my letters, he might reply to a question, or offer advice, or comment on something I'd gossiped about. His letters were mostly out of sync with mine, and I might wait a few weeks before I opened a letter that would answer a question I'd forgotten I'd asked. "I miss you. I miss Pax. I miss spring training. I miss home." Those were the salient facts; that was his litany. And I wrote back that I missed him, and that Pax was fine and missed him, too. I told him to take heart, stay safe. We'd all be reunited soon, I said.

But I was not waiting out the war in some safe harbor; I was part of it. We were all part of it. Even just being in that break room, my hands toughened up from the work I was doing, made me feel proud that I was a part of the war effort. Who would have thought that I could enjoy the satisfaction of running a machine, of producing a product that would directly affect the war? I didn't have enough backyard for a victory garden, but I had sewn blackout curtains for every room in the apartment. Because I walked to work, I was saving those gas-ration coupons for the day when Rick would be discharged and I'd drive to the ends of the earth to get him. When the neighbor-hood kids came to the door, I turned over the day's washed-out tin cans so that they could be turned into tomorrow's tanks. I helped with the St. Alban's Ladies Guild jumble sale, the proceeds going to a fund for displaced children. It was always the thought of those European orphans that pierced my heart, little children whose parents were dead, whole families gone, with no way to explain it to tiny victims. In my dark moments, I wondered if the parents of those orphans would have preferred that they'd never been born than to have them suffer the horrors of invasion, bombard-ment, and abandonment.

Yes, we were all doing our part. So the day that I opened the *Ladies' Home Journal* and saw the full-page ad for Dogs for Defense, I didn't quickly turn the page.

WANTED: WAR DOGS FOR DOGS FOR DEFENSE/ENLIST YOUR DOG NOW, the headline read.

The ad made a persuasive appeal: . . . *there's a real job today for dogs that can meet the requirements for service with the United States Armed Forces! There are duties that the K-9 Corps can perform even better than men . . . sentry duty, pack work, messenger and communication service and sledge work are but a few of the jobs many dogs are already doing for their country.*

I read every word, my glance returning after each paragraph to the illustration of a dog that looked a lot like Pax. Pax fit the bill: *Dogs may be purebred or crossbred, must not be less than twenty inches at the shoulder, not storm shy or noise shy, not less than 1 year or more than 5 years old.* Pax was a big dog, he was a little under four years old, and he'd never made a sound during thunderstorms. I'd walked him all over Boston and he took in stride the cacophony of the city streets. He defended me against drunks urinating on hydrangea bushes. He was aloof but affable, never vicious. He had heart.

The promise: *Your dog will be well-trained,*

well-fed, and well-cared for while he's serving Uncle Sam.

Purina Dog Chow, the very same I fed to Pax, was the sponsor for this ad run by the American Kennel Club's Dogs for Defense volunteer board.

My break was over, so I returned the magazine to the shelf of reading material we girls had brought for the communal room. Leaning into the small mirror hanging just next to the exit — something the female staff had requested for the once exclusively male break room — I dabbed on a fresh coat of lipstick. I may have been wearing denim overalls and had my hair pulled up out of my hard-won pageboy hairdo into a bobby-pinned pile of curls hidden by a kerchief to keep the dust and dirt out, but we all clung to our emblem of femininity — bright red lipstick. As I blotted my lips with a square of tissue, I saw behind me, reflected in the rectangle of mirror, a new poster: GIVE DOGS AND DOLLARS TO DOGS FOR DEFENSE . . . TRAINING SENTRY DOGS TO HELP OUR SOLDIERS.

I went back to the shelf and picked up the magazine, flipped the pages back to the Dogs for Defense advertisement, and ripped it out. I folded it and put it in my locker.

Everyone should do his bit.

I put the kettle on and opened up the box of cookies I'd baked for Rick. I'd used the last of our sugar ration to make them. I had pressed my thumbprint into some of the cookies so that he'd see some physical manifestation of me. In a few, I had pressed three knuckles in an attempt to represent Pax's paw print.

Lately, I'd noticed that a number of the neighborhood dogs had vanished. The big setter and the beagle no longer came up to their fences to bark as Pax and I walked by. On our way around the block that evening, we bumped into Mrs. Tingley, as we often did on Pax's after-work constitutional. She was alone, her collie, one of Pax's favorite playmates, absent from her side.

"Where's Lady?" I stopped, hauling Pax closer to me so that I could chat.

Mrs. Tingley, a middle-aged woman who had sent three sons to war, didn't answer right away, and suddenly I worried that some horrible news had come to her. Her face began to crumple, but then she pulled herself together. "We donated her, you see. To the Dogs for Defense program. She's going to be a messenger dog or a scout."

96

"Dogs for Defense. I've seen the ads."

"She's doing her bit. Just like my boys."

"Don't you miss her?"

Mrs. Tingley looked down at Pax, then up at me, and smiled. "I do. But not as much as I miss my boys. Dogs like Lady will help get them all home sooner. I believe that. You should think about donating Pax. He'd be perfect. Besides, they'll send him home to you as soon as the war's over."

"I couldn't. How could I?"

"How can you not?"

The funny thing about becoming aware of something you've never noticed before is how suddenly you see it everywhere. Now that I was aware of the Dogs for Defense program, everywhere I turned, there it was. The vanishing dogs. The posters, the ads, the newspaper stories featuring little kids handing a leash over to handsome military types. "We'll see that he gets home. He's doing his bit. You can be proud." Public-service announcements featured Rin Tin Tin as a recruiter for the K-9 Corp, and the newsreels showed the grainy images of dogs running, jumping, taking down well-padded targets, tails wagging, praised by smiling, pride-filled handlers. Saving soldiers' lives. Everywhere. And everywhere I went with

Pax, the more I imagined that everyone we passed was thinking, There's a big strong dog. He should be doing his bit. As if this were a different war, I half-expected him to be handed a white feather.

No. I had made my mind up: Pax wasn't going anywhere. I needed him too much. He was my connection to Rick, my only companion, my entertainer, and my silent partner in the darkness of my worst thoughts. If I could have kept Rick out of it, I would have. I couldn't, but I sure could keep our dog home.

And yet, in that box of gingersnaps and lemon wafers I included not only a silly love note but the Dogs for Defense advertisement I'd torn out of the *Ladies' Home Journal.* I think that I wanted Rick to know that I hadn't succumbed to pressure. I think that I wanted him to agree with me. Or make the decision for me.

CHAPTER ELEVEN

Rick Stanton shakes off the catcher's sign. This batter is better than he looks and a fastball thrown to him has the potential to tie up this game. As it is, they're losing the light and it won't be long before the game is called because of darkness. Rick winds up, kicks, and launches a curveball.

"Strike three!" Pvt. Al Hooper joyfully signals his sergeant out. With good grace, Sergeant Phillips hands the bat to the next batter and doesn't argue that, from his perspective, it had looked like a ball on the outside left corner. Only on the playing field does the strata of rank become moot. And only rarely do they get to carve a playing field out of the battlefield. Once the game is won or darkness beats them to it, rank will be restored and Phillips will be back to making the calls.

Rick tosses the baseball gently up and down. The Boston Braves had sent him a box of balls and a carton of bats almost nine months ago. Through near-constant movement of their battalion, barrages, and battles, his platoon had lost most of the donated equipment. They are down to two balls and one bat. He'd joked that maybe they should start using grenades for batting practice, hitting toward the outfield of enemy territory. They all joke. They all play this bizarre form of pickup baseball for one reason only: It keeps their minds off the next day. It isn't enough to have survived until today. There is always tomorrow and it is tomorrow that they worry about. You know you've made it today. But, will your number be up during the next advance, the next ambush, the next time the enemy fires its big guns in your direction? Baseball, sometimes played in a tiny market square or in some farmer's abandoned field a few yards behind the artillery, is something they can do and forget for nine amateur innings why they are playing on foreign soil in a danger zone. And that tomorrow may not be your day.

If they are hunkered down in a small town or village, sometimes children will show up to watch. Eyes peek over windowsills, followed by a slow emerging from gaping doorways; the gradual building of an audience who watches the game in an unnerving silence. Nonetheless, these kids often surprise Rick with their knowledge of this quintessentially American game. Or, maybe it's just that kids have an innate understanding of how games are played. They watch as intently as genuine fans while the Americans, stripped down to undershirts, helmet liners instead of baseball caps, swing and miss, catch flyballs, run the bases — generally mess kits loaned for the duration of the game — sliding headfirst into home plate, which, by invented tradition, is always the helmet of the highest-ranking officer playing the game. They watch, and sometimes Rick will call a kid over and put him in the game. Ragged children, skinny in a way a child should never be, a wariness and timidity in their eyes that looks permanent. A tiny miracle may take place when he calls a kid over, stands him beside a mess kit, and gestures in crazy sign language that he should catch the ball and tag the runner out. Sometimes, not always, that one kid will lose the wariness in his eyes, and a little sparkle will show. One little moment of pleasure, of *play* in a life spent scrambling for survival. That was how they've lost most of the balls — Rick gives them to the kids in exchange for a smile. He thinks of his own unborn children. He'll teach them how to play the game and about these kids and how much the game of baseball meant to them.

This time, there are no children watching. They end the game before dark with a quick one-two-three last inning, chalking up a two-to-one victory for Rick's team. It isn't all that different from winning on the legitimate ball field, handshakes and back-slaps, easy laughter, good-natured ribbing of the losing team. All that's missing is a tavern and a cold beer. All that's missing is the life he left behind. Most days, it is pos-sible to keep his perspective. This carnival of noise and destruction and blindly follow-ing orders is his here and now. Francesca and Pax and playing baseball live in a very special compartment in his brain, a place that he lingers over only during those rare moments when he isn't fully engaged in the hard work that war forces on him. To dwell on what is a very different plane from the one he currently inhabits is like thinking of sex while pitching a no-hitter. To think of home and his life and how much he misses it is hazardous. It's a losing proposition.

Yesterday, the battalion had gotten mail for the first time in a couple of weeks. Rick had each one of Francesca's letters bundled together in the bottom of his pack, and during the stretches when they didn't receive mail, he'd extricate the bundle and read two or three randomly pulled out of the pile. He used to keep the letters in his field jacket pocket, but the bundle had become too thick to carry there, where it weighed against his breast, pulling him to one side.

So, like all his comrades, Rick stood in the crowd and waited to hear his name called by the quartermaster, the anticipation of a letter or two like a taste in his mouth.

"Stanton!"

"Here, sir."

The quartermaster deftly snapped a bundle of letters into the air, where it sailed precisely to where Rick stood.

"You ever want to pitch, you let me know." Rick tucked the bundle into his jacket.

"I got a hell of a fastball, Stanton; you don't want to hit against me." He rooted around a little more in the mailbag. "Wait, you've got a package." The quartermaster lofted a small brown paper-wrapped box to Rick.

Rick read each of the stockpiled letters from Francesca in date order, each one decorated at the bottom with her XX's and OO's and a messy paw print from Pax. Her letters, like his, had taken on a certain rhythm. The weather, a greeting from her parents via their monthly phone call, a snippet of gossip about neighbors or one of the players who had remained behind; a report on her day at the factory. A funny story about Pax. Pax sending his love.

The box held cookies, bashed mostly into crumbs by the time it reached him. Among the remnants was an envelope. Rick licked the tip of his finger and picked the crumbs off the envelope, savoring the bite of ginger as he tasted what his wife had tried to do for him.

Dearest Rick,
Sweets for my sweet. Pax did his own paw prints. Honestly.
With all my love, your own,
Francesca

His sticky fingers found the slick magazine paper and he pulled out the enclosed advertisement. Rick had seen one, a war dog. Just the sight of a well-made American dog, so unlike the scrawny, fearful mutts that scurried away from them as they approached, too long feral to trust human beings, had made him more homesick than he'd ever been in all this time. The dog had been a casualty dog, put to use in the aftermath of a battle, locating the still-living wounded. All Rick wanted to do was pat the dog, but the soldier handler was clear: No one was allowed to do more than admire this working canine from a respectful distance. Rick's fingers had itched to feel fur beneath his hand, and the rebuff had sent him into a funk of missing Pax.

Rick held that creased piece of magazine paper in his hands, studying the photograph of the German shepherd and his proud young owner. He looked away and pressed a hand against his sternum. When the big guns thundered, it could feel like one's chest was collapsing from the percussion. Rick felt exactly as if his chest was being crushed. He crumpled the page, pitching it away from him as if it were a grenade. Lacking enough weight, the paper dropped well within the danger zone. He knew what Francesca was doing, even if she might not realize it. It wasn't that he couldn't see it; he really could. Pax, big, strong, smart, working as a scout or sentry, as a casualty dog or messenger. Rick retrieved the ad, smoothed it out, refolded it, and added it to the bundle at the bottom of his pack. A working dog. Smart and loyal, more than capable of doing the kind of work the War

Department had developed. Rick could see Pax in the K-9 Corps. He just couldn't see anyone but himself being the dog's handler. They'd be an excellent team, he and Pax. They always had been, even before Francesca. From the time he'd scooped up the wet, thirsty, hungry puppy, Pax had belonged only to him. Anyone who had ever loved a dog wouldn't easily give up that dog to war; but war was their life now. If Pax could talk, would he say he'd rather be home sleeping under the kitchen table than be doing his bit?

Rick and his platoon are called into formation, the balls and bat are stowed away, the momentary respite from action is over, and by this time tomorrow, well, who can say what may be true tomorrow. He doesn't have time to write to his wife, to answer that unspoken, implied question. He's squandered that time with a pickup baseball game. The game had gone well, but for once it hadn't given him the usual release from his present. No matter how hard he had concentrated on his pitching or his hitting, the idea of his beloved Pax being sent into the same kind of daily danger he endured obstructed his focus.

As Rick climbs up into the already-moving

troop carrier, a hand grabs his, hauling him over the tailgate and into the truck; the private who had been the umpire for their pickup baseball game grins at him. "That was a great game. We should challenge the Krauts to a baseball game; we'd be sure to beat their asses."

Two days later, Pvt. Al Hooper was dead. He'd walked off to the side of the road to take a piss, smack in front of three camouflaged Germans, who opened fire on him, killing the boy instantly.

A scout dog would have alerted the platoon to danger. That umpiring private would never have died. That night, Rick bummed a sheet of V-mail from a buddy.

Dearest,
I know that you weren't asking the question, but the answer is that Pax should do his bit, too. We should volunteer him for the Dogs for Defense program. It's the right thing to do. So, it's going to be up to you now to keep one more creature in your prayers.

Love,
Rick

P.S. Please tell Pax that I'll be looking for him.

CHAPTER TWELVE

Dear Mrs. Stanton,
This is to advise that your German Shepherd Dog, Pax, has been called into the K-9 Corps of the U.S. armed forces . . .

When the war is over and you have had an opportunity to learn firsthand from the soldiers who have benefited by these trained war dogs, you will realize what a splendid contribution you have made toward your country's welfare in time of war.

Sincerely,
Forest M. Hall
Regional Director
Dogs for Defense

Receiving that letter had been tantamount to getting Rick's induction letter. Hall's reassuring words of my future pride and Pax's inevitable glory did nothing to assuage the lumpen feeling that surrounded my heart. I shook off Connie's attagirl embrace; I didn't feel noble; I just felt sad. Pax didn't have any choice in the matter. Like a draftee, he was just being told what to do and would be sent away. Rick at least could write to me and let me know he was doing all right; Pax would disappear for the duration, and I believed that I might never know where he was. Europe or the Pacific, the Aleutians or stateside, protecting the coast with the Coast Guard. That last option was the one I prayed for. Like Rick had said, I now had to add Pax to my personal prayer list, along with my husband and brothers, cousin Sid, and all the players who had left the game, voluntarily or not, to be a part of the war.

The men came to collect Pax on an early-summer morning. I'd taken the last couple of days off from the factory, loath to lose any more time with my dog than I had to. We went for long walks, used up my precious gas ration to drive to the country, where he could run unrestrained. I'd talked to him, explaining over and over what was going on and where he was going and what he was going to be doing, and how proud we were of him, but I knew that he only heard the soft speech as soothing, not as explication. He had no sense of what was to come.

They came, and you might have thought I was a mother sending her baby into war, the way I failed to hold back my tears, the way I clung to that dog's neck so hard, he had to wriggle loose. Because I was so upset, he became upset and acted as if the two youngsters sent to collect him were a danger to me. He growled and snapped, until finally I had to order him into the wood and chicken-wire crate. And then he looked at me like I was punishing him. I'll never forget that look of confusion in those beautiful eyes. He didn't whine, though, as you might expect. Despite his confusion and upset, Pax never whined.

"He's a nice dog, ma'am." This boy in his grown-up's military uniform shut the cage door, locking it with a twist of the wing nut. "He'll be a good soldier."

My mouth went dry for a moment before a metallic taste of bile flooded it. Panic has a flavor. "Wait. I can't do this." I reached for the cage, but the kid gently blocked my hand.

"But, ma'am, you have done it. You can't back down now." No longer a boy, but a soldier, a man with orders and the authority to carry them out.

"One more minute."

He dropped his hand, but I could feel his eyes on me as I knelt in front of the door. "I won't open it, I promise, but could you step away, please?"

He did, far enough away that I was confident he couldn't overhear my whisper. I spoke so low that I was sure only Pax could hear me and that he'd understand these last sorrowful words. "I love you, you big silly boy. Come back to me. Come back with Rick."

They drove off, my dog in the bed of that military truck. In my hand was his simple leather collar, which had been replaced by his new military-issue one. I coiled the leather around my hand and went into my profoundly empty apartment. That night, as I lay sleepless in my marriage bed, I found myself listening for the sound of Pax's toenails on the bare floor, patrolling the place one last time before settling into his bed. Outside, a dog down the street barked. No other dog answered.

When Rick left for war, I was one among thousands of women enduring a wartime separation. I busied myself and found purpose in the factory. When Pax left, I had only the small comfort of a handful of other dog owners and had lost a good deal of what had kept me busy before. No evening walks, no rushing home at lunchtime, no use for the few scraps of leftovers I couldn't bring myself to eat. I picked up Pax's scattered toys and gnawed bones and his leash and put them all in his basket in the corner of our bedroom, there for when he came back. I kept his collar in my dresser drawer, in safekeeping for when he'd need it again.

CHAPTER THIRTEEN

Pvt. Keller Nicholson can't believe his luck. His application to join the K-9 Corps was accepted and here he is at the Dog Training and Reception Center in Front Royal, Virginia. He might have exaggerated his experience with dogs, confidently claiming that he'd owned several, when the truth was the only dogs he had ever lived with were the beagle Aunt Biddie owned, which kept him warm as he slept on the lumpy couch on the screened-in porch that served as his room when he lived with her, and Laddy, the dog the groundskeeper at Meadowbrook kept tied to a doghouse.

When the chance to become a handler arose, it wasn't the thought of either of those dogs that crossed Keller's mind and set him on this course. It was the fleeting sight of that dog with the couple on the station platform in Boston. The way the man knelt to say good-bye, the genuine affection, and the way the dog guided the woman through the commotion. The people are vague figures in his memory, but the dog stands out. He'd like a dog like that.

The former remount facility has only just been converted to its new purpose, training dogs to perform the services of scout, sentry, messenger, or casualty dogs. The din is deafening as the four-legged recruits voice their opinions in barks, bays, and howls.

The civilian dog trainer has given the six new human recruits to the K-9 Corps an overview of their training program. "From now on, you and you alone are responsible for the care and well-being of the dog that will be assigned to you. We'll teach you how to groom him, feed him, train him, and work with him. No one else handles your dog. No one else is allowed to so much as pet him. He must look to you for everything that he needs — from food to praise. This way, we build a team of two. Your life and his depend on his unquestioning allegiance to you."

Keller feels a little thrill pass through him, a tickle of excitement, not unlike those long-ago Christmas mornings when his parents were still alive. He follows along as the five other soldiers are paired with their charges.

A boxer for the big Indianan; a farm collie for the kid from St. Louis; a nondescript brown dog for another, an Airedale for the fourth. The fifth recruit is paired with a stunning Irish setter. Keller thinks that he would be happy with any of these dogs, each one meeting and greeting the man who would become its partner with sniffs and a general willingness to be friends.

The other new handlers are left behind as the trainer and Keller continue on down the line, passing all sorts of dogs.

"Nicholson, I got one I'd like you to try. But he's a tough one. No one's been able to handle him since he arrived, and if you don't make a go of it with him, he's going back."

The trainer leads Keller away from the rows of doghouses to a rectangle of high chain link with a doghouse in one corner and a very sullen-looking animal sitting in the exact middle of the confined space. At their approach, the dog's head lowers and his eyes narrow and fill with an unmistakable hostility. He looks to be mostly Shepherd, but some other influence is evident, his jaw a little wider than a true German shepherd's, his muzzle maybe more boxy.

"Why's he in a cage?"

"He's a biter."

"Isn't that sort of what we want in a war dog?"

"We want a discerning biter."

"What's his name?"

"Pax."

"Funny name for a vicious dog. My high school English teacher would call it 'ironic.' " Keller squats in front of the enclosure. "Here, Pax."

A low rumble emanates from the dog's throat, like distant thunder on a summer's day. The dog makes no move otherwise; his eyes are fixed on Keller. Even with the sturdy kennel door between him and the dog, he begins to feel an instinctive urge to back away slowly. Pushing the feeling down, Keller instead makes a little kissy sound as he snaps his fingers softly, poking them through the diamond-shaped chain links. Despite the fearsome behavior, this is a beautiful animal. He's the color of tarnished silver and his muzzle is etched in the same black as the saddle over his shoulders. His ears are like capital letter *A*'s. Inside one of them is a tattoo, marking him as the army's own. He uses his ears like radar to judge the sounds coming from the parade ground; but his predator eyes remain fixed on Keller's own. The dog's rumble deepens into a growl. He sounds more lion than dog. The black-rimmed lips curl back and the dog's teeth are exposed in a wolfish grin.

The civilian dog trainer puts a hand on Keller's shoulder. "I feel I should tell you that two other handlers have tried him."

"How far did they get?"

"Not far. He scared the bejesus out of both of them."

Keller meets the dog's stare with his own. He sees it, and he knows it: the hollow eyes of the disconnected, the abandoned. The anger of being powerless. Being ripped from the known and thrust into the unknown. He sees it. He knows it. You can survive only by keeping all others at bay. The other boys at Meadowbrook had eyes like these, wary and suspicious. Trust was a concept completely removed from their short lives. Fed, watered, clothed, educated, but not cared for. Even among themselves, the bully hierarchy defined respect and demanded tribute, but friendship was rare.

"You don't have to try him. It's just too bad to have to send back an animal with such potential."

"Look, give me a chance. A couple of days. I can't make any promises, but I'll give it a shot."

"Okay. You got it." The trainer claps Keller on the back. "I take it you've worked with dogs before?"

Keller shrugs. "Nah. I just, well, I just think he needs a fair chance."

What Keller can't say, and really doesn't fully understand, is that there is something in this dog that recollects his own journey. Not since the day when he was five and his parents were killed when the Portland-to-Boston train collided with their stalled car, not since the day his aunts had abandoned him to reform school, not since the day his great-uncle Clayton Britt took him out and put him to work on the boat, has Keller felt connected to any living creature. Until now. Reflected in the dog's dark eyes, Keller sees himself.

Keller sits outside of the dog's kennel, a half-empty bowl of dog food beside him, the dog's intended dinner. He's been stationed here, alternately sitting with his back against the links or facing the dog, or most of the day. He's kept up a patter of conversation, as if the dog might actually be listening. He hasn't told him anything important, just nattered on about sports or how hot it is or about the way the guys in his barracks remind him of being in his old dormitory at Meadowbrook, except that there are no bars on the windows. "You got bars, don't you?"

Keller holds another chunk of meat in his fingers and thrusts them through the links as if he's trying to feed the bears at a zoo. This one drops a bare three inches from Keller. "Bars are pretty awful. If you don't want to be behind bars, you should be nice. At least nice to me." As he talks, he's been tossing bits of meat into the kennel, hoping to entice the dog to move toward him. It's as if the dog has some invisible force field around himself; he's only snatched the bits of meat that have landed within reach, and he hasn't looked the least bit grateful.

The dog, in a sphinxlike position, doesn't move, but his eyes go to the latest chunk of meat sitting beyond his force field, then back to Keller's face. He doesn't lick his lips, but he does pant. It is unmercifully hot, and Keller's uniform blouse is darkened with sweat. Without the mitigating sea breezes of his coastal upbringing, he really feels the heat and humidity. This Southern summer heat is oppressive for a boy from the more temperate clime of New England.

The only concession the dog makes to Keller's presence is allowing him to refill the water bowl with the hose aimed at it from the safety beyond the kennel. Anytime Keller has slipped open the latch, the dog has growled and retreated behind the doghouse, not like a dog in fear, but a dog who refuses to be near a human.

"I know that it's hard to trust a stranger. Hell, I don't trust people I know." Keller laughs, and for the first time the dog inches toward the piece of meat. "Your people, for some patriotic reason, decided that you needed to serve your country, and I believe that you will. But first you have to serve me."

The dog creeps another inch.

All Keller wants for today is that the dog not growl when he opens the kennel door. He's tried six times in the last six hours and he's almost ready to call it quits. His five fellow handlers have all had their first training session and he can see them out on the parade ground playing with their dogs. All he needs to say is "Give me another dog," and he can be out there with a canine companion who is willing to be his partner, instead of trying to be a lion tamer.

"Okay, Pax. Last time. I won't deny you your dinner, but it would be nice if you were a bit grateful for it." Keller flips the U-shaped latch. At the sound, the dog leaps to his feet, head low, ears back. "No, you're right. Why should you be grateful for something when you never asked to be in this situation. That's like me being grateful to

121

Clayton Britt every time he put creamed cod on the table. He had to feed me, and I guess I have to feed you." With that, Keller swings the gate open and steps in, bowl of horse meat held out as a potential barrier should the dog actually attack.

Pax doesn't. He sits. He watches closely as Keller lowers the tin bowl. The bowl sits right at Keller's feet. In order to get his dinner, the dog must approach the man. Neither one moves. Then Keller moves the bowl closer to the dog with his foot. The dog steps a foot closer to the bowl.

"So, that's how it's going to be?" Keller pushes the bowl halfway to the dog. The dog moves to halve the distance between himself and the tempting bowl of food. "Come on, Pax, come get your dinner. I sure want mine."

The dog isn't growling, and Keller takes this as a success. It's enough for today. He pushes the bowl directly under the dog's chin. By now, the sun-warmed meat is attracting flies and a bluebottle buzzes around the dog food in the bowl. Without even taking his eyes off Keller's face, the dog snaps and the fly disappears.

CHAPTER FOURTEEN

Pax was bewildered. Boxed, freighted, handled by strangers, then brought to this place of dogs to endure the relentless cacophony of the displaced. He had no idea what was happening, or why. All the dog knew was that he had no clear mandate, no orders. Francesca had clung to him and then ordered him into a crate. She'd asked and he'd willingly entered the crate, turned around, and watched quietly as a stranger fastened the door closed. The crate was lifted into the back of a truck and Pax couldn't see over the tailgate. Couldn't see that Francesca wasn't following. The rumble of the heavy engine obscured any sound that she might have been making, calling him back.

The crate went from truck to train, and back to a truck. The air was different here, warmer and filled with the scent of other dogs and men. Pax stood in his confinement and barked out a greeting. He was taken out of his crate and he wriggled with anticipation, so many men. Surely Rick was here; surely Francesca would appear to take his leash in her hand. A veterinarian examined him, patted him on the head, and handed the leash to yet another stranger. And then another stranger attached him to a doghouse and left him there with a full bowl. But neither Rick nor Francesca appeared.

During the long night, the cooler air dragging thousands of new scents to him, Pax lay awake and grieving. He understood it now: He'd been sent away. The only people he trusted had turned him out of the nest as if he were a weanling puppy being chased off by a newly pregnant mother.

The only recourse for his battered spirit was to resist. A growl, a show of teeth, a bite, and these unfamiliar men knew enough to back away. He would not capitulate. He would not wag his tail for that bowl of food; nor would he eat it if anyone watched. He would not submit to being touched and he snapped at the hand of the first person to try to touch him. Even without the sense of abandonment, Pax's nature wasn't open to strangers. He'd tolerated Rick's pals, always polite, but always aloof. Francesca had been the only other human to penetrate that singular devotion. Rick was gone and now she had sent him away, and these strangers thought that they could lay hands on him and make him do their will. Not once in his short life had Pax ever bitten anyone until he bit the arm of the second man to think he could dominate the unhappy dog. That's when they put him in this isolated kennel.

This third man came and simply waited for him. He sat beside the enclosure, talking quietly. He tossed bits of meat to him, but Pax disdained touching any that didn't fall close by. Wounded in spirit, the dog would not be seen accepting his gifts. He growled when the man stood and defiantly opened the gate to the kennel. Pax showed his teeth and the man gave him the win when he stepped back out of the enclosure. The man came back and did it again, and again Pax growled to warn him away. The man knew that he had the upper hand, however, because he still held the food bowl in his hands. The bits that had landed beside Pax were not enough to satisfy his hunger. The man sat back down, and the two considered each other, the wires of the cage separating them.

Pax lay still on the hard ground and studied this man sitting purposefully in front of him. Their eyes flicked over each other's forms, the dog reading the man's youth easily; the man comprehending the dog's simmering rage. The dog locked eyes with the man and recognized that he, too, was a solitary creature, not given to connection. When the man didn't look away, the dog knew that they were equals. The man, like the dog, would not submit. When he came into the enclosure one more time, the bowl held out like an offering, a thin suggestion of caution came from his skin, and Pax admired that. The man wasn't afraid of the dog, but he respected him. Pax let him push the bowl to him, although he didn't eat until this patient man walked away.

The next day, it was just the same. A bowl of breakfast, fresh and still smelling like food and not carrion. The heat that reflected off his coat drove him to pant, his jaws wide, tasting the scent of the man's sweat, a scent that was working its way into the dog's thoughts. It told the story of what he'd eaten, and that he'd had beer the night before. Pax breathed in deeply; the familiar odor reminded him of Rick, who always poured a little beer into a saucer for him. He loved the grainy taste, like eating some kinds of good grass. Rick had been gone for a long time. The scent of the beer on this persistent man's skin made Pax long for the companionship of those hot summer nights when Rick would come home after a game and tell Pax all about it.

Pax had protected Francesca, and acknowledged her as his responsibility, but while Rick was there, his heart was always his. Man and dog. A dignified and purposeful relationship of equals. But Rick was gone and Pax had no way of knowing if he'd ever come back. So much time had passed, and with it the expectation of reunion, that Pax had thrown his heart into Francesca's care. Taking care of her and being loved by her. And then she, too, was gone. Like his mother so many years ago, vanished.

Here was this new man, cautious and patient, not reaching out to touch, respectful and smelling delicately of last night's beer. As long as the dog had been isolated in this hot, humid, strange kennel, he hadn't slept deeply enough to be rested. Like his wolf antecedents, he was on a perpetual high alert, ready to defend himself, a captive. But an unlikely relaxation came over him on the third day of this man's unwanted companionship. Pax fell into a deep sleep, his body shaded by the doghouse, his sense of being threatened gone for the short time he slept.

Waking abruptly, he knew that the man

was still there. He raised his head, sniffed the air to gather in the man's now-familiar scent, and, satisfied, allowed himself to go back to sleep.

CHAPTER FIFTEEN

"We've got a lot more dogs. No sense wasting any more time with that one." The civilian trainer's name is Rod Barlow and he's been working with dogs, as he puts it, his whole life. A sturdy fifty or so, he says that he's encountered dogs like Pax before and if their people don't want him back, the best recourse is to put them down. In this case, though, sending the dog home is the best option, and his donor has made it clear that if he fails, he goes home. Lots of dogs have bombed out of the program; Pax is just the first to bomb out because of aggression.

"One more day, I promise. I won't waste any more time. Just give me that." Keller doesn't know why he's being so stubborn about this. It's not like the dog is giving him any notion of a breakthrough; and, in all his life, Keller has certainly never been one to embrace personal challenges. Meadowbrook taught him about finding the easy way out. Clayton taught him that hard work does hurt. Besides, he's falling behind his cohorts, as they have already mastered teaching their dogs to sit, heel, and come. At this rate, even if he gets Pax to cooperate, they'll end up in the next group and his new pals will be assigned and gone.

Pax doesn't know that he's about to get sent home. He has no sense of failure, so why should Keller care? His buddies are already teasing him about his stubborn belief that the big shepherd will make a great war dog.

Keller stands in front of the fence with Pax's breakfast bowl. He's already decided that he's not going to spend the day waiting for this mess of horse meat and kibble to stink. He's going to go in, feed the dog, and if he growls, Keller will call it quits.

"Okay, Pax. Here's your breakfast. I'm coming in and you're going to let me." Keller lifts the U-shaped latch and steps into the kennel as if he expects a happy greeting, not a bite. He doesn't move slowly, just deliberately. He sets the bowl down and picks up the empty water bowl. "You must be pretty thirsty. Hang on." He refills the water bowl and places it beside the untouched food bowl. All this time, the dog has been standing, A-frame ears at attention, panting softly, but not growling. Keller doesn't move away from the food and water. "You want it, you gotta get past me."

There is a slight shift in the air, a barely discernible breeze that touches the back of Keller's neck, evaporating the line of early-morning sweat trickling down into his collar, and he shivers. The dog raises his nose to the air. Keller squats, snaps his fingers. The dog eyes him, and for a moment Keller feels like prey, until the dog's big ears fold back gently and the "at attention" look recedes into "at ease." "Good boy. Come on, Pax."

Keller stretches out his fingers and the dog stretches out his nose. The soft, hot breath of the dog travels up his hand and along his arm to the elbow, then to his crotch. He tells himself, This is how dogs behave; don't move. Pax continues his olfactory investigation against Keller's bent knees and, finally, to his neck and then his face. Keller's thighs are screaming at this point and he goes to his knees. He keeps both hands open and to his sides. He makes no move to touch the dog.

Suddenly, it seems like the dog is satisfied with Keller, as if he's passed some canine test of character and the dog has decided that he is sufficiently harmless. The dog walks past Keller to his food, which he bolts, then empties the water bowl. Keller stays on his knees, remaining at the dog's eye level. It isn't enough to feed the dog; he needs to leash him and take him out of the kennel. He needs the dog to be willing to be touched.

"This is your last chance, Pax. You'll get a dishonorable discharge if you don't co-operate with me. You don't want that, do you? Sent home in shame? You've got too much pride for that, don't you? I know what it's like for your family not to want you. I know how mean people can be. I do. So I know how hard this must be. No one can tell you that you're more valuable to the U.S. government than you are to your fam-ily. Maybe they didn't want you anyway, and this is a better option than some others. Maybe you scare them, too. I don't know. Maybe you were a burden to them. Are they poor? Are you yet another mouth to feed? The army will keep you fed; I can promise you that. I'm still eating a lot of chipped beef, but I can't complain. I'm still getting a lot of orders and sleeping in a roomful of men again, but I'm not complaining. At least I get a paycheck. At least I get some respect. You will, too. You work with me, boy, and we'll be top dogs in this outfit. You and me against the Nazis." He keeps talking and the dog begins to visibly relax.

"Did you have a cruel master? Someone who put the viciousness into you with a beating? That happens. I've seen that, too. Too many blows with the strap doesn't teach a boy to be good; it teaches him to hate."

Pax is still standing, but now he's standing beside Keller. Keller offers his right hand again to the dog. Pax sniffs, then lowers his head; his eyes turn away, and Keller takes that as permission. He scratches under the dog's chin, then runs his hand up to his skull. He strokes the ears down to his neck. Beneath his hand, the dog tenses up; Keller can feel the muscles in his shoulders harden. He pulls his hand away. The dog swings his big head up and sniffs Keller's face again. It takes a lot of nerve to remain perfectly still this close to the dog's teeth, but Keller knows that he has to pass some kind of test with this animal, and showing fear won't help him.

Pax sits in front of Keller. There is no longer any feral hostility in Pax's expression. He is panting, and it looks more like grinning than a hostile show of teeth. Suddenly, he yawns, a great gaping and wholly benign action. Keller reaches out again, and this time the dog raises one big paw and sets it in Keller's hand. The dog sighs, a sound less of capitulation than of relief.

Keller has never been in love, but he's pretty sure it can't hold a candle to the feeling he has as he and his one-man dog work together. Now that he's accepted Keller — and only Keller — as his leader, the dog responds to training with a joyous enthusiasm, as if it's all a game. They breeze through the basic obedience exercises: sit, heel, down, stay. They quickly catch up to Keller's pals, and he and Pax are now fully engaged in the training that will eventually determine their assignments: scout, casualty dog, messenger, or sentry.

Pax can scale walls, crawl on his belly as if under fire, sniff out a hidden "enemy," and stay put like a sculpture when asked. One of the two most difficult and make-or-break accomplishments is to ride happily in the back of the troop truck, which, surprisingly, several of the farm-raised dogs have failed. That seemingly ordinary test is frightening to them because they've never before been given the opportunity to do it. Pax bounds into the truck and acts like he expects to drive.

The second, and even more critical, test is

to stand under small-arms fire without flinching. This one, Keller has worried most about, but here again, Pax stands his ground and tolerates the noise of a sergeant firing beside them, even as he folds his ears back. His expression is one of dislike, but not fear.

Pax can leap a three-foot hurdle as if he's got a springboard under him and scale a seven-foot solid wall like a champ. Keller puts him into an off-leash long down and walks away. After a time, he signals to the dog to come. Just as the dog hits the midway point, Keller abruptly signals a new command and the dog instantly flattens himself against the ground. As if he's under fire, Pax crawls to where Keller squats waiting for him.

Rod Barlow nods at Keller. "Good work."

Keller finds himself flushed with pleasure. *Good work.* It's as if a craving has been satisfied. A craving he was unaware of having. He keeps his head down as he praises his dog. *Good work.*

Keller hasn't written to Clayton at all since he left for induction, has never planned to write to the old man. And certainly he hasn't received any letters from his uncle. But he's filled with the helium of praise and he needs to share it. No, he won't write to Clayton, but there is someone else he can share this unexpected happiness with.

Dear Miss Jacobs,
I am well and I hope that you are, too. I want to let you know that I'm on my way overseas soon. I am a dog handler in the K-9 Corps and my dog is named Pax (which I remember you teaching me means "peace".) We're assigned to be scouts, which means we'll make sure that the way is safe ahead for our troops. Because I did so well, they asked me if I'd stay on here as an instructor, but I said no thanks. I can't imagine not being with Pax after all the training we've done together. I trained him and I want to be with him over there. Pax is a big dog, mostly German shepherd, and really handsome. We work really well together and it's not like work at all, but fun. You'd be surprised at what we can do. He's the best thing to have happened to me. If you saw him, you'd understand.

Keller isn't quite sure how to end this very first letter he's ever written.

Not much else to say. Keep well and don't let those rowdy students give you trouble. They'll have to deal with me if they do. Your friend, Keller Nicholson

He examines the page for handwriting flaws and, finding none, folds the page and slips it into an envelope and addresses it to Miss Ruth Jacobs, care of the high school. It seems too impertinent to send it to her house in Hawke's Cove, although he knows where she lives — in a small house with blue shutters and a well-trimmed hedge. Slipping the letter into his pocket, Keller nudges Pax, who's sleeping the sleep of the well exercised. "Go for a walk?"

Before the last word is out of Keller's mouth, the dog is on his feet and waiting for the command to heel, ready for anything.

CHAPTER SIXTEEN

Pax is off leash, his flat leather working collar is fastened on, and his attention is riveted to the woods opposite. He is telling them in no uncertain terms that the enemy is there. Keller flags his squad and they take cover behind pines and oaks. There is no sound, and Pax understands that this means the enemy is aware of them, too. Everyone is keeping deathly still.

At Keller's signal, Pax has flattened himself against the ground and is about ten feet in front of Keller and the platoon. His ears are pricked and his nose works the air. He hears what the men cannot, the susurration of living breath in nervous men. He can smell what they cannot, the sweat of unwashed and exhausted men. Pax can tell, too, just how many of the enemy lie behind the trees on the opposite side of the rough circle of woodlot. If he could, he'd tell them there are only five to your seven, and one of those is wounded. But he's capable only of warning his platoon, not comforting them.

Their platoon leader signals for his six men to split up, half to circle to the left, the other three, Keller included, to move to the right of the woodlot. Keller nods and then signals to Pax to slowly move back to his side. Like his feral ancestors, Pax understands the exercise. To him, this is his pack. They are hunting. Race memory excites the dog, but his human training keeps him in complete focus on his man, his pack leader, just as, in the wild, he'd be focused on the alpha dog, unquestioning of his leader's orders. They are circling their prey, trapping it within the confines of their numbers. Pax becomes rigid, his very skin tense with the need for soundless movement, his muscles hardened with the exertion of moving like liquid. In moments, he is back at Keller's side; only the slight touch of his nose against Keller's hand breaks the discipline of the hunt.

Pax has become a dog with purpose. As much as living with Rick and Francesca had been rewarding, and comfortable, this life with Keller has hardened him into what his nature meant for him to be. A hunter. A guardian. A pack member with a job. Even when his feet are sore from the miles of hard terrain, his belly growling in anticipation of a battle-delayed dinner, his thirst barely slaked with the shared contents of Keller's canteen lapped out of his helmet, Pax is happy. Bivouacked in bombed-out cellars, or in the field, or against the crumbled walls of a village, Pax presses his long body against Keller's, settling his muzzle against his partner's neck, keeping them both warm. Like littermates, they play and eat and sleep and work in constant companionship, excluding all others. Their exclusivity suits Pax; he has only Keller to worry about. The others may surround them, and Keller interacts with them in their human language, but touch and comfort and food and grooming come only from Keller.

Pax loves his work, his purpose, and he has come to love Keller for giving it to him.

Now Pax alerts his pack to the presence of the enemy. The game is on.

CHAPTER SEVENTEEN

It's been more than a year, but Keller has lost track of time. It seems like he and Pax have been together forever, been in this war all their lives. They've seen action in Italy and in Morocco. Now they're back in Italy as the rumblings of a major offensive can be felt. They've come a long way since those first few months, when he and Pax were viewed with suspicion at best and considered a waste of space and supplies at worst. Until Pax alerted him to the sniper barely visible in the bell tower of a village church. The dog's clear warning got the squad out of harm's way, and Big Sully, the most vocal skeptic regarding the usefulness of a war dog, took the sniper out.

After that, Keller and Pax were welcomed any time they showed up, ready to make the way safe for the squad or the platoon or the division. Everyone wanted to pet Pax, or feed him scraps, but Keller and the authority vested in him by the K-9 Corps strictly forbade such overtures. Pax is a one-man dog, he told them. One man's partner. His.

Another night patrol. Each patrol has the same purpose — to seek out the hidden enemy and get him before he can get them, and there is a certain rhythm to it, a dance of hide-and-seek. The dog is in his point position a few feet in front of Keller. The rest of the squad is fanned out behind the man and dog. As always, they are aware of the intensity of their task and the certainty that they will succeed.

They move, knowing that every step they take is fraught with the potential to reveal their presence to the enemy before they can locate him. For those who have been in this squad for more than a day, they are certain that the dog will give them the edge over that unseen enemy. He is their good-luck charm, their guardian angel. A quarter mile, a half, and the dog will freeze; no statue was ever as immobile and yet so expressive. Like a bird dog, he'll point out the machine-gun nest or the sniper. They'll protect their flank, fire, lob a grenade or two. Maybe take a prisoner, maybe simply pull the fallen enemies' Nazi-version of dog tags from beneath blood-saturated shirts and put them into slack-jawed mouths. Someone will come and claim these dead. Then, the signal to the platoon that the way is safe. Pax has made the way safe. They have become complacent.

The first shots ring out over their heads. The next round comes closer and the members of Keller's platoon fire their weapons toward the covert, where the Nazis lean around the trunks of pine trees and fire back at them. The veiled moon breaks free of its gauzy web and casts a silvery light down on the woodlot, filtering through the trees and giving shape to the dozen men engaged in this skirmish for possession of land none of them wants.

A bullet whizzes past Keller's ear and splits the thin sapling behind him. Even before his mind can register the nearness of that bullet, Keller is on his belly, crawling through the pine needles in the direction that every sensible bone in his body is telling him is wrong. Pax is beside him, slinking silently along the pine needle–strewn ground. Keller fires again, aiming at shapes, at the firefly flicker of rifle fire. He knows that every time he discharges his weapon, he, too, is betraying his position. The cross fire intensifies.

Keller is hit; the violence of the bullet

throws him backward. He fights the pain and the insult; fights against panic. He is face up in the pine needles. Pax is beside him, whining and grasping at Keller's tunic with his teeth as if he could pull him to his feet. Voices fill the night, loud now, orders shouted in two languages; more gunfire and then the crash of boots pounding through the woods — whether running away or chasing, he can't know.

Keller stares up at a patch of starry sky no bigger than a handkerchief, visible between the trees. He misses the clear open sky above the cove, the stars and the constellations pinned to the velvet of a pure winter night. Pax stands over him, panting, growling. Keller feels the blood seeping out, touches the place with one hand and holds it up to the unfiltered moonlight. Pax licks that hand. Pain blurs his senses, blinding him to everything but the white-hot pain. He feels himself losing consciousness and fights it. He's got to make sure, make sure of something, but he can't recall what it is. Is he late for school? Is he out on the water, his boat wallowing against a beam sea? Is he impaled on the spear-point finial of the wrought-iron fence surrounding Meadowbrook?

Keller hears voices coming closer, thick

with the incomprehensible speech of the enemy. His dog growls, a throaty savage sound, feral. Pax's blood lullaby. But the voices don't move away; they grow louder, closer. The growl becomes a snarl. Keller struggles to open his eyes, struggles to his knees and claws the ground for his rifle. He sways a little, and his rifle feels ten times heavier than it did. He can't quite get the muzzle up to point it at the Kraut who is coming at him, a trick of the moonlight making the blade edge of the German's fixed bayonet glint.

With a sound more roar than growl, Pax flies through the air.

Keller can close his eyes; his dog will keep him safe. The velvet darkness of oblivion takes Keller away.

"Pax? Where's my dog?"

"Nicholson, just take it easy."

"Where is he?"

The medic is fiddling around with a syringe, tapping it with a dirt-rimmed fingernail.

"Is he all right? Was he hurt?"

"I have no idea." The medic presses a fresh compress on the bullet hole in Keller's left shoulder.

"He won't eat. He's trained not to take

food from anyone."

"That's not my problem. My problem is that I've got to evac you to a field hospital and I don't have room on the transport."

"Not without Pax."

"Without Pax."

Keller struggles against the soporific and lovely effects of the morphine that the medic has just injected into his arm. "Get him. Please."

The medic doesn't respond, and as the arms of Morpheus descend, Keller whispers Pax's name over and over, terrified that the medic is lying to him.

CHAPTER EIGHTEEN

The hot scent of his partner's blood explodes in Pax's nostrils; the scent of being quarry, not hunter. As the shooter charges, bayonet fixed, Pax vaults from a standstill and knocks the German to the ground. He is trained to hold a prisoner in any fashion he can, and he holds this one down with the weight of his body and the tensile strength of his jaw, ignoring the man's screams and flailing. He overpowers this sinner, expecting that Keller will point his weapon and call him off. He doesn't, and the mingle of human voices in the woods grow closer, angrier, louder, and gunfire spits from every direction. Pax ignores it and keeps his jaw locked on the fallen enemy's arm, penetrating through the wool to the skin, muscle, and bone. He bears down; this is the man who hurt Keller.

So consumed in defending his partner, Pax doesn't hear the sound of the shot,

doesn't feel the penetration of the first bullet. The second shot takes him down.

Chapter Nineteen

Keller opens his eyes, to see Big Sully looking down at him. Roger Sullivan, late of South Boston, is the one guy Keller knows will tell him the truth about Pax. "Is he dead?"

"See for yourself."

Keller is suddenly beneath a mound of wriggling dog. Sully helps hoist Keller upright so that he's neither crushed beneath the weight of the dog nor his shoulder wound reopened by the vigorous reunion. "Pax. Pax. What did they do to you, boy?" A slightly grungy white bandage is wrapped around the dog's middle and a thin line of missing fur mars the perfection of his skull.

"Bastards shot him, but he was moving so fast, they only grazed him. You should see what he did to them. When we got there, they were gabbling like they'd found themselves faced with a werewolf. Practically asked us to take them prisoner."

Keller recognizes bullshit when he hears it, but he's grateful to Sully for lying to him. "Thanks for taking care of him."

"Medics did a good job. He's a grunt like the rest of us, but nothing but the best for him." Sully is quiet for a moment, his usual glibness put away. He looks tired, as they all do. Maybe even a little discouraged. "Look, we lost Carson. Almost lost you."

"I'm sorry about Carson. He was a good kid."

Sully runs a hand down the length of the dog's back. Keller doesn't say anything; for sure, Sully deserves to break the rules. "Nicholson, your dog saved you. That Kraut would have finished you off if Pax hadn't attacked him. He's a lucky dog, but so are you."

Sully gives Pax one more forbidden pat and leaves Keller and his dog to rest.

"If anything had happened to you . . ." Keller cannot complete the whispered thought. His relief in having Pax here, alive and hogging the cot, brings hot tears to his eyes. Keller hasn't wept since he was a little boy, not since his first night at Meadowbrook, a thrown-away child, alone and confused.

This dog is his family. And the only other thing as frightening to Keller as having Pax killed, is the fact that, at the end of this endless war, Pax will go home to his real family. And Keller will be, once again, all alone.

CHAPTER TWENTY

"I had your baseball card. Still do if my mom hasn't chucked out all my stuff." The private is a skinny kid from Lowell, all freckles and brown hair so thin that his scalp shows through his buzz cut as if he didn't have any hair at all.

"This war goes on much longer, that may be the only baseball card with my picture on it, so you'd better hope she hasn't thrown it out. It'll be a rare one." Rick runs a cleaning cloth over the barrel of his carbine, a gesture faintly reminiscent of rubbing pine tar on his bat. The wind is picking up the higher up they go in the mountains and he's glad that it's summer, not winter; that's for the mountain troops, not him. Rick is squad leader, and it's his job to get this bunch of kids up and over the mountain to join their armored division as it collects these strung-out groups of five or six infantrymen slowly making their way along the narrow mountain trail. Sometimes the trail takes them into the woods; sometimes it leads them up toward the sky. Sometimes, like now, it meanders along a series of ledges, wide enough for only one at a time to pass. Above them, already ensconced, the German army. At midday, Rick could hear the sound of artillery bouncing off the other side of the mountain, the vertical assault beginning.

"You had good stats that last summer you played." The kid is still chattering about ancient history. He won't admit it, but Rick is flattered by the kid's interest. Baseball was a lifetime ago. He's even lost track of how the Braves are doing, struggling to field a decent team with old-timers and the increasingly rare player with a high draft number and no qualms about not enlisting. Sometimes Rick wonders if he's still got it, his arm. He's muscled up, that's for sure, but does he still have the distance? The ability to put a small spherical object into an invisible box exactly where he wants it? It took years to develop that skill, and now it's been years since he's really used it, the little intersquad pickup games notwithstanding. He never throws his good stuff at amateurs; that would be like throwing a smokin' fastball at a Little Leaguer.

"Okay, everybody up. Let's move." Rick puts an end to the conversation.

The ledge trail is like a ruffle along the bald side of the Italian mountain, dipping in and out as the contour of the hillside folds in on itself, then bells outward. There is a stark beauty to the view, looking down on the green of vegetation, up at the azure sky. Lone pine trees cling to the hillside, tenacious and scrawny.

When they finally meet up with their division, Rick is hoping that he'll find a few letters waiting for him from Francesca. No, he knows that he will; she's a faithful correspondent. Through her letters, he feels like he is there for every little bit of her day, from her distaste for chicory coffee to the gossip at the wire factory. He knows that, so far, her cousin Sid is all right, and her brothers, too. She has no news for him about Pax. Pax has been in this war for more than a year, almost two. The only thing they know is that if anything had happened to him, they would have been informed. So, as he writes in his letters back, no news is good news. Their dog is doing his duty, his bit. Secretly, Rick wonders how long before this streak of good luck will run out for those Francesca loves. Five loved ones in a war is not good odds. What talisman does she keep in order that they remain safe? As a ballplayer, Rick has seen plenty of superstitions acted out before every game: the same socks, turning three times around before leaving the locker room, never letting a wife say "good luck" before a game. His own game-day nod to Lady Luck was to slip a few dog hairs into his cap. Whatever other superstitious belief she might have, Rick knows that for Francesca, it's mostly just prayer.

The trail rises and falls, rises again. The rocky hillside becomes sheer cliff, a hardened wall they keep to their right as the trail once again puts them on a narrow ledge. Rick wants to hurry his men through this all-too-exposed place.

It's the skinny kid from Lowell who falls first, victim to a clean shot from the precipice above them. The rest hit the ground, crab-crawling their way to the relative safety of the rock wall, keeping arms and legs close so that the Germans have nothing to aim at from above. Rick cranes his neck to see what their options are. The next squad will arrive in no less than half an hour. To retreat from this narrow ledge will open them up as targets as surely as moving ahead would. They are pinned down.

Rick fingers a grenade dangling from his

belt, unclips it. The rock face is maybe thirty feet high and angles back slightly. Baseball is geometry. He's fired a ground-ball hit to the pitcher farther than that to get the double play. Slowly, Rick, keeping his back to the rock face, stands up. He has the grenade in his hand, and he tosses it gently, as if waiting for the catcher's signs. He briefly wishes that he were a left-handed pitcher; this toss would be easier if he were. But he's not. He's a strong righty, accurate and unhittable. Rick pulls the pin, steps away from the rock face, and fires the grenade, putting just enough arc in it that the explosive should curve right into the Germans.

Instead of diving back against the safety of the wall, Rick waits, watching in horror as the grenade, subject to the immutable laws of gravity, falls back toward him, where it will blow them all off this ledge.

As if he's watching a flyball coming his way, Rick instinctively reaches up to catch it.

■ ■ ■ ■

PART TWO:
1946–1947

■ ■ ■ ■

CHAPTER TWENTY-ONE

"Come in." I held back the screen door to let Keller Nicholson and our dog, Pax, into our house. I felt nearly faint with relief at the sight of him, the dog. Our dog. Even before Keller Nicholson had gotten out of the mud-spattered car he and Pax arrived in, I was out of the house and down the walk to pull the passenger door open and release Pax into my arms.

When Pax didn't jump out, but looked to Nicholson for orders, I felt wounded. Snubbed.

"It's okay, Pax. At ease, boy." And with that, Pax bowled into me, licking my face and wagging his tail so hard, he nearly took himself off his feet.

"Ma'am, before we go in, there's something I'd like to say." He didn't step one foot over the sill, although Pax straddled it, forelegs in the house, hind legs still beside Keller.

"Rick has been waiting. He's been waiting for this dog a long, long time. Please come in."

"Mrs. Stanton, I want to keep him. I can't imagine life without him."

That froze me to my spot. How dare he say such a thing to me? "I guess that you'll have to try."

The litany of our prayers to keep them safe were intoned with fervent belief Sunday after Sunday, and still our boys died, or came back, like Rick, wounded, changed forever, their spirits crushed.

They found me at the wire factory, those crisply uniformed harbingers of disaster. Bright young men, charged with the unforgiveable duty of informing family members of their soldier's change of status from unharmed and alive to wounded or lost or dead. As if, in the formality of their words and posture, you might respond less emotionally to the news that your husband, who once wanted only to play ball in the big leagues, is now grievously wounded and simply to survive will be as close as he will ever get to living his dream; that your response will be contained by the choreographed manner in which these boys dressed as men have regretfully informed you that your life is never going to be the same.

My supervisor didn't send anyone for me; he came himself, taking me back to his office, where the soldiers waited, their white-gloved hands behind their backs, their caps tucked precisely under their arms; the weight of their duty not bowing them, but keeping them upright. Mr. Towne had also beckoned my pal Barbara, who shared a spot on the line with me. Maybe he felt that I needed to have a woman there. That I would behave with womanly weakness.

Seeing them, expecting the worst, it didn't quite penetrate when, instead of informing me of Rick's death, they told me he was wounded, and suddenly not in Europe, but in England. I think that Mr. Towne caught me as my knees buckled and slid a chair beneath me. "Rick is in England; that's wonderful news. He's out of it." I started to laugh. Whatever had happened, he'd be fine. He was in England. He was alive. These crisp young men had said so.

Barbara finally got my attention, shaking me out of my hysterical euphoria. "Francesca, he's seriously wounded. You understand that, don't you?"

"I just know that he's still alive."

Barbara took my hands in hers. Her nails were freshly painted, a bright bloodred, at complete odds with our factory work.

"They've given you a telephone number. They don't know any more than what they've told you; you need to make that call."

The two soldiers bearing bad tidings were clearly waiting for some sort of civilian dismissal from me. Mr. Towne kept a hand under my elbow and I stood up. "Thank you."

The pair made a stiff about-face, one fell in behind the other, and they left the office, moving on to deliver more bad news to other families whose lives would be forever changed.

Keller Nicholson leaned his back against the screen door, keeping it open, neither entering my house nor leaving it. The dog was sniffing the air, his tail beating a rhythm against the copper screening. He danced on his front legs. He knew that beyond the hallway of this new house lay his man, the man who had always been Pax's one true master.

I hadn't told Rick that Pax was coming home until I was absolutely certain. I had no desire to get his fractured hopes up, only to find out that Pax hadn't survived, or, maybe worse, hadn't been able to be rehabilitated from war dog back to pet dog. If that had been the case, I think I would have gone to wherever they had taken him and stolen him back. If he'd changed from the loving, tractable dog we'd known three years ago into something else, something the army called "unsuitable for home placement," I would still have wanted him for Rick. Rick had lost so much, I just couldn't bear it if the dog was lost to him, too. With every week that went by postwar when Pax's status was unknown, Rick lost ground in his own rehabilitation. And then, after an eternity that was reminiscent of the eternity I'd waited for Rick to come home, we got word that Pax was safe and doing well in the retraining program. He could come home. It was the first genuine smile I'd had from Rick since the day he was returned to me.

"Let him go."

Keller bent and unclipped the leash from Pax's collar. The dog stayed where he was. He was still connected to his handler, unused to thinking for himself.

"Send him."

"Pax, go ahead." Keller's words held no command in them. They might have been nonsense syllables, meaningless drivel.

Pax looked at Keller, as if he, too, hadn't understood the softly spoken words. He wanted clarification. In that almost human desire for clarity, I could see how close these two must have been in the battlefield, dependent one upon the other for their lives. One misunderstanding and everything would go horribly wrong. The dog eyed Keller and waited for some better instruction. Even as his eyes studied Keller, his nose twitched, and I could see that the distraction of what he surely knew lay at the end of this short hallway was tantalizing him. So close to his beloved Rick, one command away from reunion.

"Pax. Go to him."

The dog's trot was soundless along the runner that led from the front door to the room that Rick occupied. Keller and I didn't follow, but waited in an awkward silence, which I finally broke. "Come meet him."

CHAPTER TWENTY-TWO

Pax ambled down the corridor to a room where the door was not quite shut. He nosed it open, already certain that behind that door was the person he'd once been adhered to. It had been a long time ago, and the memory of that person was as faded as the dreams that he'd dreamed when opportunity gave him a chance to enter deepest sleep. But the scent had remained imprinted in his memory. A scent he would never have forgotten and one that he would have been able to discern among a thousand others. Keller was his present, and the bond he had with him was soldier-deep. If he had once trusted Rick with his daily requirement of food and exercise and play and affection, with Keller he had survived when others had not. It had been an atavistic existence, surviving by wit and by clan. Pax had acknowledged Keller as leader; Keller had depended on Pax to hunt and to defend.

This recognizable skin scent was overshadowed but not obscured by the other odors of this human body, urine and seeping fluids. A rotting that informed the dog that this human, this scent that he remembered in the same way he remembered his mother's, was not exactly like the man he had longed for until Keller came into his life. And then Rick spoke and all the strangeness fell away. Saying his name like breathing a prayer out loud: *Pax.* Out of this mouth, the word that had been the first word Pax had ever recognized for its true value sounded so different to his sensitive ears. It was as if, when identified by Rick's "Pax," he was a different creature from the one that Keller called Pax. Gentleness and play versus the serious business of war.

The big dog instinctively knew better than to throw himself into the arms of the man in the chair. He sat, then quietly lowered his head to Rick's lap. One hand stroked his head. The other, truncated and bound in a white gauze sleeve, lingered over the dog's head. The dog sighed. He didn't have the capacity to wonder how it was that, after all this time, after being sent away, after being befriended and given a purpose, after months in constant danger and after being solely Keller's own, he was here, in this strange house, with his head in the lap of his once and beloved master.

Rick was weeping into his fur, and Pax didn't know what to do to help. He'd never known Rick to be unhappy. His entire experience of Rick was one of optimism and joy. This casualty — for that's what he smelled like to a dog who had spent a lot of time behind the front lines of the battlefield — confused him, and he had only one option. He pressed himself deeper into Rick's lap, until only his hind legs remained on the floor. He whined, a guttural assurance that whatever it was, he would fix it. He would make it stop. The hand gripped the nape of the dog's neck, and Pax was filled with grief for his long-gone mother, who held him just so. Finally, Rick lifted his head and batted the tears away. "Good dog, Pax. You have no idea how much I've missed you. My good dog. Thank God you made it."

Words instead of tears were a good thing. Pax pushed himself off Rick and sat, his tail still swishing against the floor, his jaws open with the excitement of reunion, and his eyes on Rick's face. His ears, though, were turned back, listening for Keller.

CHAPTER TWENTY-THREE

Keller really doesn't want to meet this Rick Stanton, this other claimant to Pax's loyalty. It was easier for him to have no face to imagine, no wheelchair-bound casualty of the same war he and Pax had emerged from intact. After nearly half a year in Germany with the occupation forces, Keller and Pax had finally accumulated the points needed for redeployment back to the United States. Keller had taken the dog to the retraining center and convinced the authorities that he should be the one to work with Pax. His excellent record of dog handling, and the earlier recommendation that he stay at the Front Royal Dog Training and Reception Center as a trainer worked in his favor and he was granted his wish. Besides his own dog, Keller was assigned to work with other dogs there for rehabilitation. Lots of play-time, lots of long, sauntering walks, no full-body crawl, no hunting down the enemy, no small-arms fire, no aggression against strangers. Keller was amazed at how these animals adapted to new circumstances, as if able to compartmentalize everything they had learned earlier. Better than some veterans he knew, who woke in the night in a sweat and had no tolerance for noise.

Keller had expected that the hardest thing for Pax would be to accept being touched or handled by others, to revert from being his one-man-dog to a dog it was safe for anyone to be around. He was a little disappointed at how easily Pax slid from war dog to pet. If Pax had retained his hostility to strangers, he might have been rejected for rehoming. And it would have been so easy to take him for himself. But Pax, surprisingly, seemed to understand that the threats and dangers he'd been trained to locate no longer existed. The edict came down: His people wanted him and he was rehabilitated. Discharged with honor from the U.S. Army, Pax needed to go home.

When Francesca had written that it would be impossible to leave her husband to collect the dog, Keller, on the verge of his own honorable discharge, volunteered to deliver the dog to the Stantons. Lucky for Keller, Rod Barlow was still involved, and he got the CO to agree to let Keller make the trip, highly unusual as it was. The CO was no fool; he knew that Keller was too attached to this Dogs For Defense volunteer. "Go, but don't think for one minute that they'll change their minds."

"I won't. I don't." But he'd rehearsed his plea aloud all the way from the retraining center. *I really think that the best thing for this dog is to remain with me. I'm thinking about joining the police force, and he'd make a great police dog. He's too well trained to be a pet dog again. He needs stimulation. He needs. I need. I can't let him go.*

Every mile of the journey from Virginia to Massachusetts, Keller fought against the temptation to simply change routes and disappear into the vast country that he and his comrades had defended. Only feeble honor kept Keller from doing it.

"Come meet my husband." Francesca steps into the hallway and Keller, empty leash in his hand, has no other choice but to go into the house and follow her down the corridor to the room where Pax has gone, his nose and ears homing in on his target precisely like they honed in on the enemy.

The room has been converted from a den into a hospital room. The drapes look less like something meant for a quiet retreat and more like a remnant of the blackout rules, heavy and drawn against the late-afternoon sun. On one wall, built-in shelving above a cupboard holds a set of encyclopedias and a tattered dictionary, but the rest of the room is furnished with the antiseptic materiel of illness and barren of homely comfort. Stateside, Keller has visited many a wounded friend, and this room smells as if it is inside a VA hospital, not inside a modest home in a neighborhood in peacetime America.

"Sir." Keller extends his hand and then balks, impulsively throwing up a salute as if belatedly realizing that Stanton's battlefield promotion was to staff sergeant. He feels foolish; both of them are civilians now, all honors and ranks behind them. The salute was meant only to compensate for the fact that Rick Stanton wouldn't be shaking hands ever again.

Stanton says nothing. Not looking at either Keller or his wife, he is focused entirely on the dog.

"Darling, Corporal Nicholson brought Pax back to us." Francesca's tone is cajoling, and Keller feels slightly embarrassed for her. Stanton continues to ignore them both.

The room is so still that Keller can hear

the tinny sound of a radio playing in another house and, from a tree in the backyard, a raucous jay warning off a crow.

"Sir, I asked your wife —"

"Don't." Her tone isn't cajoling now; it is razor-sharp and a warning. She shifts her shoulders back, deflecting his attempt to ask that her husband give up the only thing he loves.

Which means that he is the one who must give up Pax.

Rick Stanton finally looks at him. "Nicholson. Thank you."

"He's one in a million, sir." He's going to be unmanned if he doesn't leave this room right now. He needs to turn around and walk out of this house and get into the secondhand car he's bought with his savings and drive away. He needs to figure out what to do with the rest of his life. But Keller remains where he is, waiting for dismissal. Waiting for the moment when he'll have the strength to leave behind the only creature that he's ever loved, and that, he's certain, has ever loved him. A bitterness fills his mouth like a suffocating lump, forcing him to swallow, leaving him speechless. Only once has he ever felt this kind of pain, and to equate the death of one's parents with the return of a dog to its rightful owners seems wrongheaded, but that's how Keller feels. His parents are shadowy figures, remembered only vaguely; this dog has been by his side every moment for three years. What they have endured together isn't something that time will diminish. Privation, danger, terror, and courage. These will not fade.

"Corporal Nicholson, can I offer you something? A cup of coffee? You must be hungry; it's well after lunchtime." Francesca puts a hand on his arm, gives it a slight tug. She wants him out of here before he can say anything more.

"We ate on the road. We're fine." *We.*

"All right. Thank you again," she says, the hostess ready for the party to end.

"The thing is, he's my dog." The words come, flavored by the bitterness he feels.

Pax lifts his head from Rick's lap. He casts a sideways glance at Keller, then back to Francesca. His tail is no longer wagging. Rick's hand slips to hold the dog's collar, as if he's afraid Keller will order the dog away and the dog will go. But Keller has no stomach for a heartless demonstration of loyalty that he and Pax would inflict on this couple. And, right now, he's not sure that Pax would obey him. The dog looks like he's found heaven in Rick Stanton's immobile lap.

Francesca suddenly puts herself between Keller and Stanton. Her green eyes fix on him, her hand rises, and she points a finger at him. "No. Pax is our dog. Rick's dog. That was the agreement. We are very grateful to you for keeping him safe, but you need to leave."

"Wait." Rick pushes himself against the back of the wheelchair, sitting fully upright. For the first time, Keller notices that one side of his face bears the smooth scars of healed burns. His right ear is twisted, as if it had partially melted. "Fran, would you mind leaving us alone for a moment?"

She drops her hand, and her shoulders shift again. She steps away. "Fine. I'll be in the kitchen."

Stanton lets go of the dog's collar. "Why don't you take Pax out? As you say, it was a long trip, and I'm sure he needs to go. Right, Nicholson?"

Keller nods.

"Pax, come."

All three wait to see if the dog will obey her. The dog looks from man to man.

"Go ahead, Pax." Rick and Keller speak together and the dog follows Francesca out of the room.

Chapter Twenty-Four

Sometimes, in the last few seconds of sleep, when the night's dreamscape still feels real, Rick Stanton can forget that he is no longer the man whose waking dreams had come very close to being fulfilled. He wakes always to the truth that his once-within-grasp dreams are now and forever reduced to memories. Memories of almost succeeding. Of not quite. Close but forever just out of reach.

Not just the dream of pitching in the majors but all the rest of what he had wanted — expected — to achieve in his life. He made it to the majors, and would have been in the starting rotation the spring after the war. He married a beautiful woman, and he would have treated her to a good life, a life of travel, a nice house, and a family. Rick Stanton wakes up to the reality that he is useless as a man, a provider, and a burden on this woman who never lets him see her struggle to cope. He is more or less locked up in this tiny room, living out his life, calling out to her to help him with the most humbling of tasks. She has become his nurse. She smiles and tells him jokes, and tries so hard to pretend that she's happy. In return, he has become *difficult.* Snappish. Frustrated by the effort of the simplest of tasks, he has turned gratitude for her help into resentment. She pulls his blanket up and he shoves it away. She strokes his hair back and he looks away from her. Rick wishes that she would storm out on him, allow him the dignity of getting angry with him. Her patience is wearing on his.

Getting Pax back has been the chief goal they've shared, besides keeping nonhealing wounds clean. Having him here was their holy grail, if only to have something else to think about besides his schedule at the VA hospital or whether it was finally time for another pain pill. They'd been made to wait, and the wait had become the ballast keeping their rocky boat from capsizing. "When Pax gets home," they said to each other, implying that things would improve. There was never any finish to that phrase, no complementing fantasy of a sudden return to health, or magic moment when they would look over the dog's beloved head and smile at each other like they used to. "When Pax gets home" was sufficient unto itself as the dog spent additional months in occupied Germany, while he was in the retraining center, while they waited for someone to bring their dog home.

Keller Nicholson has brought Pax home and, with him, an attachment that is so obvious, Rick can nearly smell it. They should never have let Pax's army handler bring him home. It isn't doing anyone any good. Not Nicholson, not Pax, and certainly not them. Like so many who come to visit, Keller looks past Rick and fixes his gaze on the thick drapes, or the shelf of encyclopedias. Anywhere but at him. Rick is glad that he insisted that Francesca get him up and into his wheelchair. It's bad enough being helpless, but being in that bed just exacerbates the impression that he's an invalid. Which he is, but not one who can't grasp at a last shred of self-esteem when another man is present. A fellow veteran. A subordinate, a mere corporal to his battle-won staff sergeant's stripes. "Sit down, Corporal."

There is a kitchen chair that serves as the guest chair in this tiny room filled with the paraphernalia of his physical needs. It's modern tubular steel, with a padded vinyl seat and back in a hideous turquoise-and-orange pattern that defies definition. There is a little tear in the vinyl and a fluff of stuffing pokes out. Keller pulls the chair away from the wall and sits opposite Rick. Now he is looking directly at him, and Rick looks for the pity that most visitors can't hide. To his surprise, Rick doesn't identify pity in those deep-set brown eyes; he sees something else entirely. Keller looks at Rick not with pity or sympathy, but with anger.

"I want him. He's been with me a long time. We're a team. He's not a pet any longer." The brown eyes widen and the pupils dilate until the brown is occluded by the black. His mouth is a tense line, his hands fisted on his knees. "I'll pay you for him."

It is so refreshing that Rick nearly laughs. Finally, someone who won't mince around just because he's a one-armed paraplegic former ballplayer. "Well, you can't have him. And there's no amount of money in the world that could buy him from me."

Keller gets to his feet so suddenly that the chair tips over with a crash. "I owe him my life. I can't just leave him behind."

"Nicholson, we know he means a lot to you, but you have to understand what he means to me." In the world of his pre-waking dreams, Rick often runs. He feels the air on his face and he feels the dirt beneath his feet. He doesn't know if he's running from or toward something. Right now, seeing this other man's distress, Rick wishes uselessly for the ability to run away from this scene. "You think that you need him, but *I* need him. I've had everything taken; he's what's left."

There is no change in Keller's expression, no softening into empathy, no lessening of the anger. "The only good thing I've ever had in my life is this dog. I don't have a wife, or a home, a family, a job. He's it, my life."

Rick knows that if Francesca hears the crash of chair against floor, she'll be back in the room in moments. He doesn't want her in here, and he doesn't want Pax in here, either, until they settle this. He doesn't want to see the dog choose Keller. Even while the dog's head was in his lap, Rick was painfully aware that he didn't have the dog's full attention and that when Keller entered the room, the dog relaxed, a softening of the excited tension in his shoulders, a lighter sigh.

Rick shifts a little in his chair. The place above where his spinal cord was severed is sore and he's afraid that Francesca is going to have to tend yet another break in his fragile skin. He needs to be lifted back into bed, to be rolled over so that she can salve it. "You have no job? No home to go to?"

"No, sir." Keller bends to pick up the kitchen chair. He sets it carefully back against the wall where he'd found it. He won't be detoured from his determination to win this argument by niceties. "But he'll have a home, you can be sure."

"Then what are your plans?"

Rick can see him thinking about his response, weighing the merits of telling the truth against a plain civil lie. "The thing is, I plan to keep this dog, maybe go into police work. It would be a crime to waste his talents."

Rick recognizes the challenge in Keller's blunt statement. He's challenging Rick to fight for this dog. A flicker of some vestigial machismo surges in Rick, the urge to take this subordinate and shake him, shake him until he understands that he's never going to take Pax from him. He feels like he can stand up and grab Keller and beat him to the ground, and he's boundlessly grateful for the redirection of his simmering anger and resentment. It's good to feel mad with someone besides himself.

"Not possible. I won't let him go."

Keller smooths the brim of his new hat,

puts his hand on the doorknob. If he chooses to walk out, call the dog, and disappear, there really isn't anything Rick can do to stop him except cry "thief!" If Pax obeys Nicholson, heeds his orders, then Rick thinks that his heart, already crushed with the heaped losses of career and hope, will break.

He shifts in his chair again, the sore spot pulsing. Last night, when Francesca tried to shift him from the chair to the bed, she slipped, cracking her knee against the metal bed frame. She smiled and mocked herself, stubbornly refusing to admit that caring for him is difficult. That she isn't up to the task, that a five-foot-two-inch, hundred-pound woman is capable of lifting a six-foot-something man. "Look, Nicholson, my wife needs help. With me."

"I'm sorry to hear that." Keller lifts his hat to his head. He's said what he plans, and in the next minute he'll walk out that door and call the dog and the dog will go with him.

"Wait. Hear me out. I have an idea that might work for all of us."

CHAPTER TWENTY-FIVE

After Rick was shipped stateside, we spent nearly a year in Washington, D.C., while Rick was in the Walter Reed General Hospital there. Once he was discharged, we decided that we wanted to go back to the Boston area. There was a good VA hospital there for him to continue with his therapies and we both felt like it was home. It was the place we'd met and married and dreamed our big dreams. During those long months at Walter Reed, we focused entirely on getting Rick healed and rehabilitated enough so that I could bring him home. Bringing him home was goal enough; all our other prewar pipe dreams had gone up in smoke.

My cousin Sid — who'd made it back safe and sound and very nearly untouched by a war spent in England — found us a single-family house to rent in Quincy, not far from the shore at Squantum. I think he imagined that I'd be able to wheel Rick along the shore drive to enjoy the view of the Boston Harbor islands and eat takeout from Ray's Clam Shack like a normal couple. Of course that didn't happen. Our days were housebound, my only excursions to the grocery store and his to the hospital, where it seemed like he was continually being admitted because I had a hard time keeping up with the bedsores and the wound that just wouldn't heal where his arm, his pitching arm, had been blown away.

The house came with a one-car garage, conjoined to the main building by a glassed-in breezeway. Passing from the house to the garage always felt like being underwater as the light filtered through the glass blocks. The doorways weren't wide enough to get Rick and his chair through, so he ended up having to endure all weathers as I loaded him into the car from the front walk. We didn't have a ramp, either, so my biggest challenge was to ease him down the three steps, as if his wheelchair were a giant baby carriage, then anchor my weight against the forward motion of the chair as it rolled down the slope to the sidewalk. My fear was that someday I'd lose control and he'd go careering into the side of the car or, worse, into the street and oncoming traffic.

When Keller Nicholson brought Pax

home to us, we'd been in that rental house a little more than six months. Rick had been hospitalized about five times in that period, and the little house didn't look appreciably more lived in than it had the day we moved into it. Rick was in what had been the den, and I slept upstairs in the larger of the two bedrooms. The second one, the one that still had nursery wallpaper from the previous tenants, I used to store everything I hadn't had time to unpack; most of our life together was contained in cardboard boxes with labels that described how life had been: *Wedding Presents, Photo Albums, Baseball Equipment.*

In another life, I'd have washed that charming babyish wallpaper and planned where to put a crib. I hated that room, a reminder of the end of our first, best goal.

In all that time, Rick had never told me what happened and I believed that he couldn't remember. It wasn't unusual, after all. Traumatic amnesia. All I knew was that in the ambush, all of his men were lost, Rick the only survivor.

Rick kept Keller in his room, leaving me to fiddle around in the kitchen, craning to hear their voices, wondering what could be going on. Pax panted and paced the hallway from Rick's room to where I stood, useless, in the kitchen, too late for lunch, too early for dinner. The dog looked at me with a clear concern and all I could do was pat him and mutter words meant to soothe him. "It's all right, big guy. It's good to have you back. Will you be happy here? Did you miss us? Can you go back to being our dog?" My questions left my mouth unattached to any thought. "Will you miss him?" Him, Keller.

Finally, Keller appeared in the archway. He still had that military bearing about him, shoulders back, chin lifted, hands rigidly at his sides, the right one clutching the brim of his hat. I looked at his face for the first time, really looked at him, at the angular planes of his face and the aquiline nose suggesting an old Yankee heritage. What I saw was a man moving into the next stage of his life. His mouth was drawn into a military scowl, but his eyes, a deep muddy brown, glinted with enough hope that I felt my own burn.

Pax immediately went to him and sat at his left knee. I never saw a signal. Keller made no overt sign, but without hesitation the dog planted himself where he belonged. I saw the truth clearly now: This dog had formed an attachment as deep as an attachment between lovers. No part of Keller touched the dog, but the connection was as visible to me as if they'd been chained to each other. I wanted to hate him, and yet I couldn't. I understood him.

"What are we going to do?" I whispered, as if I thought myself alone in the room.

"Mr. Stanton wants to talk to you." Keller moved aside, the dog gracefully moving with him. I pushed past them to go to Rick, my hand reaching deep into my apron pocket to find a handkerchief. I was already in tears.

I expected to find Rick hunched down and devastated, and every inch of me pulsed to comfort him; but instead, he was sitting in his chair, straight and confident, his good arm crossed over his bad one. Without preamble, he laid out his idea. Keller Nicholson would stay on as Rick's aide. Room and board, and a small weekly salary in exchange for lifting and dressing and bathing and all the tasks that made up my day. In exchange for Pax.

"Franny, it's up to you. It'll take the physical burden off of you, but I know that having another person in the house means more work for you in other areas. But he's big, he's capable, and he's rootless."

"And we avoid having to argue about Pax."

Rick nodded. "Yeah. At least for a while.

It'll give us all a chance to adjust."

A stranger in my house. We knew nothing about him except that Pax was a big fan. I felt like we were trusting a dog as a reference for an employee, a star boarder, an interloper.

"I haven't struggled. I haven't complained. I *want* to take care of you."

Rick reached out his hand and grasped mine. "I know you do."

I pressed the crumpled handkerchief up to my eyes. He hadn't touched me in a long time, and the feel of the soft skin of his palm against my more work-worn hand was too warm and I worried about a new infection starting. I'd forgotten how warm a kind hand can be.

"We give him a month." He squeezed my hand and let go.

"All right."

And so Keller Nicholson came into our lives and nothing was ever the same again.

CHAPTER TWENTY-SIX

As it goes, it's not as bad as it might be. The garage is fairly well ventilated and the roll-out cot isn't the worst thing Keller has ever slept on. It's better than sleeping on the lumpy couch on the enclosed porch at his aunt Biddie's house, and certainly more private than Meadowbrook or a barracks. They've given him a three-drawer bureau with an attached mirror and an old-fashioned pitcher and bowl. He's got bath-room privileges, but he prefers to shave in the garage rather than take up time and make a mess in the house bathroom. His second-floor bedroom at Clayton's was smaller and, like this garage, unheated. He's on trial, he knows, and heat in the garage is the least of his concerns. If this situation doesn't pan out, well, Keller doesn't like to think of what might happen if it doesn't.

No, the accommodations aren't bad, but all the same Keller feels a lot like he did as a kid, living in someone else's house, on someone else's terms. Not exactly welcome, not exactly family, not exactly friend. At least he gets a paycheck and his free time is his own. The job is physically demanding, and at night he aches in places he never has before, not even after hauling pots and nets and gear from boat to shore. Not even after sleeping in a foxhole dug out of the rocky soil. The struggle to get Rick from bed to bath to chair and back again is a challenge even for someone as used to hard work as Keller is. Mrs. Stanton suggested that he visit the VA to get some pointers on how to lift a body, and maybe he will one day.

Pax spends most of his time in what Keller thinks of as Rick's sickroom. He's not sick, at least not in the sense of enduring a disease, but it is clear that this room has become his whole world, that to venture out of it is a labor-intensive struggle to get the clumsy wheelchair over the sill and through a door that barely accommodates its width. Leaving the house is worse, requiring Keller to throw his weight counter to the weight of the man and chair and roll it down step by step. He thinks it would almost be easier if he lifted Rick out of the chair and carried him, but Rick balks at that, the indignity of it. So, for most of the day Pax sits with him, his head on Rick's lap, eyes closed as Rick strokes his head over and over. Sometimes Keller hears him talking to the dog, whispering words that are meant for the dog's ears only. The dog patiently takes these confidences in and never reveals what they are.

But every night, Keller is quietly joined in the garage by his dog. He never orders Pax to come, but in the hour after Rick has been put to bed and Mrs. Stanton has gone upstairs to her room, the dog, having surveyed the property and deemed it safe, comes through the half-open door to crawl into Keller's narrow cot. Stretched side by side, they both drift into sleep.

"I don't see any shoes." Keller has gotten Rick up, toileted, shaved, and into a short-sleeved shirt and loose trousers.

"No point in shoes."

"You still have feet. You need something on them."

"Why? It's not like I'm walking out of here."

Keller abandons the search for shoes, kneels down in front of Rick, and slides on a pair of open-back slippers. The left one falls off. He puts it back on. "All set. How 'bout we get you into the kitchen for breakfast?"

"Just have Francesca bring it in here."

"She's set the table."

Rick says nothing.

Pax bangs the den door open with his head and Rick finally smiles. "Hey, big boy." The dog bounds in, tail swinging. He plants his head in Rick's lap, eyes up, ears up, doing his morning greeting routine. The dog fills up a lot of the space in the tiny room and Keller has more than once had to rescue pill bottles and teacups swept off the low tray table beside Rick's chair.

Keller leaves to tell Francesca that she needs to set up the breakfast tray again. He's batting zero as far as getting Rick to leave his room. He tries every morning, and every morning Rick ignores him or gets mad. "I didn't hire you to pester me. I'm comfortable and it's not worth the struggle. I'm in the way. Leave me alone."

"I don't know why you keep trying." Francesca has already set up the tray with juice, toast, scrambled eggs cooling off too quickly. She picks it up. "Grab some eggs for yourself. The coffee's ready." She gracefully swings the tray up like an experienced diner waitress and disappears down the hall.

There is one place set. Francesca's used plate and fork are in the sink. Keller pours himself some coffee and helps himself to the rest of the eggs. He doesn't sit, but leans against the counter, forking cold eggs into his mouth and sloshing black coffee after them. He can hear her voice, but not distinctly. It always sounds the same to him, like she's mollifying a child. She doesn't treat Rick like a man anymore; she treats him, in Keller's opinion, like a truculent ten-year-old.

This is a house with very little thought given to decor. Keller knows that they moved here hastily. She's told him how it was. After months of waiting, Rick's discharge from the hospital seemingly happened overnight. Francesca has been so consumed with caring for Rick that she's done little to make this small house homey. Furniture, sure; curtains, yes. But only a picture or two on the walls. One picture in particular tells him more of their story than he's been able to figure out from the bits of conversation he's had with either of the Stantons. Rick in a baseball uniform, in mid pitch, his back leg kicked, his pitching hand just unfurling across his chest. It's telling, he thinks, that this photograph is in a room where Rick never goes.

Keller has fashioned a clothes rack in one corner and his uniform and fatigues hang there, at the ready for his one-weekend-a-month service in the Army Reserves. This will be the first time he'll be away from the Stantons, and the first time since boot camp that he won't have his dog by his side. It's just a weekend, and not far away, just down on the Cape at Camp Edwards. It's been a bit of a surprise, how guilty he feels. Having just gotten the Stantons to where they are comfortable in having him around to do all the physical work and now leaving her to struggle with it for two nights. Guilty because he's really looking forward to being among healthy, fit men, even if it's only to drive a truck from one base to another in simulated maneuvers. Rick wears on him.

The other night, Keller brought up the subject of baseball, like any two guys sitting in a room might do. "What do you think of the Red Sox's chances this year?"

"I don't. I don't think of that at all and I'd prefer it if you wouldn't talk about it."

Rick slammed the door on that topic, which frankly leaves very little for the two of them to talk about during those uncomfortable moments while Keller bathes Rick or lifts him from chair to toilet. War talk isn't anything either of them wants to discuss, and, without the masculine conversational safety net of sports talk, that only leaves Pax.

She's not much better. At least calling her "Missus" has worn off. She's got a couple of years on him, like she might have been a senior when he was a sophomore, just about that much. Caring for her husband has prematurely aged her. Not in appearance, except for the dusky circles beneath her eyes, but in spirit. Maybe it's just that being married to an older guy, you can't be a kid. Keller was never a kid, either, but he's pretty sure that Francesca has become this way, not been raised to it. He understands Francesca's seriousness, and, coupled with the weight of her burden, her gravity.

But it's not a bad situation. After all, he's still got Pax.

CHAPTER TWENTY-SEVEN

Rick! Keller! Francesca! All together, some-times even in the same room. To Pax, it feels like all the uneven places in his life have smoothed out. It's as if everything that had gone before was leading to this. Early life with Rick. The Rick-less time with Fran-cesca. The exciting time with Keller when he had a job with commands instead of a job, like now, where he is allowed to perform tasks of his own invention. He is busy all the time. Mostly, he keeps Rick company. This isn't the Rick of old; this is a sedentary Rick. He never throws balls or sticks or leashes him to run along the streets. He no longer takes him to the park, or along the Charles River to walk for miles and miles. If Rick no longer requires active company, he more than requires inactive companionship. Pax gives himself over to this new dynamic. As long as he is nearby, within reach of Rick's hand, he is on duty. If Rick is in his bed, Pax lies alongside him, even when Francesca makes him get down. If Rick is in his chair, Pax sits with him. He waits while Rick goes into that place where he doesn't move, doesn't speak, breathing only shallowly. Pax has figured out that if he nudges Rick, or drops a heavy paw on his lap, Rick will emerge from this fugue state. *Good boy.* Job well done.

It might have been a joy to have both of his men in the same room, but there is this thread of tension that corrupts the perfection of it. He goes from one to the other, as if to tell them that he isn't divided between them, but is holding them together. But they don't understand. Francesca doesn't understand, either, and sometimes all Pax wants is to leave all three of them behind and spend a solitary hour in the backyard, waiting for the squirrel that lives in the cherry tree to come within reach.

At night, without orders, Pax divides his time unequally, finding Keller a better bunk mate. After all, they had kept each other warm during those long, harsh months of cold and commotion. Sleeping outside or under the precarious shelter of broken buildings; huddled together with backs against stone walls. Keller's body spooning his, each taking a turn enjoying deep sleep.

Not once has Keller ever ordered him aside for a mate, locking him out of their shared sleeping quarters, like Rick has. Even though Rick and Francesca now sleep in separate places, Pax still prefers his wartime buddy's warmth to stretching out beside either of the other two. Not that Francesca would ever let him on her bed.

But, on occasion, Pax leaves Keller, his acute ears hearing some small anguish coming from Rick. Then he goes back to Rick's room, places his cold nose against his first man's cheek, and waits for the grasp of his unsteady hand to tell Pax that he is helping. That he is doing a good job.

CHAPTER TWENTY-EIGHT

I extracted a straw, inserted it carefully between the floating lumps of vanilla ice cream and deep into the soda. I took a deep draw of the concoction and then caught a look at myself in the soda fountain's mirror. Foolish, girlish, I gave myself a pinup girl wink and took another sip. I'd had my hair cut, and it fanned my face in effortless curls. Unlike so many others, I never had to submit to the heat and stench of a permanent. My fair hair was always curly enough to avoid chemical interference and responsive enough to obey ordinary rollers and bobby pins. Maybelline carmine red banded the straw where my lips pressed. My indulgence. My vanity. Hair done and lips painted, I could have been any wife going home to a husband who would appreciate that she was taking care of herself. For all the good it did me.

This was luxury. An hour without guilt

because Keller would give Rick his lunch and then bring out the chess set. Miraculously, he had managed to get Rick to play the game with him, when all other attempts at the distraction of cribbage or poker or rummy had failed. Maybe because it was something easily played one-handed.

In any event, Keller's presence had given me the opportunity of an afternoon to myself. If I'd had any friends, I'd have gone visiting or talked one of them into going out to lunch. Living as we did, in near isolation in a town where we knew no one, hadn't bothered me at first. But once Keller was there and I was allowed some guiltless free time, I began to miss the easy companionship of the other baseball wives. But it had been too long, a lot of the players had changed, and the truth was, I didn't live that life anymore. I didn't want to gossip about who might be traded, or whose wife was pregnant. Especially who was pregnant.

I might have called on Clarissa, Sid's wife, but to be honest, I hadn't taken to Clarissa. She was nice enough, but I didn't have the urge to pull her into my confidences. He'd married a Boston Brahmin Vassar girl and I wasn't her kettle of fish, either. We smiled at each other at our occasional family dinners, but we'd never be the kind of friends who chatted for hours on the phone.

I wrote often to my high school pal Gertie, now Mrs. Donald Richmond, proud doyenne of five hundred acres six miles beyond Mount Joy's town limits and mother to three little boys. Gertie's life was full of farm talk — crops, cows, and corn prices — and kids. I had nothing to offer but medical updates. I had half a dozen stock sentences and I alternated them so that it didn't look like I was writing the same letter over and over: *Rick is doing well this week. We had a good visit with the VA docs. We had a little setback with his catheter, but all is well now. The leaves are turning beautifully. We've had three big snowstorms in the past two weeks. The summer is proving to be rainy.* Blah, blah, blah. Life's just peachy.

My erstwhile boyfriend Buster Novak had been killed in action in the Pacific. I confess that sometimes I wondered what it might have been like had I accepted him. After all, my life hadn't turned out a whole lot different from that of farmwife. My daily concerns, with the exception of corn prices, pretty much came to the same thing as any farm wife dealt with: feeding my men, keeping the household running, looking out for the windstorms that blew through my existence every time Rick succumbed to a depression that never quite lifted. The adventure and culture and *excitement* were long gone, subsumed by the daily struggle to survive.

When Keller appeared with Pax, that gave me something interesting to tell Gertie. "Rick is really happy to have Pax back. Nicholson is such a big help. He's taken over all the heavy lifting for me. It's made such a difference." I was one gush away from making it sound like Keller was a willing participant in the Stanton drama, instead of a man who was there because we'd held his beloved Pax hostage. A little variation on the wisdom of Solomon. Everybody wins, right?

Corporal Nicholson. Keller. Shy guy. Rarely spoke until spoken to, which was difficult for me because I found myself shy around this perfect stranger in my house. If he'd been one of those easy sorts of guys, like Rick's former teammates, all full of jokes and playfulness, it would have been easier for me. But Keller was quiet and respectful and clearly trying hard to keep himself out of my way. Once a week, he asked if he might use the bathtub. Once a week, he asked if he might use my washer. I told him I'd do his laundry, and he blushed, as if the thought of my handling his BVDs was humiliating. Frankly, I was just as happy to have him take care of his own washing for exactly the same reason. It was just too *intimate* between male and female strangers.

"I can't have you do that for me. I'm fully capable of doing my own laundry, and you've got enough to do without my becoming a burden to you."

"Mr. Nicholson. Keller, you've taken a burden off me." The minute I said it, I regretted it. I sounded like I thought my husband was a burden. I'd meant the physical burden. "I don't mean it like that."

"I know what you mean." He lifted his army duffel bag full of dirty clothes up onto his shoulder. "Thank you."

I didn't know if he meant for the compliment or the use of my Maytag.

Our days passed into something resembling a routine, and I realized one afternoon as I handed Keller a stack of folded towels and shooed him upstairs to the linen closet that I had overcome my initial unease with having a strange man in my house. What helped was that I had begun to see him not as a full-fledged grown-up, but as a younger brother. Like my younger brother, Kenny. Kenny was a tease and a pest and a disappointment because, if I'd been destined to

have a younger sibling — effectively pushing me into middle-child status — I'd
wanted a sister. Like Keller, Kenny was
eighteen when he joined the service. He
survived the Aleutians and came back just
as pesty and teasing as ever, although it was
only in letters and during the quick hello he
was afforded during the once-a-month
phone call my parents made. "Hey, Knuck-
lehead, you still bossy as ever?"

"You still being a brat?" My riposte was
never as clever as I wanted it to be. I'd lost
a little of my edge.

I didn't know if Keller had come back
from the war the same as he had been or
whether he'd been changed by it. He had
no relatives, he said, so he had no experience of being a younger brother, pesty or
not, but that's how I saw him, or, rather,
how I chose to see him — well, not the pesty
part. Keller was as considerate as anyone
could want. But I chose to look at him as a
kid brother. Keeping him at a safe remove,
but a couple of degrees up from employee.

"Keller, I was going to sit in the living room
and listen to the news," I said one night.
"Would you like to join me?" Typically, Keller retreated to his garage space as soon as
he'd gotten Rick into bed for the night.

Usually, I sat with Rick until he shooed me off to bed, but on this night he'd wanted to read and sent me out of his room early.

"Sure." His dark brown hair had grown out of its military clip since his obligatory Reserve weekend. Since then, he'd let it grow, and its poker straightness defied the Brylcreem he dabbed on it, falling against a natural center part and flopping across his brow like a little boy's. He shoved it back and it fell forward.

I resisted the urge to comb it to the side, like I did with Rick's when he, too, let his hair grow out of his summertime clip, when the three or four curls on the back of his head would appear and I would tease them into life with my fingers and then he would tease me into life. "How about I make us a bowl of popcorn? I think that there's a variety show after the news."

The living room held only a three-cushion couch and a wing-back armchair that had belonged to my grandmother and that my parents had shipped to us as an anniversary gift the fall before Pearl Harbor. When I brought the popcorn into the living room, Keller had already warmed up the radio and was sitting in the armchair. Pax was on the rug, stretched out full length, so that his head was under the coffee table. I stepped over him so that I could sit on the end of the couch closest to Keller and we could easily share the popcorn, over which I'd generously drizzled real butter — a luxury even then.

The minute I set down the bowl, Pax popped up, his amber eyes on the bounty. "No begging, you."

"When he was in the service, he was taught never to take food from anyone but me." Keller grabbed a handful of popcorn. "Now look at him."

I did and saw that the velvety black of the fur on his muzzle was fading with the onset of gray hairs. Even the sooty tips of his A-frame ears were threaded through with this immutable sign that our dog, our baby, was growing older. Rick had found Pax in 38, a tiny puppy. Our dog was almost eight years old. Still fit, still lively, but no longer young.

We'd been married almost seven years. By this time, we might have had two kids, maybe three. Sometimes lying awake in my solitary bed, I thought of those never-conceived children and felt hollowed out, dried up, and no longer young.

I finished my ice cream soda and reapplied my Maybelline carmine red lipstick. A thin paper napkin sufficed as a blotter. Time to go home, time to go back and see if Rick had trounced Keller once again at chess.

CHAPTER TWENTY-NINE

Keller is standing outside the glass-block breezeway, contemplating the angle of doorsill and ground.

"You look like you're solving a puzzle." Francesca comes up beside Keller. She's been out for the afternoon and he notices the fresh haircut. She looks nice. She looks relaxed. "I am. I'd like to build a ramp here. You know, to get the wheelchair out of the house easier." The wheelchair, not the man. "I can build one for the other side, too, so that he can get out to the backyard."

"It would help. Do you think you can do it?"

"I'm sure that I can do it. It's a matter of geometry. But, listen, I also want to widen the doorways, get rid of the sills. So he can wheel himself out of his room." Even though Keller suggests this, he wonders if Rick will ever leave his room. Being around Rick reminds Keller of the World War I veterans sitting outside the nursing home in Great Harbor, slumped in their wheelchairs, heads down, Sometimes they hadn't been seriously wounded, but their spirits were shattered. Their outward wounds had healed, but their spirits never would. Rick is like them, staring at the wall day after day, refusing to be grateful that he is back home. Frankly, it kind of pisses Keller off. It stinks, being crippled, but at least he made it out alive.

Bucky Carson didn't make it out, killed in the same action where Keller and Pax were both wounded. Neither did Dick Adams, and Keller still feels that sharp, disbelieving grief whenever he thinks of this particular death. Dick and his war dog, Rudy, both gone in an instant.

"I just don't know if the landlord will go for it. He might not be keen on making that kind of dramatic change to his structure. Maybe just the ramp for now."

Francesca slings her handbag up over her arm and goes into the house through the open breezeway door. Her shadow drifts over the thick glass blocks like an undersea creature. Keller thinks that he'll go in and check on Rick, see if he wants anything — except another game of chess. One humiliation a day is enough for Keller. After that, maybe he'll go to the lumberyard and get started on the materials for the ramp. He closes the breezeway door behind him and enters the kitchen. Francesca is there, still in her light coat, her handbag open on the table, its contents spilled out.

"Keller?" Francesca starts shoving the coin purse and checkbook and comb and lipstick back into her bag.

"Ma'am?"

"It's good you're here." She snaps the handbag shut and walks out of the kitchen.

He feels himself flush. He's not sure how to respond. No one has ever said that to him before.

"I'm glad to be of help." But she's in the hallway and his words fall into empty air.

Then she's back. Her coat and bag put away, she reaches for an apron. As she does, she steps closer to Keller. One hand keeps him from backing away. "Keller." She's more than a head shorter than he is, so she lifts herself up on her toes and leans toward his ear. "He's very glad you're here. He might not say it, but he is." Her breath is close to his ear — she doesn't want Rick to know she's talking about him — but the effect of her soft whisper against Keller's cheek incites in him the urge to place his hand on her waist and press his cheek against hers. She smells of laundry soap and fresh air.

Once when on patrol, Keller and Pax had come upon a small farmhouse, a crowded clothesline strung out behind it into the rare spring sunshine. The woman who lived there boldly walked out her door and left it open, as if to invite inspection. Pax was unconcerned as they walked the perimeter, so they left the yard quickly. But before they did, Keller, weeks from his last bath or clean uniform, walked between the lines of drying sheets and shirts, inhaling the idea of being clean and freshly clothed. Just like having a loving family, the concept seemed unattainable.

Keller swallows and closes his eyes. "I know he is. And I'm very glad to be here."

Keller uses the bathroom before he goes in to check on Rick. He needs a moment; he can't go into that room with the feel of Francesca's hand on his arm still there; with the desire to touch her back still evident in the pink of his cheek.

Pax is flopped on the bare floor, stretched out full length, taking up most of the space not already taken up with bed and tables and wheelchair. His head is beside the wheelchair; his tail is under the hospital bed. The room is stuffy and the dog is softly panting. He raises his head when Keller comes in, and Keller can hear the *flop-flop* of his tail against the hardwood floor beneath the bed. The tail bangs against a spring with a little chiming sound. Rick's lap blanket is on the floor, and Keller bends to pick it up. Rick doesn't like to sit without something across his knees; he's always cold, even in this closed-up room. "You should have called me." Keller settles the blanket back in place.

"It's all right. I can't keep you running back and forth like some deranged butler."

"I don't mind."

Pax extricates himself from under the bed and sits with the two men, his fond eyes addressing first one and then the other. His muzzle cracks open in a wide pant like a smile. He is perhaps the happiest creature Keller knows. Hours on patrol, or enduring endless hours of barrage as the big guns went off in near-ceaseless repetition, and the dog happily settled wherever Keller was. And now he was happily settled between the two of them. Keller thinks that the dog is bound to be bored. His life for the past three years had been one of work. Good work, important work. The only restlessness Keller sees is late at night, when the dog wants to patrol the perimeter of the tiny fenced-in yard. He isn't satisfied to do it by himself like a regular dog; he noses Keller into line and the pair of them walk around the yard. If Keller doesn't adhere to the dog's sense of performance, he gets a look as if to say, *You're asking for it, grunt. Fall in!*

Pax is like a retiree, a warhorse put out to pasture. Except that he's taken on the role of companion with the same dedication as he did scout. And then Keller is struck with an idea.

"You know, maybe we can teach Pax how to pick things up for you."

They practice with medicine bottles and chess pieces. Rick knocks something off his tray and Keller points at it. They've decided on the command "Pick it up" slurred together: "Pickitup." As used as he is to learning tasks, the dog figures it out in less than six tries. Proud of himself, he waits impatiently for Rick to drop something else. And Keller finds himself proud, too, not only of the dog but of himself for coming up with the idea. He loves it, this ability to communicate ideas between species. The moment when the dog looks at him with complete comprehension. As if they *are* speaking a common language.

It was like that in the war. Sometimes it

spooked Keller, how well the dog understood him.

CHAPTER THIRTY

"You're going to have to be clumsy every ten minutes to keep him happy."

"I don't see that as much of a problem." Rick says this without irony. He's infernally clumsy, and he still hasn't, after all this time, figured out that he has only one hand. He keeps instinctively reaching with his absent right hand, frustrating himself and his occupational therapists. Relearning how to do everything with the wrong hand has been difficult. He still fears soup, although forking the pieces of meat that Francesca has kindly precut for him has become easier if he thinks of the British fashion of left-handed eating and tips his fork with tines down. He doesn't say so, but Rick longs to be able to cut up his own meat. What a simple lost talent. His missing fingers itch to take up the knife and slice off a big thick piece of ham from a picnic shoulder. Sometimes he thinks he misses being able to do that more than getting up out of this chair and walking out the door. But not as much as feeling the smooth surface of a baseball, reading its individual personality in the stitching, the weight of it balanced tenderly in the palm of his hand before he settles it into position for a curve or a sinker or a fastball.

No amount of success with a fork in his left hand can compensate him.

Even with the windows closed, Rick hears the sound of sawing and hammering. Keller is building him a ramp so that it will be easier to get from the house to the hospital. Keller doesn't say exactly that; he just says it'll be handy, a quick slide right to the door of the car. No more teeth-jarring thumping down steps, no more humiliating reminders of his helplessness. Keller thinks that if it's easier to leave the house, Rick will. Except that he can't think of any place he might be taken other than the hospital. No other reason to struggle to get into the car. No place he wants to go.

"What do you think of this?" Francesca twirls into the room like a debutante. She's wearing a new dress, very fitted at the waist, and a lot longer than the dresses she wore before he went to war. The sleeves are a little puffy, trimmed with a white band. It's a blue-and-white print. She looks very pleased with herself, and it's so nice to see a genuine smile on her face.

"Very nice. You've been shopping?" Lately, with Keller there, Francesca has been going off almost every day, and she doesn't always tell him where she's going. It's like she's slipping out, a teenage girl secretly meeting a boy on the corner, hoping her parents don't notice that she's gone.

"No, silly. I made it." She gathers up the skirt, examines the hemstitching, tut-tuts. "See, I'm uneven here."

"It looks very nice, and you could have fooled me. Looks like something you'd pick up at Jordan Marsh."

Francesca twirls again, obviously enjoying the swish of a full skirt. Her trajectory puts her beside him and she plants a kiss on the good side of his face. "Keller's almost done with the ramp. What say we get out of here tonight and get some dinner out?"

"And then what? Go dancing?"

"If you'd like." She doesn't hear his sarcasm, or she's ignoring it.

"No. I don't think I'm ready for that. For going out."

"Rick. This isn't good for you. It's time to —"

216

"Time to what, Francesca? Time to do what, exactly?" He turns his face away from her.

"Time to get on with your life. You're doing much better. I know what your occupational therapist told you. He told you that you need to get out, and you do."

"He's not the one who will be subjected to the pity stares." There, he's said it. The festering notion that he will be unable to abide being looked at with pity. He doesn't want the pity of those who came back from the war whole, or the "there but for the grace of God" pity of those who never went, to the curious stares of the rude and the innocent fear of monsters in the eyes of children.

"That's in your head, Rick. Yes, people may give you a look; that's natural. But they understand and maybe even admire you." She touches his unblemished cheek with her hand. "I admire you."

"Please don't." Even Rick doesn't know if he means that she shouldn't say any more or that she should stop touching him. Her touch is a taunt, a reminder of his other disability.

"Okay. So, I'll just go change and get lunch started." Francesca has gotten so good at keeping her voice modulated. She never lets him see her hurt or mad or frustrated. She tips the door half-closed on her way out.

Rick puts his face in his hand, so sorry, so very sorry for being the man he has become.

A cold, wet nose pokes through his fingers. Pax seems intent on spreading Rick's fingers wide enough that he can then give him a consoling lick on the nose. Rick leans his forehead against the dog's brow. "Pax, what would I do without you?"

Pax has nothing to say about that. He settles beside Rick, gives his front paws a freshening up.

One of Rick's slippers has come off. He's just noticed. "Pax, pickitup." He points to the footwear. Pax seems overjoyed to perform this small request and retrieves the slipper as if it were a rabbit dashing away. No Labrador had ever retrieved something as exuberantly or as gently. Now all he has to do is teach the dog how to put it on his foot. Rick takes the slipper out of the dog's mouth and praises him, as Keller instructed, with a scratch on the chest. It seems such a little recognition of the vast service the dog performs, but Pax seems pleased. It's true that the dog seemed to come to life as Keller was teaching him to pick up the things that Rick knocked to the floor, that his canine enthusiasm for learning is unbounded. He's a dog with a brain, and one that revels in performing his tasks. How did that happen? Before, Rick had a hard time getting him not to pull on the leash. Francesca could barely control him. All that energy had been funneled into the war machine and out had come this obedient, talented dog. But Pax's attachment to Keller is still jarring, still capable of creating a spurt of jealousy that makes Rick have to turn his face away from this guy who has proved to be such a godsend. Pax will spend all day with him in this room, but if Keller comes to walk him, the dog literally leaps up with joy. A kid going out for recess couldn't show more excitement. Is it the exercise or the time with his other master that incites it?

And yet, although Rick knows that the dog sleeps in the garage with Keller, if he wakes in the night, he finds the dog with him, as if he's been there all along.

As has become their habit at lunchtime, the three of them cram into Rick's room. Francesca has changed out of her new dress and is back in her workaday housedress. She moves the rolling over-bed table into the middle of the room to accommodate Rick's wheelchair and two kitchen chairs, and places a plate of egg salad sandwiches on it so that they can all reach.

Keller comes in with a bandage around his left forefinger. "Stupid mistake. Thought my finger was a nail."

Lucky for him he has his right hand and it doesn't impair his ability to eat his sandwich.

"Any requests for dinner?" Francesca touches up the edge of a sandwich with her finger and puts it in Rick's hand. As she licks the extra mayo from her finger, an image of her in bed flashes through Rick's mind, until he slams the lid on it.

"I have an idea. You suggested going out, so why don't you and Keller go?"

"No. I don't think that would be a good idea."

Keller is shaking his head as if the idea is apostasy. He is adhering to some protocol of his own invention.

"It's fine. You two both need a break. Go get some fried clams. Bring some back for me."

"What if . . ."

Rick puts his half-eaten sandwich down, takes Francesca's hand. "Nothing is going to happen for the hour it may take you to eat dinner. You're not leaving me in danger.

Besides, I have Pax. He'll keep me company."

Francesca and Keller look at each other with almost the same expression of skepticism. Or, is it something else, a nervous shyness? Like two adolescents. Two wallflowers suddenly forced to dance? Rick realizes that he has no idea what kind of relationship these two have with each other. She speaks of him only in terms of how much he's helping. Keller never speaks of Francesca except to say she's in the kitchen or running an errand. It's obvious to him now, the way they seem to exist only on the periphery of each other. Coworkers, not companions. He doesn't know why that bothers him. It seems like they should be better friends than that. It means that Keller may yet be an imposition on Francesca even while he's giving her enough freedom to go get her hair done.

"I mean it. You both deserve a break."

Keller slips a crust to Pax. "I could do with a clam plate. It's been a long time since I've eaten clams."

"We'd only be gone a little while."

Rick can't tell if Francesca says that like a decision, or if she's trying to convince herself he can be left alone even for an hour. Has he become that much of a child that he can't be left? Life has become such an if/ then equation. If they had had a baby before he went to war, would he then have come back infantilized? If he had died, would she then have been able to move on with her life instead of being trapped here with him? If he had come back whole, would the unspoken fact of their earlier failure to conceive been finally addressed? Maybe, if there had been no war, they would have conceived. It's a stretch to blame God for not giving them a child when they'd had the opportunity, but sometimes Rick does. And then he thinks that it's probably for the best. How would Francesca have coped with an active child's needs and those of a needy husband?

Keller points to the remaining half sandwich. "Anyone?"

"I can make more; I have more egg salad made up." Francesca looks ready to jump out of her chair.

"No. I'm done." Rick sets his unfinished half back on his plate.

Keller finishes the sandwich in two bites. He starts to wipe his mouth on the back of his hand but stops himself and uses his napkin. "I should get back to work." He grabs the back of the extra kitchen chair and leaves Francesca and Rick alone.

Pax looks after Keller but remains where he is, at Rick's side, patiently waiting for another crust. Rick hands him the rest of his sandwich.

"I think that maybe it's a good night for lamb chops. The butcher has them on special."

"Francesca, go out. Take Keller and go out.

"Rick, I feel a little awkward about . . ."

"It's not a date, Fran, it's a little break from cooking."

There is a faint tinge to her pale cheeks, not quite a blush, not quite embarrassment. It's as if she's been thinking about Keller and has been called out on it. Either she's uncomfortable with him or she's not. "All right. You're right." She stands up, gathers the plates into a stack. "But just be sure I'd rather be going out with you and that I'm going to keep pestering you until you say yes."

"I need time, Francesca. I need more time."

"You can have all the time you need, but you have to promise me that you'll try." She drops a kiss on the top of his head. "Promise?"

"Yes." The word has the sooty taste of a lie.

CHAPTER THIRTY-ONE

If he had the capacity to put into words what he feels, Pax would think himself a lucky dog. If being safe and warm and well fed is one part of what a dog needs and wants, having the companionship and affection of his best people is three-quarters of perfect. One friend to be with as he dozes in the narrow patch of sunlight that ekes its way between the former blackout curtains in the small Rick-smelling room. The same friend to ask him for favors like picking up dropped things. Another friend to keep his training sharp, heeling, fetching, sniffing out potential threats to the home. Sit, stay, and even, when out in the woods, scaling barriers. Finally, the woman who gives him the best of the belly rubs, her fingers equipped for deep scratching and an instinct for the right places.

Yes, Pax is a lucky dog indeed and his sense of well-being tempers his still-youthful energies. He's been through the toughest of times — separation from those he loved, a time of required aggression and wariness — and come out mild-mannered and willing to accept this triumvirate of masters.

There is only one thing that puzzles him: why these three don't seem to be as content as he is. They are like a small pack lacking a leader. He's tried to step into that role, but their humanness limits their comprehension. He's taking as good care of them as he can, but they still insist on a separateness from one another. They don't snap at one another, and if they are jockeying for position in the pack, it's too subtle for him to detect. Instead, there is this *deference.* Keller was admirably alpha when they were a pack of two. But his position in this group is unclear. Francesca, as a female, is a likely candidate, but she, too, refuses to take the lead. If he had to, Pax might give Rick the leadership, but his ability to hunt or protect or mate is clearly compromised, and that should remove him from the head of the pack. So Pax watches out for all of them, not entirely comfortable in his role, finding it hard to interpret from day to day exactly what it is these three humans want from one another. At least he knows what they want from him. To be there for each of them.

Yes, he's a lucky dog.

CHAPTER THIRTY-TWO

I think that it's still there, Ray's Clam Shack. Across Quincy Shore Drive from the beach, back in those days they served food fried in a deep fat fryer filled with liquefied Crisco, a maxed-out cholesterol feast and absolutely divine. I was a kid from the Midwest. Fresh seafood was a treat, and that fried mess of clams and french fries and tartar sauce was exotic to me. Keller insisted we get clams with bellies, suggesting that clam strips were akin to eating margarine instead of butter — just not good enough. I admit that it took a bit for me to get used to the taste and feel of the contents of a clam belly, but once I did, I never went back to the untutored Midwesterner's version of clams.

Even though the place was only a few blocks from home, we took my car. Partly because Rick's take-out dinner would be cold if we walked it home and mostly because neither one of us was interested in prolonging this excursion, leaving Rick home alone and potentially helpless. What if something happened? That sentence should be in all caps. Pax was there, at the ready to retrieve anything Rick could point to. Keller had refined the dog's mission to include getting Rick's sweater, which lay at the foot of his bed, or dragging his lap robe up and over his knees. Should the evening paper arrive when we weren't around, the dog would push his way out the front door and take it in to Rick, this last without a command or, to the best of our knowledge, anyone training him to do it. We still hadn't seen him open the front door to get back in. But, with all that, the dog couldn't dial a phone or put out a fire. Worst-case scenarios plagued me.

The other reason I thought we should take the car was because we were still very shy with each other and this whim of Rick's was best accomplished quickly. Without the third party of Rick, or even Pax, we were only a little better than foreign dignitaries without a common language.

We took our dinner to the beach, finding an empty bench to sit on side-by-side, the greasy bags between us. And we talked, as parents of young children do, of our two common interests. Rick and Pax. How funny Pax was with that squeaky toy hanging out of his mouth. How much better we both thought Rick was using his left hand.

Conversation petered out and we sat back to admire the view of the Boston Harbor islands.

Keller scuffed his feet in the sand. "This is lousy sand."

"What do you mean?"

"Kind of, well, kind of city sand."

I laughed. "You're a beach sand connoisseur?"

"Sort of. Spent a lot of time standing in it."

"Where?"

"Little place called Hawke's Cove. Up north of here. I lived for a while with my great-uncle." Keller lifted a whole clam dipped in a coating of tartar sauce to his mouth, chewed. "He's a commercial fisherman, mostly close to shore."

"That must have been nice, being on the water."

Keller didn't say anything for a moment, then shook his head. "It wasn't vacation. It was hard work."

There was no nostalgia in his voice, as there might have been with a lot of men. Even hard work has its nostalgic quality —

a pride of purpose, of accomplishment. With Keller, it sounded more like he had survived something. He didn't elaborate then; only later did I learn about his virtual slave labor and understand that he had indeed survived something.

"Is that where you learned to eat clams with bellies?"

Keller gave me one of his infrequent smiles, and for the first time I saw that he had a really nice smile and wished that maybe he'd use it more. "That and how to make a mean chowder." He pronounced it in that quintessentially New England manner: *chowda*. "I'll make it some night if you want."

"Rick would love that. It was always what he ordered when we went out." And then I remembered that Rick avoided using a spoon. "Well, maybe not yet."

Keller knew what I meant. "He will. I promise."

The scenery recaptured our attention. A small boat was powering its way toward one of the islands, and I couldn't imagine what reason it might have for such a journey. As far as I knew, there were no inhabitants on the tuft of island that the boat was headed toward.

"That's a lobster boat; he's out checking

traps. He's probably got them set where there're rocks. Lobsters like cover." *Lobstas.*

"Another thing your uncle taught you?" I crumpled up my empty cardboard clam boat and shoved it in the paper bag.

"Yeah." Keller followed suit, and grabbed both empty bags. We needed to pick up the order for Rick. "Can I ask you something?"

"Sure."

"Rick was a ballplayer, right?"

"Yes."

"So, why won't he let me bring in a radio so we can listen to the games? You'd think that he'd want to keep up."

Hadn't Keller noticed the fact that Rick left the sports section unread? I chalked up his insensitivity to youthful callowness. Of course, he wasn't a youth and it wasn't callowness. Eventually, I figured out that his bluntness had more to do with his upbringing, or lack thereof. "It's too painful. He was slated to become a starting pitcher with the Boston Braves, but instead he went to war and lost his dream."

"I'm sorry. I shouldn't have said anything."

"If you want to listen to the games, feel free. But don't think that you're going to get him to."

"I thought that if he'd listen to the radio,

he might, I don't know, start to feel better."

"By being reminded of the loss of the thing that meant the most to him?"

"Look, he's in there all by himself, staring at the wall. Unless you're in there, or I'm making him play chess, he's probably *only* thinking of his loss."

The thing Keller couldn't know is that I understood Rick exceedingly well, including his aversion to the topic of sports. For a long time, I felt the same aversion every time one of my ballpark acquaintances or a friendly neighbor down the block announced that she was pregnant, something that was happening postwar with startling regularity. Or I stood next to a mother with a pram beside her in the butcher shop, watching out of the corner of my eye while she tucked the baby in more securely and smiled down with that Madonna smile all women are capable of. I tossed out the baby pictures my Iowa girlfriends kindly sent to me, inviting me to share in their joy.

Maybe making Rick listen to ball games *was* a good idea. After all, I was a little better now, having a new focus forced upon me with Rick's challenges, so that the sight of a pregnant woman on the street corner no longer made me avert my eyes. And there were so many of them. It was as if the world had gone procreation crazy in order to make up for the staggering losses of war.

"At least now he's got Pax. And you. Before it was . . ." I couldn't go on. I couldn't admit that those months of being Rick's only caregiver had been anything other than a privilege.

"Just you. Yes, it's a good thing that I'm here to help. And it's really good that Pax can at least get him to smile once in a while. But, Francesca, it isn't enough."

I was done with this conversation. I know he hadn't meant to, but he was making me feel like I had somehow failed Rick by not making him listen to baseball on the radio, forcibly reminding him that life and baseball had moved on without him. Well, they also recommended rubbing dogs' noses in their messes to punish them. "Let's go get the order and go home."

"I'm sorry. I didn't mean to stir up trouble."

"It's not like I don't see what's wrong, Keller. You never knew him as the man I married. He was charming and funny and sexy and full of life. He was *full of life.*" I hated the way my voice broke. I hadn't cried in a long time, not since I realized that tears really never relieved. They just pushed my thoughts inward, until I felt sorry for myself.

"The war took that from him, didn't it? I get it. But he's got the whole rest of his life to live, and if he can't even leave his room, what kind of a life is it going to be? For him, and for you."

The little lobster boat had moved out of sight around the curve of the island. A pair of seagulls had landed close by, attracted by our impromptu picnic. I had nothing to toss to them. We had eaten every bite. "Do you plan to stay on?"

"Do you want me to?"

"We do, but the question is, do you want to stay?" It came to me that Keller was done with taking care of a man who hadn't come through the war in the same way he had, with his limbs intact and his spirit undiminished. He didn't answer right away, and I could feel my heart hammering at the fear he would say good-bye and leave me once again alone with my husband.

"I do."

I didn't know I'd been holding my breath until I released it. "Oh, good. Good."

"But it's not enough." A coincidence of words, or had this been what he'd meant earlier about it not being enough?

"We can't pay any more, honestly." It was a pittance, eked out of Rick's benefits. We were feeding Keller, and providing a place to sleep. Even living with us, he had expenses — a car, clothing, and so on. Here he was at the beginning of his postwar life, living like a Victorian servant.

"No. That's not what I mean. I'm thinking of taking advantage of the GI Bill and going to college in the fall. I can do both, go to school and help out with Rick. If I can stay on with you, I mean."

"Of course you can." I almost giggled in relief. He'd stay. I felt reprieved and I knew that Rick would be pleased, even if he didn't say so.

Keller tossed the bags into a trash can and we dashed across the street, back to where Rick's dinner was waiting to be picked up. I don't know why, but we dashed hand in hand.

Chapter Thirty-Three

"Pax, pickitup." Rick points to a medicine bottle sitting on the edge of the bedside table. It holds his painkillers — fifty little white pills guaranteed to take the edge off his continuing pain, if not cure it.

Pax watches Rick's gesture, identifies the target, and goes to the table. He lifts the bottle gently, glances back at Rick to confirm that he has the right object, and then brings it to him.

"Good boy." Rick scratches the dog's chest, then runs his hand over his head. "Really good boy."

Unscrewing the cap with his teeth, Rick shakes out two of the pills. He slips the morphine into the pocket of his sweater. Now his problem is how to put the vial back on the nightstand so that neither his wife nor Keller will notice. He is stockpiling, week by week, a dose of morphine he hopes will put an end to this nonsense. He's tired, really tired, and he could just take everything that's in this vial now, but he doesn't. He doesn't want it to look like a suicide. There, that's the word. *Suicide.* Death by personal choice. A death that would disqualify Francesca from his life insurance. One of these nights after Keller gets him settled into bed and Francesca has kissed him good night, he'll swallow his purloined hoard of morphine pills, send Pax out of the room, and fall asleep for all time, putting an end to this half-life.

But right now his problem is how to get the little bottle back to where Keller left it. Rick is facing in the wrong direction. After the laborious morning routine of getting him out of bed and cleaned up, Keller always leaves him facing the door. They've been working on a new command, one invented to give Rick a little more freedom of movement within his room. Folded up on the tray table is a terry-cloth towel. He grasps it and shakes it toward the dog. "Pax, pull me."

Pax loves this new game and cheerfully mouths the end of the already-shredded towel.

"Pull me," Rick repeats.

With Pax's teeth gripping the towel and his weight sunk into his back legs, Rick keeps a resistance on the other end like a game of tug-of-war, until the chair slowly revolves and Rick is facing the bed instead of the door.

Perfect. Except that the space between the hospital bed and the wall is too narrow to navigate in the chair. He needs to get the dog to replace the vial, or at least get it onto the table. "Here, Pax."

Pax is at the ready, his tail swishing across the bare floor in anticipation of further usefulness. Rick gets the dog to take the bottle in his mouth. "I have no idea what to ask, so let's try: 'Put it down.' " Pax happily holds the vial and wags his tail, but his eyes are pure doubt. "Okay, whole new command for you. Pax, put it." He points to the table, but the dog puts the bottle in his lap. "Good boy." Rick has the dog take the object back and then touches the edge of his bed. "Put it." The dog puts it in his hand. "No. On the bed." This is stupid. He doesn't have Keller's innate ability to communicate with this animal. He doesn't have the right words or the right tone of voice. Like everything else in his life, he can no longer make it work.

Rick hears the connecting door between the kitchen and the breezeway open and then the sound of drawers opening and shutting. The smell of fried food precedes Keller and Francesca down the hall. In the half a minute it takes Francesca to gather a plate and napkin, Rick has to figure out what to do with the vial. Reflexively, he underhands it toward the bedside table. It bounces with a glass-on-wood clang and hits the bed. Rick wishes he'd used a curve.

"Is everything all right?" Francesca is behind him. "What happened?"

"Nothing." Rick hopes she's referring to the fact that he's facing away from the door. "Pax and I are just working on our commands. He's turned me around. So, what did you bring me?" Francesca turns him back around and gestures to the dog to leave the room. "Pax, out." The dog bolts out, as if he's been held captive. Francesca settles a dish towel across Rick's chest, tucking one end of it under his useless arm. He feels like a child and he peevishly pulls it off. "No utensils necessary for this dinner; you don't need to put a bib on me. I won't get sloppy."

He hates it when he speaks to her like that. But, honestly, the mothering thing is beginning to wear thin. She treats him like, well, like an invalid. At least Nicholson has the good grace to *ask* if he needs something done before assuming he wants it.

Francesca lifts a cardboard boat of whole-belly clams out of the bag. "Keller's going to stay with us. He told me so tonight."

"I thought it was our decision, not his."

Francesca looks stunned, then mad. It's a new expression for her, and he's perversely pleased with himself for inciting a wholesome emotion for once. "I said he could. It's what we want, isn't it?"

"As long as you're still okay with it. I know this hasn't been easy."

"It's all right. It's fine."

Rick sees that it is. This having a stranger in their midst has moved from odd to ordinary. "So where is he?"

Francesca looks away from him, her chin tilted a little, and Rick remembers how it once felt to take that chin in his hand and lower it so that their lips met. "He's listening to the baseball game."

"Oh." Of course he is. It's August and the season is building toward the World Series.

"He wants to know why you never listen."

"What did you tell him?"

"The truth. It's too hard for you." Now she looks back at him and the sadness in her eyes is more painful to him than his physical hurts; it splinters him. He has six pills in his sweater pocket. He needs to find a better place to keep them, but there is nowhere in this room that isn't touched by the two other people in this house. No privacy.

CHAPTER THIRTY-FOUR

Keller has arranged things so that part of the garage looks like a bedroom — the cot, the bureau, and mirror — and part looks like a sitting room. He has a radio plugged in on what doubles as his workbench and he can listen to the baseball games that Rick refuses to listen to. Keller rescued an easy chair from a neighbor's curbside trash and he's positioned it with an upended ammo crate for a footstool so that he can comfortably drink a beer and listen to the game or read a few pages of *Le Morte d'Arthur* under the light from his new pole lamp. With his first paycheck, he sprang for the radio and lamp, and in a couple of weeks he'll find himself a rug remnant so that when cooler weather comes, he won't be walking on cement. In his whole life, Keller has never before enjoyed having a place of his own, the privacy of an empty room. He'd been in isolation, sure, but that wasn't solitude; that was punishment. A windowless room at the top of the third floor in the administration building, no light, no food, no blanket. This is privacy. No one to interfere with him, no one to bully him.

His experience of women hasn't been one of maternal care and kindness; his aunts were resentful of his extra mouth and the extra work, more quick to slap him than to praise him. He learned to keep out of the way, stay in the corner, not ask for more. Matron Willis at Meadowbrook looked the part of a kindly lady, a bit overstuffed, never seen without her apron, loose bun twisted on the top of her head; however, she was anything but. She and her husband, whom the boys called "Willie Whiskers" behind his back due to his walrus mustache, were the houseparents of his dormitory at Meadowbrook. Fifty truants and thieves, miscreants and the dispossessed lived in each of the four buildings charmingly called "cottages" by the founders of Meadowbrook School for Boys. There was nothing parental about their oversight. Matronly Matron Willis had a quick hand with the wooden spoon, and more than one boy was deafened by a blow to his ear with it. The boys were treated essentially as prisoners, and corporeal punishment, or being locked up in isolation, was the rule of the day.

Francesca takes care of him, making sure that he gets enough to eat, and that if he has a favorite, she cooks it. She brings him clean sheets every Monday. She seems happy to do it, even though he's said he is fully capable of washing his own sheets. It makes her seem like a landlady, as if this is a boardinghouse, except that they're paying him to be here. He's stopped her from actually making up his bed. He makes sure he joins her in the backyard when she's bringing in the sun-dried clothes. He carries the basket in for her.

Keller never entirely closes the door between his space and the breezeway, and at least for now, while it's still warm, the house door is also kept open so that he can be summoned at a word. The open doors don't diminish his sense of happy solitude, but it's nice to be within call of people who seem to want him to be there.

Pax comes in, tail wagging gently. "Hey, bud. Time for a walk?"

Roof.

"I'll take that as a yes." Keller ties the undone laces of his shoes. As he does every night, he heads down to the beach so that he can throw sticks for the dog. Tonight, the simple exercise of heeling off leash is the only reminder of their war work. The dog sticks like glue to his left leg, sitting as Keller waits at the curb for traffic to pass; never allowing himself to be distracted by the admiring glances of passersby. They pass Ray's Clam Shack on their route and Keller thinks about what he told Francesca about wanting to take advantage of the GI Bill and go to college.

Keller pulls a thick stick out from under a set of cement steps leading down to the beach from the sidewalk promenade. It's a particularly good one and he keeps it hidden so that they have it every time they walk to Squantum. He puts Pax in a sit-stay and then flings the stick as far as he can into the water. "Get it." The dog bounds after the stick, snags it, and crashes through the shallow water back to Keller. Imagine how much the dog would enjoy the cove below Clayton's house. Keller shakes off the thought. This city beach is just fine, thank you. The idea of going back to Clayton's house still has the power, after all this time, to squeeze his heart with dread.

The truth is, he hadn't really thought about going to college; it wasn't something that had ever been suggested to him as a goal. Not even Miss Jacobs had ever suggested that he apply, probably because she knew Clayton would never approve of such a lofty ambition. She was lucky to get him to allow Keller to finish high school. Keller can hear Clayton's voice in his ear, as if the old man were standing behind him: *Don't be getting above yourself, boy. Fisherman don't need no college.*

Francesca had beamed at him, asked him what he might want to study, *encouraged* this crazy out-of-the-blue idea. Saying it, that he wanted to go to college, wasn't anything more than a ploy to ensure that he can stay where he is, here with Pax. The money is scant, true. But the alternative would mean that he'd have to fight over Pax with the two people he's come to feel responsible for. He can't do it to them or to himself. Or to Pax. The dog is so content. All the months they spent during the war, and yet he never saw the dog's tail wag so much as it does now. Oh, there were times when a mission was accomplished and everyone could relax and the big dog would get a little silly. But they were never 100 percent safe, and so, never 100 percent relaxed. Neither one of them slept a full night until now, although Keller knows that Pax makes the rounds from room to room a couple of times a night. Still, it's a home-front kind of patrol. No real threats.

Francesca's reaction to his plan had been so genuine, as if she'd been worried that he might leave them. He's become necessary and welcome. Keller suddenly blushes at the thought of his grabbing Francesca's hand to run across the street last night. There wasn't even any traffic bearing down on them. It was impulsive, and the memory of it judders through him. Her hand wasn't as smooth as he had imagined. Her fingers linked through his were stronger than he might have expected from such a little woman.

"Pax, get it!" He whips the long stick as hard as he can. It tumbles end over end, and the rocketing dog is nearly there when it hits the sand.

She hadn't pulled it away in horror; she'd laughed and run with him like they were little kids. Maybe they looked like sister and brother. Keller finds himself smiling at the softheaded idea. She's so small and fair, and he's not. No one would take them for siblings.

Funny, Rick's insistence that they go out to dinner last night. It wasn't so much that he wanted them to leave him alone, but more like he hoped they'd work a little on improving their own association. He was right. Even in that short time alone —

without the buffer of Rick or the dog — a little of the reserve that Keller and Francesca keep between them was sanded off.

It's getting dark so early these waning days of summer. Looking away from the glow of Boston in the night sky, he sees a sprinkling of stars has emerged. Keller can pick out Sirius, the dog star, always at the heel of his master, Orion.

Pax bounds up to Keller, shaking the stick as if it's a living creature whose neck he wants to break.

"Leave it."

The dog places the heavy stick at Keller's feet.

"Time's up, Pax. Let's head home."

Home.

CHAPTER THIRTY-FIVE

His two men confer and now Pax is being taught something new to do for Rick. All of his new accomplishments take place in this space. It's quite a change from the field work that he and Keller had done, long runs, lots of energy burned off, the flinty scent of danger overhanging every action. In comparison, these new accomplishments are really pretty tame. With Keller, he was part of a hunting pack. Lead dog, his followers flanking the prey and then taking it down for him. Here, he is domestic, nest building without a mate. *Pickitup. Pull me.* And now a two-part exercise: *Take it. Put it.* The men use a rubber ball as the training object, so he takes it in his mouth and then moves to a spot that Rick points to with his forefinger. Keller has taught him that *Put it* means to carefully put the object in the spot that he thinks Rick wants him to. It's not an easy task. Sometimes it's really hard to determine where Rick is pointing. He's dropped the ball on the floor, on the bed, on the table and had to go retrieve it when it bounced away and under the hospital bed. Crawling under the lowered metal frame isn't an easy thing for the big dog to do and makes him think of his war experience, crawling on his belly beneath rifle fire. Rick gets impatient and says *no no no no* a lot. Finally, Pax masters the nuances of Rick's gestures and has a perfect run of placing the object on the table when Rick points to it, on the bed, and, yes, on the floor as directed. Then they try other objects, like the little bottle.

Keller is pleased with him, but Rick keeps asking him to repeat the same exercise long after Keller has left the room. It has gone beyond mere practice and is sliding out of the realm of a game. Rick's repetition of the series of commands to retrieve an object, give him the object, take the object, and then put it where Rick indicates has taken on the same intensity as those exercises with Keller as the big guns thundered over their heads and the men around them depended on them to secure the way. Rick's aura suggests life and death even though the object isn't to locate an enemy hidden in a thicket, but to bring him a glass vial.

Rick's praise goes beyond a mere touch. Pax doesn't understand his words, but he knows that the tone of Rick's voice means that he is extraordinary.

CHAPTER THIRTY-SIX

We had a ramp, thanks to Keller. He'd also appealed to my landlord, played the veteran card, I think, and had gotten grudging permission to widen the doorways and remove the sills to accommodate Rick's chair. A few days of noisy carpentry and Rick was, in our minds at least, set free. In his mind, it made no difference. He wouldn't budge.

"It's a beautiful day, and you haven't been outside since your last doctor's appointment. Come on, we'll go for a ride, maybe get some ice cream."

He looked at me as if I was treating him like a child. Which I was.

"I'm fine in here. You go."

"Keller's made this possible for you. At least come out into the yard. You haven't seen my lilies." My tone had tensed up, so that I wasn't so much cajoling as badgering.

Keller glanced at me and I could see the

warning to be patient. It was hard. I'd been patient with Rick for months. More than a year. Would I be damned if I got a little impatient now and then? No one understood better than I did the magnitude of his loss, but it was my loss, too. It was, in my mind, the way life was now, and no amount of hiding in a darkened sickroom was going to change that. He needed to accept that things weren't going to go back to the way they had been. I didn't want him to spend the rest of his days like this, a self-incarcerated captive.

"Pax will keep me company. No need for you two to sit inside on such a nice day."

"Rick. Please."

My husband looked at me with a dull stare. Even his eyes had changed since the war. Eyes I'd once said were the blue of a Delft tile were now the color of distant shadows. He no longer looked at me with bright eyes, with happiness and anticipation, with humor or mischievousness. With desire. The war not only had taken his arm and left him wheelchair-bound but had also stolen his spirit.

"Okay. That's fine. But I'm opening these goddamned curtains." I pushed his chair aside and yanked open the dark drapes that kept his tiny room in a state of perpetual gloom. Sunlight burst in, revealing dirty streaks on the windowpane. I unlocked the double-hung window and raised it. Fresh late-August air, bearing the faintest tinge of a sea breeze, pushed into the room, ruffling Rick's hair. He looked like an underworld creature exposed to the light of day, squinting against the sudden brightness.

I'll never forget it, what Pax did then. He picked up the rubber ball that they used for training and poked it into Rick's left hand. Reflexively, Rick took it, and I could see the habit of squeezing a ball hadn't been amputated with his pitching arm. Pax stood back and barked as if to get Rick to throw the ball. Which he did, in an awkward throw, as if trying to rid himself of a nasty object. He threw the rubber ball right out the window and, to our amazement, the dog leaped out after it. In seconds, he was back in the house, ball in mouth and dancing on happy front feet, as if to say, *Do it again!* And Rick did.

"It would be easier on him if you went out in the backyard with him." Keller kept one hand on the back of Rick's chair. He'd come running at the sound of our excited voices, skidding into Rick's room as if he thought we were on fire. "He'd love it if you would."

The dog came pounding back into the room, nails skittering on the hardwood floor, ball clutched in his jaws, tail beating from side to side. He'd let himself in through the open breezeway door, open because we had hoped that we'd be wheeling Rick out of the house for his inaugural ride down the new ramp. Pax then took it in his head to tease Rick, to play a little game of keep away with him, making him reach for the ball, stretch a little.

"Gimme that, you mutt!" Why was it that the only time my husband seemed amused was with this dog?

Pax pranced around, shaking the ball like prey. His tail swept a metal washbasin off the bedside table, and the stainless steel clanged against the bare floor. In the next moment, he knocked the pile of magazines off as well, the *National Geographics* flopping to the floor like dead fish.

"I think he's telling you something, Rick." Keller grasped the handles on the back of Rick's chair and swung him around so that he could back him out of the room. Rick made a token protest, but Keller ignored it and kept going. "You'd better get outside with him before he wrecks this room any more."

And so we four rolled out of that sickroom

and through the kitchen and out the newly widened door to slide Rick down the ramp Keller had built to give him access to the backyard. Pax led the way, the rubber ball firmly between his teeth.

I know now that Pax had been a hero during the war. I didn't know the story then; that would come later, as Keller and I became better acquainted. It was still too early to have begun asking those questions, questions about his service, about his experience. Keller's and Pax's, I mean. But that August afternoon, that dog became a bona fide hero in my eyes. He'd done what we hadn't been able to do, break Rick out of his self-imposed confinement.

Rick and the dog stayed outside until even Pax was exhausted from the game. Rick kept tossing the ball for him, and I sat on the back steps, watching. I might have cried a little. With every throw, it became more like a pitch. Slow underhand became an overhand toss, evolved to a slider, a curve. A sinker. No fastball, but I think that was more because our small yard wouldn't accommodate a long throw. As it was, Pax twice scaled the back fence to retrieve an inaccurate throw. With each pitch of his left arm, Rick's right stump rose in an echo.

CHAPTER THIRTY-SEVEN

Sometimes Rick wakes up in the night, or out of a diurnal doze, thinking that he's late for practice. It is so real, so immediate, that he imagines that his legs twitch and his right fingers are flexing. His heart beats, pumping blood through his veins as if he's been running bases. Then the fear of being late for practice — he's been late too many times; they'll fine him — transforms itself into the greater fear that his reality won't dissolve like a bad dream.

Francesca is so good to him, but even he can see that her patience is wearing thin. She wants him to accept his new dynamic and return to being the man she fell in love with. She's told him, whispered it into his good ear. "You're still the man I love. I fell in love with you for you, not because you're a ballplayer. That's like saying I only love you for your pitching. I'd have fallen in love with you even if you were a pipe fitter." She nuzzled him on the cheek, the wrong side, the side with the skin grafts, the side that feels invisible, as he has no feeling in it. "Whatever that is." She'd been in here an hour ago, coyly sitting on his lap, as if she might expect a response. He is loath to wrap the remains of his right arm around her in a quasi-hug. She kissed him, wanting something from him he cannot give. Rick wants desperately to desire his wife.

And the only thing he could say was, "I *was* a ballplayer. It was the only thing I ever wanted to be." He keeps beating the same dead horse. He knows it and there doesn't seem to be any way to prevent himself, to pretend that he's getting over it, to put on a brave face, to convince himself that he'll be fine. Instead, he's begun to snap at every suggestion that he accept this turn of events. He's a war hero, she says. Francesca doesn't know that, far from being a hero, he was simply a fool.

She slid off his lap and asked him what he might want for dinner, chicken or hamburgers. The minx replaced by the hausfrau.

It's nearly dark already. Francesca has replaced the blackout curtains with new white ones that allow the room to fill with daylight when Keller tilts the venetian blinds open every morning. Rick can watch the passage of time by the way the sunlight circles the perimeter of the room. Sometimes the metal blinds rattle in the late-afternoon breeze, chiming like a halyard on a flagpole and setting his teeth on edge. Rick can't maneuver his chair close enough to the window to close them, and he wants Keller to train the dog to pull the cord to raise them so that they stop clanging.

"Interesting idea, but you know that you can always ask me to do it. That's what I'm here for." Keller has finished bathing him and now carefully adjusts the pajama top so that the long right sleeve is pinned back and won't get tangled in the humiliating side rail of the bed. They're afraid that he'll roll out of bed like some little kid. You have to be able to flip yourself to roll out of a bed. You can't flip out if half of you is dead-weight.

"It would be nice not to have to depend on you. Or Francesca. Pax is so smart, and he likes working with me." The list of tasks that the dog can now perform to ease Rick's immobility has grown. He can now fetch a long list of items by name. It's as if he's memorizing vocabulary. He's conquered the "Get it/Put it series of commands, and when Rick is enduring the sharp phantom pains in his missing arm, Pax stands rock steady as he clings to the dog's nape. When the memory of pain eases, Pax licks Rick's nose, as if to say, *That's that, then.*

"Just try."

"Okay. Let me figure out how to do it. I'll come up with something."

Pax is sitting, watching, his golden-brown eyes following Keller's every movement; he's licking his lips in anticipation of the next thing that will happen — the nightly walk. Keller will disappear for an hour with the dog, and it is then that Rick feels most betrayed. Even if Francesca comes in with her knitting or mending and they turn on the radio to listen to the news or a broadcast from Symphony Hall, he doesn't relax until he hears the slam of the door and the dog comes back in to spend the rest of the evening with him. It isn't so much the fact that Keller gets to *walk* the dog; it's more that the dog is so happy to go with him. It's foolish to be jealous of Pax's attachment to Keller, but he is anyway. Pax was his dog, his rescued puppy, the boon companion of those happy, ignorant days before the war. Even before Francesca. How this dog can smile every time Keller reappears, really smile, a great happy canine chuckle coming out of his mouth, his eyes lit up, doing his puppyish happy dance, which once belonged only to him but is now being danced for this other man? Even if Keller has only been gone half an hour. What kind of experience forged this bond?

"What did you and Pax do, during the war, I mean?" Rick puts his hand out to stop Keller from sliding the chair to the bedside. "Scout, right?"

"Yeah. We were part of the advance team tasked with clearing out the enemy."

Rick slides his hand down the dog's side. Beneath his fingers he can feel a nub of scar tissue. "How did he get this?" It isn't so much a question as a demand. As if Keller failed somehow to protect the dog while Pax was in his care.

"He took a bullet. He was fine." Keller has his eyes on the dog, a liar's avoidance.

Rick takes a deep breath. "And what happened to you?"

"Are we trading war stories now?" Keller grabs the wheelchair and muscles it over to the bed. It's after ten o'clock, clearly past Rick's bedtime.

"Yeah. Don't you think it's about time?"

"Nothing like what happened to you. Is that what you want me to say?"

Rick feels a hot blush rise on the good side of his face, and he absently wonders if

261

both sides of his cheeks turn red or whether the smooth, shiny new skin stays waxy. "I just want to know what happened to my dog."

"Our platoon came under fire."

"And he was out front?"

"We were. In the woods, pretty deep forest. We'd spread out; Pax and I were on point position, as always. He did his job. He alerted us, real quiet, real accurate, and we got down. The Krauts didn't know we had a dog, so they aimed high. We kept moving forward and, I don't know, all hell broke loose. I got hit." Keller drops a hand on the dog's head. "He defended me."

Rick hears the catch in Keller's voice. "Go on."

"Last thing I remembered was him giving it to some Kraut. A day later, I woke up in a field hospital, absolutely panic-stricken, wondering where he was. What had happened to my dog."

"My dog."

"Your dog." Keller takes his hand off Pax, aligns the chair, and removes the arm so he can lift Rick into the bed. "He's one lucky dog. He was all right. My buddy Sully got him tended to right away. If they passed out medals to dogs, he'd have gotten the Purple Heart."

"Did you?"

"Yeah. Would rather have gotten a promotion."

"He saved your life."

"He did." Keller settles the blankets, docks the wheelchair in the far corner, out of the way. "You want the light on for a while?"

"Leave it on. I may read."

Pax, as he does every night at this time, gets into the basket that they've put in Rick's room for him. He licks his nether parts, yawns, stands up, circles three times, and curls up. Rick knows that as soon as the dog senses he's asleep, he'll leave that cozy spot and search out Keller. Keller, whose life he saved.

CHAPTER THIRTY-EIGHT

Keller tries to be as considerate as he can be regarding Francesca and Rick's privacy. He doesn't eat supper with them unless asked. He takes his plate into his garage bedroom instead of eating alone at the kitchen table. He doesn't want them to feel like they have to invite him to join them in the tight confines of Rick's room, and if he's sitting in the next room, it's just too awkward for all of them. He's a third wheel, for sure, but he's not complaining. If Rick ever decides to come out of his room to eat, that may change. Three at a kitchen table is different. Still, he's aware that he needs to allow them husband and wife time, time when they can feel unobserved, uninhibited. That's another good reason to take long evening walks with Pax. Keller has signed up for an English class at Quincy College, so that will give them three afternoons a week without the presence of a star boarder

264

in their house. Keller tries not to think about what kind of physical relationship Rick and Francesca may have. It's none of his business. Besides, they've been married a long time, so maybe it's not quite as important as it might have been. As important as it would be to him.

Betty Ann Carlin was his first. A quiet girl in his math class, completely unaware that she was very pretty behind those truly ugly spectacles. Clayton didn't hold with a social life, so he and Betty Ann said they were staying after for extra help and instead took long walks along the beach, finding themselves nestled into the concavity of low dunes. Maybe if there hadn't been a war, he'd have ended up marrying her; probably would have had to, the way they were going at it in the shelter of that cold sand. She never wrote to him, not even a Dear John.

Then there was the occasional war-destitute Italian girl willing to trade sexual favors for cigarettes and chocolate bars. Stateside, discharged and living with the Stantons, it's been a long time, and Keller is finding himself thinking all too often of sex. He's hoping that maybe he'll meet a nice coed willing to take a chance on an older man. At twenty-three, he's likely to be five years older than most of his incoming freshman classmates. Most of his fellow GIs will be attending the night classes, but with his odd little job, day classes make more sense. Rick needs him here at night to help him get ready for bed, to be available.

Sometimes it's hard to remember that Francesca isn't that much older than he is. Maybe it's part of being married to a man so much older; more likely, it's the life they have ended up with that has forced an early maturity on her — the weight of it.

Lately, he and Francesca have found a nice balance, no longer shy with each other, more relaxed and working smoothly together. He reaches for the dishes in the cupboard before she asks; she tosses him the can opener before he's got his hand on the dog food can. Once he has Rick settled for the night and she's been in to say good night to him, sometimes, not always, but some evenings when the weather is nice, they slip out onto the back stoop to share a lager and smoke a cigarette. They talk of other things besides Rick — light conversation about the news or the nosy neighbor who is perplexed by their living situation; whether Francesca should look into one of those freezer plans; if he should take an accounting course or test the collegiate waters with English literature. He's told her a bit about his past; she's talked about life in a small Iowa town and coming to the big city to find love.

Francesca taps at the open garage door. "I'm going to walk down to the market. Is there anything you need?" The weather has turned a bit cooler and she's wearing a sweater set he's never seen before. It fits so well that it makes him look away.

"How's Rick?" Keller closes his book, ready to do whatever might need doing.

"Fine. Pax is keeping him company. He said to tell you not to go in." She brushes a fleck from the front of her sweater.

Something about that little unconscious brushing stirs him. "Do you want me to go for you? Stay here and relax, put your feet up."

Francesca shakes her head no. "What, and read a French novel and eat bonbons?"

"If that's what you want to do, sure."

She taps a knuckle on the doorjamb. "Do you want to come?"

"I can carry the bags."

"And help me figure out what to have for dinner. I'm fresh out of ideas."

Keller has never eaten so well. Having gone from Depression-era make-do to institutional food to bachelor cooking and back to the institutional food of the army, he finds that home-cooked is something that amazes him pretty much every day, and when beef stew cycles back into the menu, he's as happy to see it as the very first time she made it. Roast chicken, pot roast, all manner of Iowa country-girl fare. And she seems to do it all effortlessly. Every single day.

"I tell you what. I'll cook tonight." Keller grabs his jacket. "The chowder I promised."

He is rewarded with her smile. A simple gift of a smile. The heady feeling of making Francesca happy travels through Keller's body. He's never made anyone happy before. He follows her out of the house, a silly grin on his face, and all he wants is to do it again.

"We should let Rick know we're both out of the house." The smile is gone. The weight that keeps Francesca grounded is recharged. The slight alleviation of that weight has evaporated in an instant. It is constant, this inelastic attachment of her responsibility to Rick.

"I'll go in and talk with him. If he needs me to, I'll stay. I can give you a list of what I'll need to make chowder." Magically, the smile comes back. He's taking a task off her shoulders and all he wants is to keep doing that.

Rick doesn't want him, waves him out of the room. Pax whines a little, knowing by Keller's body language that *outside* is going to happen. But he doesn't move from his place beside Rick. Keller unkindly thinks that it's because Rick has his hand on the dog's collar, but he knows that Pax won't leave Rick's side during the day unless one of them orders him to. It's uncanny, this attachment. On the day that he arrived here with Pax on the end of his official K-9 Corps leash, Keller would have bet the farm that Pax would have chosen him over Rick. Now he's not so sure. Francesca buckled on Pax's old civilian collar, and that old expression "A dog can't serve two masters" is proved wrong every day. Pax has figured out a way to do it. And it's been both challenging and fun to train him to be of use to Rick. The issue with the venetian blinds was fixed when Keller attached the rubber ball to the cord. Now all Pax has to do is grab the ball and pull. The blinds go up. A quick jab to the right and they lock in place. That was the hardest part of the exercise, and after a number of crash landings, he finally got it right.

"We won't be long."

"Take your time, Kel. Pax is here." Rick tugs gently on the dog's nape, and Pax seems to grin.

"Are you sure . . ."

"Keller, knock it off. I can be trusted to stay put and not get into trouble. My catheter is clear; my chair is positioned right; you've talked me into the radio, so I can listen to WBZ news. I've had lunch, dessert, and I can reach this week's *Life* magazine. Go out. Take Francesca and, for God's sake, forget the store. Take her to the picture show." Rick shifts his weight in the chair, half-lifting himself with his good left arm. "If the house catches fire, Pax will call it in."

Keller throws his hands up in the universal sign of surrender. "Okay, okay."

"And Keller. I mean it. She needs some fun. I know she doesn't have any girlfriends around here, so you're it. Show her some fun, and I don't mean just this afternoon."

"He's fine."

"What did he say?" She's put a hat on, a little lozenge of a thing that nestles among her curls. "Out with it."

"He'd like me to make sure you have some fun. More fun than going to the grocery

270

store. Like seeing a film."

She doesn't say anything for a moment, then gathers her handbag and shakes her head. "He's being generous. He can't be left for that long."

Keller shuts the door behind them. "Francesca, he thinks we treat him like a baby. And you're what we called in the war 'collateral damage.' He knows that you are as trapped by that wheelchair as he is."

"I'm his wife. I want to be with him."

"He knows that. But, don't you see, maybe all this attention is overwhelming. Too much of a good thing."

Francesca spins around to face Keller. "A good thing? It's all we're ever going to have."

Keller shoves his hands into his jacket pockets. "I'm sorry. I've said too much. It's none of my business, except that he was adamant that I get you out of the house and show you some fun. That's all. You're all he has and he wants you to be happy." Keller doesn't offer his arm to Francesca; he keeps three feet away as they walk down the cracked sidewalk.

"That ship sailed, my friend. My happiness and his. All we can do now is take care of each other." Abruptly, Francesca turns around and goes back to the house. Keller is left standing on the sidewalk, his hands in his pockets, wishing that he'd kept his mouth shut.

CHAPTER THIRTY-NINE

Pax rests his chin on Rick's knees. He waits patiently until he senses Rick's heartbeat slowing down. Some days they go through this exercise eighteen times, except, of course, the dog has no sense of counting. He just knows that Rick's blood pressure is up and that the only way it will go down is if he stands or sits next to him, on his left side, as if aligning himself in a proper *heel,* and places his head in the man's lap. To an outside observer, it would look like simple human/dog affection. No human could possibly detect the curative effect that the dog has on the man. Rick cannot feel the weight of the dog's head in his lap, but he always knows when it's there, even if his eyes are squeezed shut and his good hand is wiping away the tears that threaten his dignity.

Nothing hurts; everything hurts. Pax always knows when this psychic pain occurs. He is instantly at the ready, and he will go so far as to drape his long front legs over Rick's dead ones and press his body against the man's chest until he gets the response he wants, the embrace of both arms. Hunching over, Rick will lay his cheek against Pax's skull, his breath tickling the dog's ears. Pax will stay motionless until Rick shucks off the spell of phantom pain and panic. Then he'll jump down from Rick's lap and grab a ball or a squeaky toy and transform himself from merciful spirit to mischievous sprite.

Eyes bright, he'll tease Rick with the object until Rick gives the order to put it in his lap. With the bedroom door fully open, Rick can throw the ball or the toy down the hall. Lately, he's managed to pitch it far enough that he bangs the front door. The big dog skitters down the hallway, rucking up the carpet runner into a roller coaster, catches the ball or the rubber mouse on the rebound, and runs back to Rick. It's his reward for doing his job. Pax has come to do his job very well.

CHAPTER FORTY

We'd settled into a good routine, Rick and Keller and I. And Pax. Pax was a godsend. Keller did all the heavy work, and I was given the freedom to act like a normal housewife, planning meals and changing the curtains with the change of season. I think that Rick was showing improvement. During the late summer and early fall, we got him out into the backyard a few times, or I should say that Pax did. He'd tease with the rubber ball, poking it at Rick until Rick finally took it and tossed it. If Pax teased enough, Rick might allow us to get him outside and he'd throw the ball for the dog like he had on that first evening. But the weather turned colder and I didn't want to risk letting Rick go outside and sit. He was so delicate in so many ways. Prone to infections. Every day that went by when he didn't show symptoms of a bladder infection or a wound infection or a cold coming on was a good one.

Keller started school, testing the waters with a class in English literature. He had that book, the one about King Arthur that he'd kept on his nightstand as long as he'd been living with us, and it turned out that *Le Morte d'Arthur* was part of the syllabus for that class. I'd never read it, so, because he had a paperback edition from the college bookstore, Keller offered to lend his hardcover copy to me so that we could talk about it and help get him ready for the class discussion. The first thing I noticed was the inscription on the flyleaf: *To Keller Nicholson as he begins the journey of a lifetime.* Miss Jacobs. Keller was so closedmouthed about his past, whereas I found myself talking about mine, telling him about life in a small Iowa town, about my friends and what high jinks we used to get up to. Things like lighting May baskets filled with horse manure on fire and putting them on the front porch of the school principal's house, then running like mad, so we never actually got to see the look on her face. Picking all the new lilies in Mr. Bernardsen's garden and taking them home to appalled mothers. Keller had no such anecdotes, as if he'd passed through his early life, arriving fully formed on the shores of World War II. He chuckled at my exploits but never shared any of his own.

"So, who's Miss Jacobs?" I asked one day.

"My high school English teacher."

"You must have been pretty smart in school to earn this."

"I was. Smart enough."

It was like pulling teeth. "Was this a graduation present?"

"No. She gave it to me the day before I left for induction." He looked at me with what I'd come to recognize as his "Ask me no questions and I'll tell you no lies look, but not before I saw a flicker of memory soften his eyes. Whoever she was, Miss Jacobs meant something to Keller Nicholson.

Keller finally made that chowder that he promised. I took some in to Rick, knowing full well that the challenge of eating left-handed with a spoon was going to be hard. Keller, as usual, didn't join us for dinner. "Gotta study." A good new excuse for him to keep to himself, allowing us a privacy we didn't really need.

As dignified as Pax was, he was a terrible beggar and sat watching us, me on one side of the tray table, Rick on the other, the dog's eyes following every mouthful. "Go lie down." I wasn't usually the one to order the dog around, but that night I wanted no distraction for Rick. Pax gave me one of his "You've broken my heart" looks, but he went to his basket. I tied a tea towel around Rick's neck, set another one in his lap. He might not have been able to feel it, but hot chowder in his lap would have been very bad.

Rick didn't say anything, just stared into the shallow bowl filled with Keller's beautiful traditional New England clam chowder. Not thick. A thin cream broth with chunks of potato and clams. He'd bought the clams and shucked them himself, disdaining to buy minced clams.

"Try it." I took a mouthful. "It's really good."

"I can't. Give it to the dog."

"I will not." I set my spoon down and took his, dipping it into his bowl. "Here." I offered it to his mouth like a mother offers a spoonful of baby food to a child.

Like a child, he screwed up his mouth and turned away. "I'm not a baby. Stop treating me like one."

"Then pick up your own spoon and eat your dinner." I don't know why I got so mad then. It wasn't a particularly unusual refusal on Rick's part. It was just that Keller had made this chowder, made it because I said

278

Rick liked it. Rick was being rude. I was glad that Keller wasn't in the room to hear him, but it would be hard to lie to Keller and tell him that Rick had gobbled it down. "Stop being a baby. You've got to learn to use your left hand sometime, and this chowder is worth it." I set his spoon beside his bowl, took up my own, and commenced eating the rest of my dinner.

Rick sat there, the soup spoon at a right angle to his full bowl. I'd inadvertently put it on the right side. I grabbed it and put it on the left side of the bowl, handle toward him.

"You don't have to hold it correctly. Remember that's what the occupational therapist said. Just grip it. Lean in, and eat this damned chowder."

Keeping my eyes on my own dinner, I didn't watch as he lifted the spoon left-handed, clubbing it in his hand like a little kid struggling with his manners. He dipped it, catching a little in the bowl of the spoon. Somewhere between the bowl and his mouth, the spoon tipped and the mouthful of chowder went right down the front of him. Slowly, Rick set the spoon down, pulled the tea towel from his neck, and placed it carefully over the still-full bowl. "I'm done."

Rick refused to try, so I gathered up those bowls, nesting my empty one beneath his full one. I grabbed the napkins and spoons and the waxed paper–sealed rectangle of pilot crackers and fled that room, my head roaring with the unspoken. Chowder slopped over the edges of the bowl, dotting my path from sickroom to kitchen. I didn't care. I stalked into the kitchen, the brightness glaring down from the ceiling light after the evening dimness of Rick's room. I was shaking, and that inner vibration of anger thrummed so intently that the chowder left in Rick's bowl trembled like a lake in an earthquake. A dollop crested the edge and ran down my wrist. It was cold, but I reacted as if I'd been scalded, and slammed the bowls from our wedding china hard into the porcelain sink, and I was glad at the destruction. Shards and chowder flew, spattering the window over the sink and the floor and the counters. One shard struck me on the cheek.

"Are you all right?" Keller was beside me, pulling me away from the sink. A towel dangled from the back of a chair, and he grabbed it, dabbing it gently against my cheek. "What happened? Did you slip?" He sat me down on that chair and knelt to examine me for more damage.

"He wouldn't eat it." I was crying, and the words came out in individual bursts.

"Oh, Francesca. Don't take it so hard." Keller turned my face toward his. "It's all right."

"No, it's not. Don't you see, Keller, he's just not trying."

Keller pulled me to my feet and, I don't know if it was instinct or impulse, but he held me in a hug. A hug is such a simple thing, and yet can mean so much . . . affection, sympathy, joy. I felt the length of his strong, healthy, complete body next to mine and gave in to the urge to lay my head against his chest. I hadn't been held by a man in such a long time except for Sid's cousinly embrace or my father's paternal one. This was both and neither. I look back now and imagine that he rocked me a little, but I'm not sure that he did. I put my arms around him and felt an equal contentment in the relaxation of his shoulders and back muscles. It would only hit me later, when I knew more of his story, that Keller had not had a hug himself in many a year. Maybe most of his life. I don't remember how long we stood like that, under the glare of the overhead light, chowder and china all over the place, maybe twenty seconds, maybe an hour. My arms around him, his around me.

I could feel his breathing slow. In and out, in and out, until my agitated respiration finally matched his.

Finally, we did let go of each other, laughing a little in that embarrassed giggle of humans who have given into temptation, filing the moment away under things never to speak of. Keller got a mug out of the cupboard and filled it with chowder from the pot still warm on the stove. He buttered two pilot crackers and walked Rick's dinner down to him.

I should have thought of that. A mug. So simple an answer for a man not converting to left-handedness easily. If I had, that evening's meal would have been so ordinary. Things would not have been set in motion. Even now, I don't regret it. Even now, I remember how good it felt to be held.

CHAPTER FORTY-ONE

They've gone out. After dinner, which Keller thoughtfully put in a mug so that he could handle chowder — which was really good; Francesca was right — Keller came back in and asked if he would be all right till ten o'clock or so, when they would be back from the picture show. "I will. Go. Have a great time and be sure to buy her a box of popcorn. She loves it."

Keller didn't respond, just made sure that anything he might need for the hour and a half that he would be alone was at hand. "Pax, you stay, keep Rick company." It was such an unnecessary command in Rick's opinion, and annoying. Like Pax would ever have to be *ordered* to stay with him.

It feels surprisingly good to be alone. Completely alone. Like the first time he was left home alone when he was nine years old and his mother had an altar guild meeting and his father was at work. A litany of "don'ts" and a list of "dos." He spent the afternoon poking around his parents' closet, looking for clues to their life before him. He found a shoe box of letters, but they were mushy and he didn't read them all; a pair of shoes from the last century, old-fashioned and surely too tiny for his mother's feet; a mink stole he didn't know his mother owned.

"Pax, get it." Rick points to the vial of morphine on his bedside table. Just sitting there, just out of reach. He's been asking for morphine every night and then palming the pill so that he can add it to his growing collection. The pain is real, and sometimes he retrieves the hidden pill because he can't sleep without it. Hide three, take one. It's a box step he's losing ground on. "Pax, get it." Rick has to repeat the order because the dog is unclear about the target. "Vial."

Cocking his head, Pax picks up the vial in his jaws as tenderly as a retriever picks up a duck. He brings it to Rick, placing it in his hand. "Good boy." Rick inserts the vial's screw top between his teeth, but Keller has it screwed on so tight that he's afraid he's going to chip a tooth. He then wedges the vial between his useless leg and the side of the chair, but the glass is slippery and turns with each twist, offering no purchase against the threads of the cap. There's a damp washcloth in the stainless-steel bowl he uses to wash up in the morning. "Pax, get it." Rick points to the cloth dangling over the edge of the bowl, and miraculously Pax cottons on to his meaning instantly, snagging the cloth in his teeth and carrying it over to Rick. Wrapped in the damp cloth, the bottle stays put and Rick finally gets the cap off. After all this, he extracts two tabs to make up for the effort. And he immediately drops them both on the floor.

The two little pills bounce twice and scatter like mice.

"Shit."

Pax cocks his head and then scratches vigorously at his side. He gets up and sniffs at the pills.

"Get it." Rick whispers the command, uncertain whether or not he really wants the dog to put morphine pills in his mouth.

Pax's sniffing pushes one of the pills into the middle of the floor, visible to anyone coming in the door. Rick maneuvers his wheelchair a little left. Maybe he can roll over the pill and crush it. It'll look like a little talcum powder carelessly spilled, instead of a clue revealing his exit strategy. The other pill has rolled under the bed; nothing to be done about that.

By now, he has squirreled away fifteen morphine pills. He really doesn't know how many it might take to, as Shakespeare once suggested, shuffle off this mortal coil, but he's guessing it's closer to twenty-five. Every one counts. Losing these two will set him back. In the quiet of the late afternoon, when he is just waking from a nap, before he needs Keller to come in and help him up, he sometimes hears the low rumble of two people in ordinary conversation. They talk back and forth, their words mostly indistinct. A little laughter. Rick tamps down the spurt of useless jealousy and makes himself be glad that Francesca has someone to make her laugh, even a little. He knows that he behaved abominably tonight. She's only trying to help him.

Francesca deserves so much more out of life than being chained to a man like him. She tries so hard. Kissing him. Putting her hands on him as if she expects the mere power of her touch will fool the demons and put life back into his desire. He's tried. The only unwounded thing left to him is his imagination, and when he pictures her as she came to him so often, seductive and beautiful and innocent and mercurial, nothing. Not even frustration. Dead to the world. The images that inflicted near-pubescent physical agony on him as a grown man are only images now. Pretty pictures. Not a eunuch. Not a gelding. Intact but impotent. Not a flutter. They had hoped, of course, that even insensate, he could still — what was the word the doctors used? *Perform.* Do his duty.

They should have tried harder, back when he was waiting to go to war, tried to have a child then. How utterly egotistical and naïve they were to think that they had all the time in the world. That having his child and then losing him would have been a bad idea. Who could have ever predicted that, with him, she was saddled with both: a perpetual child, a helpless man.

"Pax, grab it." Rick holds out the knotted rope he now uses with Pax to move the chair around. Francesca jokes that they should get the dog a harness, like a sled dog would wear, and let him pull Rick down the street. Pax takes the knot in his mouth and helps Rick aim toward the renegade pill until the wheelchair tire hovers close to it. Rick hesitates. The loss of this addition to his collection is too dear, so he leans forward, stretches out his good arm. His own legs block his reach. Rick lifts his left leg over his right, clearing a path. In trying to reach it, his fingers accidentally move the pill just far enough that he can't pick it up and he can't move his chair any closer. "Pax. Good boy. I just need you to get it a little closer to me." Rick points to the pill but can't come up with a command that might make the dog actually push the pill closer. "Get it?"

It's as if the dog is contemplating what to do. Does he understand what Rick wants? He looks at Rick with those wise amber eyes, flooded now with the darker dilation of his pupils in the evening-dim room. He looks at the object, the target Rick aims his finger toward. There is a moment of stasis, of complete quiet, when even the street sounds fade into silence. Rick can hear his own breathing and the soft puzzled sound the dog is making. *What what what?*

"Get it."

Using the tiny teeth between his long wolf-ish incisors, Pax delicately lifts the tiny object up from the floor. His lips close over it and for a moment Rick panics. What if he swallows it? Would human-grade morphine kill a dog Pax's size? "Give it!"

Pax's dewlaps curl up in a comic mask of distaste as he drops the slightly wet ball of compounded morphine into Rick's open hand.

The slam of the front door startles Rick and he nearly loses the pill. Quickly, he hands the vial to Pax with the whispered command "Put it." The dog is his ally. The dog does what he needs, then helps Rick spin the chair back around, so that when Francesca appears in the bedroom doorway, he's right where she left him, Pax's head on his dead knees.

"How was the show?"

CHAPTER FORTY-TWO

Pax doesn't like it when the three humans are in separate places. Some herd-dog instinct survives in him and he's only really happy when the three of them find themselves together. However, that isn't the usual dynamic, and the dog has had to content himself with dividing his time unequally. He knows that his primary function now is to stay with Rick. That's a role he loves and is proud to have. He delights in being able to carry out Rick's requests and it is his best task ever to absorb Rick's darkness into his fur. But he really likes it when he can pester Rick into going outside and throwing the ball for him like he used to. The ball doesn't go as far as it did long ago, when they'd play in the park and Pax might have to run half the length of the field to get the ball, but it is the only time Rick seems like the old Rick. If, in the old days, Pax might take the ball and run away, playing his version of keep away while Rick chased him, laughing and cursing, he knows better than that now and is willing to return the ball to Rick with dependable speed. Throw, catch, return, over and over, until Rick hands the ball to Francesca and Keller wheels him back into the house. Pax is never ready to quit the game, and he tries not to let his disappointment show. He trails along, hoping that maybe Keller will pick up the game later.

The good news is that Francesca and Keller seem willing to be in the same room together a lot more now. It's easier, not having to go from living room to garage all afternoon long while Francesca irons and Keller reads. Now they sit together, reading and talking, in the living room while Rick naps in his room. Pax settles on the braided rug and dozes, listening to their low voices. He doesn't understand one word, but the soft human vocalizations lull him. Francesca's voice has lost some of the tautness he'd grown used to hearing. Keller is using his voice more. They vocalize like crooning littermates, and Pax enjoys the sound of effortless companionship. He's one of them, Keller's sock-covered toes scratching at his belly, Francesca's fingertips finding the nirvana place at the base of his tail. *Good boy, Pax.* They smile over him, pleased with

him. He's keeping everyone happy.
He *is* a good boy and life is sweet.

CHAPTER FORTY-THREE

Keller chalks up that spontaneous hug to the emotion of the moment. She was upset, and he just wanted her to feel better. He tells himself that it wasn't any more significant than had Francesca been his sister. Or cousin. Except that he's never had a sister, or had any desire to touch either of his female cousins, who lodge in his memory as tormentors, not pals.

If it meant only a quick dash of human kindness, why are they assiduously avoiding physical contact now? If her hand bumps his in passing the salt, she apologizes. If he accidently grazes her with his arm as he is reaching for a screwdriver out of the utensil drawer, he backs away like he's been scalded. If it meant nothing, why does he think about it all the time? The feel of her cheek against his chest, the way she sank into him, as if climbing into a life raft. How good it felt to have his arms around another human being. It wakes him up at night.

After a warm early fall, the weather has turned more seasonable, and even with two extra army blankets over him and the dog's warmth, it's getting pretty hard to imagine staying in the garage bedroom much longer. At the very least, they'll have to start closing the connecting doors to keep the cold out of the house, and that will make it difficult to hear Rick if he needs Keller in the night, and Pax will have to chose one place or the other to sleep. They haven't talked about it yet, but they'll have to. Not counting the den, which has been made over into Rick's sickroom, the house has only two bedrooms, both on the second floor.

The thing is, Keller hates giving up the privacy, or the illusion of privacy, that the garage apartment offers. If he moves into the spare bedroom, there will be no separating himself from the Stantons. Even retreating to an upstairs bedroom to read or do homework won't give him the psychological break that going into his "apartment" lends.

But it's not just a loss of privacy that makes moving into the house an uncomfortable idea. After all, he's said good night to her any number of times and watched her mount the stairs to bed. Greeted her as she comes down in the morning, housecoat tied neatly around her waist but her curls tousled and her cheeks rosy like a child's. If she's slept well, he can see it in her clear eyes; equally, a restless night and he can read in the shadows beneath her eyes the thoughts that have kept her awake. Once, she greeted him exactly as she does Rick: "Good morning, sunshine." She blushed at her mistake, but throughout the day he kept smiling at having been so greeted.

Keller just can't imagine being across the landing from her all night long. It's just too intimate. It just doesn't seem — what's the word? — *proper* for him, as a single man, to be sleeping across the hall from his landlady. Sleeping, or not sleeping, a mere two yards apart.

Landlady. Keller laughs at his choice of word. What is she really? His boss? No. Rick's wife. He would be sleeping in close proximity to Rick's wife. What would the neighbors think? "What do you say, Pax? Will the neighbors talk if they think I'm sleeping on the same floor as a married woman? Will you chaperone us?" Pax just shakes from nose to tail, stretches fore and aft, and utters nothing useful.

Maybe he'll go to the hardware store down on Hancock Street tomorrow and see if they have any space heaters he'd feel safe using. During the worst of the winter months, when the woodstove in the parlor was inadequate to the task, Clayton would haul out a cylindrical kerosene heater and fire it up. Keller remembers sleeping with one eye open on those nights, the noxious fumes of the burning kerosene leaving a bad taste on his tongue, and the fear of burning to death in the night.

It's easier to think of tomorrow's errands than it is his task of tonight. It's decidedly the oddest request that Rick has made of him, and he's still not certain how to handle it. Francesca kicked about it, too, but in the end Rick, as always, made a good case. It's their anniversary, the Stantons. And Rick wants Keller to take Francesca out to dinner and to the Totem Pole Ballroom out in Auburndale. "Be my surrogate."

Keller had to look the word up. *Surrogate,* meaning "replacement." A willing replacement.

"It's what I would be doing, and why should Francesca be denied a little fun just because I can't do it?"

"I don't dance." That seemed the most reasonable way to refuse. "I mean, not since they forced us to learn the box step in gym class."

"Francesca is a wonderful dancer; she'll

help you out."

"Rick, don't do this." Francesca twisted a tea towel in her hands, and the smile on her face failed to suggest that she thought he was teasing, that Rick was having them on.

"Honey, come on. It'll be fun."

Keller put his oar in. "Rick, you take her. I'll drive you there. We can go early, get a good seat for you close to the floor."

"And do the jitterbug with her? No. I want her to dance and I want you to take her."

Rick keeps doing this, throwing them together, as if their eating at the Clam Shack or taking a walk or going to a picture show somehow *entertains* him.

"But, Rick, it's *our* anniversary. I want to spend it with you." Francesca had that tension in her voice again. The tension of not saying what she wants to.

Keller left the room; this was just too marital for him. Later, she came to him, smiling, shaking her head, as if Rick were a naughty little boy getting his way. "Have you ever been to the Totem Pole? We used to love to go. Good music. And, Kel, we don't have to dance if it makes you uncomfortable."

Keller wondered if she meant dancing in general, or just dancing with her might make him uncomfortable.

"Francesca, we can do whatever you'd like to do."

"I think I'd like to go." At once, Francesca looks young, girlish.

"Then we'll go." He points at her, smiles. "As long as you don't ask me to tango."

"You kids look beautiful." Rick shifts in his wheelchair. "Where's the corsage?" Keller hands him the box with the flower in it, ordered, exactly as Rick wanted — pink and blue chrysanthemums with a white ribbon. Rick gets the box open, but they all realize at the same time that there is no way he can pin it on his wife. Keller awkwardly fashions the arrangement to Francesca's dress. It flops and she unpins it, walks to the hallway mirror, and fixes it for herself. "They're beautiful. Thank you." She doesn't look at either of them, so it's hard to tell whom she is thanking.

In order to make this less like a date and more like a night of bowling, they've had dinner already. Before he took his plate into his room, Keller got Rick out of his and to the dining room table, where he had put two place settings, a little bouquet of fall flowers in the center to mark the special occasion of their anniversary and Rick's grudging willingness to sit at the table. Rick insisted that he not be put to bed, that he'd be up waiting for them with Pax. He and Pax would listen to the live broadcast from the Totem Pole on the radio. He'd be fine, he insisted.

By the time Keller and Francesca arrive at Norumbega Park, the Totem Pole Ballroom is crowded and the dance floor swarming with people dancing to a small combo warming the crowd up for the next act. Black tuxedos and gowns in jewel-like colors blur and spin below them. Keller is dressed in his only pair of good trousers, black merino wool, his only dress shirt, and a tie borrowed from Rick. His jacket is borrowed, too. He's never owned a suit, never before felt the need, but here he stands with Francesca, in the dress that she made herself. She'd chosen the material well, with an eye toward what's fashionable, and she looks every bit as sophisticated as anyone else on that dance floor in the bell-shaped skirt and narrow belted waist of her blue-and-white dress. He offers his arm and they descend to find an empty seat.

"Can I get you something? A martini, maybe?" A martini sounds as sophisticated as she looks, he thinks.

Francesca tilts her head, nibbles her lower lip. He can see the thought process behind her eyes. Should she relax enough to say yes? Should they keep this as simply fulfilling a bizarre whim of Rick's? "Sure. Why not."

It takes nearly fifteen minutes to get through the pack lined up at the bar, and then he loses some of the expensive drink as he maneuvers his way through the crowd back to where Francesca waits, her gaze on the dancing couples, a smile on her face, as if she knows she needs to look like she's having a good time. But Keller recognizes that wan smile as one she so often wears when Rick has been difficult. "Here you go. What's the expression? Mud in your eye?" He wants to get that wan smile off her face and replace it with a genuine one.

"Something like that. I'm afraid I've never been one of the toast-giving crowd."

"Me, either. Seems like something they only do in the movies." Keller sips the martini, fishes out the olive, is uncertain if he's supposed to eat it, puts it back in, leaning the tiny sword that skewers it against the rim of the glass.

They watch the crowd in silence for a bit. It seems obvious to Keller that he should ask her to dance. They can't keep sitting here all evening drinking expensive drinks, ignoring the intent of being in such a place;

it's not the sort of place where you go simply to sit and drink martinis. Rick is listening to the WNBC broadcast and will grill them later, want to know what music they danced to. "I have to live vicariously now. Do it for me." That's what he said as they went out the door.

Keller starts to speak, when Francesca sets her drink down and says. "So, tell me, how do you know so much about carpentry? You were a fisherman, right? Before the war?"

Maybe it's the unaccustomed martini, or maybe it's the music surrounding this conversation; maybe it's the fact that, in asking him about himself, Francesca has laid a hand on his arm, just above his wrist. Whatever it is, he is drawn into telling her the truth. "I went to reform school when I was nine. I learned carpentry there." He sits back, pulls his arm away, and waits for her reaction.

"Nine. Oh my, what could you have possibly done to get sent to reform school at that age?" She doesn't look at him with distaste, but curiosity, maybe even a skeptical amusement, as if she doesn't believe him.

"Truancy. Well, I decked a truant officer and the state took that as a sign of my delinquent nature."

"That seems very harsh."

"In a lot of ways, it was better than getting passed around from relative to relative who didn't want me. I got three squares a day and clothing that mostly fit. And a trade."

"But you were smart. I saw the inscription on your book that your teacher wrote. She thought a lot of you."

"Miss Jacobs? Yeah, she did. But that was when I was living with Clayton. He claimed me when I was sixteen. Put me to work."

They sit quietly, letting the old war tunes work a little nostalgia on them. Keller tosses back the rest of his martini. "Hey, we're here to dance, not reminisce."

CHAPTER FORTY-FOUR

The radio is tuned into WNBC's local affiliate. At nine o'clock, live music from the Totem Pole Ballroom begins. The announcer introduces the band, no one Rick has ever heard of, and the guest singer, also no one Rick has ever heard of. No Dinah Shore or Dorsey Brothers. But the music is nice and they play a lot of tunes he remembers from when he and Francesca thought a good night out on the town was when they went someplace and danced. For a little Iowa girl, Francesca knew how to do all the modern dances — jitterbug, Lindy hop, and even the East Coast swing. She was fun to sweep off the floor in his showboating exuberance, swinging her up feet-first toward the ceiling. Keller may take her out on the floor, maybe even now as the band plays a Duke Ellington song, but Rick doubts he'll have any of those moves. Too bad. Francesca deserves to have a great partner on the dance floor.

Pax stands up and shakes himself, shoves his nose beneath Rick's resting hand so that Rick can give him a good ear scratch. It's well past the point in the evening when Rick is put to bed, if only to lie there awake. Long hours in the chair, longer hours in the bed. The band finishes up "Cottontail" with a flourish, and the sound of applause fills the airwaves. The band leader introduces the next song, and a bouncy tune Rick doesn't recognize comes out of the boxy radio. His fingers begin to tap out the rhythm on the dog's skull, gentle six-eight taps, as if he's playing drums. Pax wags his tail and laughs his doggy laugh. Rick dances his fingers up and down the dog's long back and Pax motors his back leg as if he's being tickled. The music changes to a swing rhythm and Rick rocks from side to side, patting the new beat on his paralyzed knees. He can hear it but not feel the slap. He slaps his face on the bad side. A different sound than hitting terry-cloth-covered dead knees. Sharp and snappy. He slaps his good cheek and says, "Ouch!" He does it again. Pax has stopped laughing and watches, his eyes on Rick, his nose working and his ears, determined to comprehend Rick's behavior. He's making the sound of violence but laughing at the same time. Puzzled, but convinced there is no danger, Pax sits facing Rick.

"Let's dance, big boy." Rick thrusts the knotted rope toward Pax. Obligingly, the dog grasps the end and tugs left, in the direction Rick is looking. Then Rick quickly looks right and the dog tugs him right. The wheelchair swings left, then right, but not in time with the music. Pax can move him only a foot or so in either direction. It's more a slow waltz than dancing to the thumping beat of the high-energy trumpet solo being played now.

The plaintive first notes from a clarinet take the place of the energetic piece and a slow and sensuous music fills the room. Whatever it is, the key provokes a musical nostalgia in Rick. Every rising note reminds him that he is not listening to this music with his wife on their anniversary; he's playing with his dog and his wife is maybe dancing to this very sweet and sensual music with another man. Dancing in the very place where he got down on one knee, just like in the movies, and asked her, their acquaintance barely a week old, to marry him. And she said yes. He has cheated Francesca of the life she deserved.

Every descending third in the clarinet solo reminds him of how much he loves her. And how often he treats her like a servant, an annoyance. "Pax, why do I do that?"

Pax has let go of the rope. He has no answers.

The radio is on the built-in shelves that house the encyclopedias and the dictionary. The glow from the tubes casts a candlelike warmth into that dark corner. The music has grown too much to bear, but no one has taught the dog how to turn the radio off. Whenever the band takes a break, in that few seconds before the band leader or the announcer or whoever he is introduces the next song, Rick can hear the crowd noises — applause, laughter, the clink of stemware against stemware. People having fun. Francesca and Keller, having fun. It's what he wanted, to give her a good time. Is that her voice he hears, laughing like she used to in the days when the Totem Pole was *their* place? Touching him just so, so that he knew when it was time to leave; to go home and continue the dance. How soon would she suggest to Keller that they leave? How soon before her fingertips graze the back of his neck?

He has got to shut this radio off. It's enough to have made them go; it's suddenly too much to listen to it. He's like a blind man imagining a elephant.

"Pax, pull me." Rick tosses the end of the knotted rope out to the dog as if he's throwing himself a lifeline. "Pull." The dog is so astute to his gestures that Rick has only to look at the radio to get the dog to aim for it. The dog has to back up. If he were wearing a harness, he could pull Rick by moving forward, a more natural and effective method. But, as it is, the big dog literally has to back himself into a corner in order to get Rick where he wants to go. Which means that he can only get him within a foot of his objective, because the dog's own body is in the way. "Good boy." Pax slips out from the alley made between Rick's chair and the shelves. Rick can get himself close enough now; his good left hand is enough to propel the chair forward that much more. Except that the radio isn't on the lower shelf. It's placed on the third; no one took the time to move the books, instead just setting up the radio in the most convenient place. Keller drilled a hole in the shelves so that the cord, attached to an extension cord, runs down the back of the unit and disappears behind the closed doors of the built-in cupboard that makes up the base. Rick's fingers don't quite reach to the knob. No one has ever thought that Rick might want to shut the goddamned thing off. It's become such a habit, this leaving him out of things, making sure he wants for nothing and, by doing so, turning him into a hopeless invalid.

Rick stretches as far as he can reach. The music continues to taunt him, louder, livelier, sexier. She looked so beautiful tonight. Keller's hands on her as he struggled with the corsage. Shy or desirous? Rick pushes his chair back a foot. Examines the geometry of his helplessness. In therapy, they want him to get to the point where he can push himself up, be of more help to those helping him. Rick grips the armrest and pushes himself toward the radio; he lifts himself half a foot, maybe more, and then is struck with the truth. If he lifts himself with his only hand, he has nothing to shut the radio off with. He starts to laugh, a dry, hacking, chest-deep sound that brings Pax to his side. Even the dog knows that there is no humor in the sound he's making.

If he can grasp the cord, maybe he can jerk the plug out. The band leader introduces the guest singer, and suddenly the room is filled with the throaty crooning of a woman lamenting her lost boyfriend. She's lost him to another. It's pure blues, and tears spring to Rick's eyes. "Pax, let's try something else." Together, they position him so that he can grab the latch on the cupboard door. It sticks a little, but he gets it open. Inside the cupboard, replacing the games and puzzles of previous tenants, are the medical supplies that he uses — tubing and sponges, basins and bandages.

Rick has to reach across his dead legs in order to feel around inside the cupboard for the cord. He thinks of them as ballast, that they'll hold him steady in the chair as he reaches. Because he can't move them, or feel them, he's perfectly assured that they will stay put. Because they don't move, he can't quite reach far enough into the deep cupboard to touch the cord plugged into the hidden wall outlet. He needs to get a little lower, a little closer. He pushes his chair backward and leans forward, but he's blocked by the length of his unfeeling thighs. The electric cord is a tantalizing inch from his reaching fingers. Rick tries moving his legs apart, lifting one, then the other and placing them against the sides of the chair, but the wheelchair is too narrow and the best he can do is a mere five or six inches of freeboard. Even with that, bent nearly in two, the solid roof of the cupboard obstructs his getting any closer. Rick bangs his head on the edge. It's hopeless; he's stuck here listening to the music that his wife and his *caretaker* are no doubt dancing to. Keller's hands on her waist, she's reaching up to place her left on his broad shoulder, her right hand — he pictures it bare, not gloved — in Keller's, palm to palm, fingers linking at some point in the dance.

The lament is wrung out to the last note and the song is over. She wasn't betrayed; she's betrayed her lover. She's done him wrong.

Rick tries one more time, lunging past his dead legs and reaching deep into the cupboard. The next thing he knows, he's facedown on the floor; the wheelchair has catapulted backward, where it knocks into the tray table, upending it with the force of its empty trajectory. Everything on the table flies off; his water glass smashes on the bare floor, his magazines scatter, and his empty coffee cup rolls out into the hallway.

Pax is there, standing over him as if he's a fallen soldier on the field. The dog is upset, and keeps pawing at him. "I'm okay, Pax. I'm okay." The dog doesn't seem convinced. He barks, paces, comes back, and settles only when Rick touches him. "Francesca is going to kill me." Pax must agree, because he lies down beside Rick and heaves a great sigh. His normally upright ears are flattened side to side like immature puppy ears.

"Maybe you can get me rolled over. Let's try. It's going to be embarrassing enough for them to find me like this, but at least I can be looking up." Rick runs Pax through his lexicon of commands to get the dog to fetch the knotted rope, then use his weight as leverage so that Rick can flip over. On his back, Rick looks right into the cupboard and, finally, reaches the plug.

CHAPTER FORTY-FIVE

If I had been reluctant, and maybe even a little mad, about going to the Totem Pole with Keller on my seventh anniversary instead of with my husband, that reluctance finally gave way to a relaxed enjoyment that I hadn't expected. I admit it, it was *fun.* It was fun to be in the company of a crowd of happy people, to have a drink or two. To dress up and feel pretty and desirable. To dance. Being there was a reminder of what I had rejected poor Buster for.

Keller wasn't the best dancer, and my shoes took a beating, but he improved as the night went on and we got over the shyness of two wallflowers on a forced date and let the music and the momentum carry us. An hour. That's all we stayed, a hour, maybe an hour and a half. Just long enough to have some fun, a laugh or two. An hour when our strange confederacy faded and a new dynamic emerged. Not employee and employer, or caretaker and the cared for, but a couple of friends out for a night on the town. We didn't speak of Rick, at least not after we started dancing. For this golden hour, we weren't two of three; we were just the two of us.

"We should go." I don't remember which one of us whispered this first. Between us, I think we said it twice or three times. And each time the band would launch into another terrific song and we stayed on the dance floor. My second martini grew warm on our table, untouched. We'd sat down between sets, Keller stealing the olive out of my glass, biting it off the sword-shaped pick with a smile.

To tell the truth, I was a little shocked at Keller's admission that he'd spent seven years in a reform school. Truancy. Hardly armed robbery, but still. If my initial reluctance to have him live with us had been based on nothing more than a primitive fear of strangers, this confession underscored how instincts are sometimes valid. It's a good thing he hadn't mentioned it at first, or I would never have let him into our house. But now I knew him. I saw every day how he had risen above such a rough beginning. My own growing up had been so effortless. Oh, sure, filled with bumps of childhood and the foibles of adolescence, but I was secure and educated and loved. Keller was not. The little I had gleaned about his early life had chilled me. After he'd been orphaned and passed around from relative to relative, reform school and the harsh life with his great-uncle might have turned him into a monster incapable of kindness. Here was this perfectly nice man, and the only affection he'd ever had was from the dog we all loved. In some way I understood that, although I don't think I had articulated it to myself at that point. All I knew was that I was glad he was there, that he was a gentle man who had somehow become a part of our lives. Part of our family.

"We got engaged here." I had finished my second drink and suddenly it felt necessary for Keller to understand why this place had significance; that it wasn't just Rick's whim that had sent us there.

"He told me."

"We barely knew each other, but I was sure he was the one."

"How did you know?"

How to answer that question? "I just knew."

Keller didn't say anything, and I wondered if he was thinking that I regretted my choice.

"I love him. He's not the same, and everything we planned on has been changed, but that doesn't change how I feel. I just wish I could convince him of that."

"He knows it." Keller gently took my two hands in his. "He knows it."

Those big hands holding mine were so warm, heated up by the warmth of the ballroom and the dancing, maybe the alcohol. I left mine in his and closed my eyes. "The thing is, sometimes I wonder." I couldn't finish the thought. I couldn't say it.

"Wonder what?"

"No. It's a terrible thing to say. I just sometimes wonder if it would have been better . . ." I trusted this man sitting there, but not with my worst thoughts.

"If he'd been killed, would it have been better? Is that what keeps you awake?"

It was, and Keller's saying it out loud shocked me. A tear leaked out, threatening to spoil my mascara. "No. Not exactly." I scrambled to deny it.

"Francesca, it's a natural thought. It doesn't mean anything." He handed me his folded handkerchief. "You'd be a saint for not thinking something like that now and again. And, as much as I admire you, I'm thinking you're probably not really a saint."

That made me laugh and gave me the knees to get up and go to the ladies' room to collect myself. Maybe I wasn't a saint, but I was beginning to think that Keller Nicholson was. No, certainly not a saint. A reform school angel sent to me.

Keller offered to fetch the car and pick me up at the door, but I refused. We'd been gone longer than I had wanted, and suddenly I was filled with a need to get home, to make sure that we hadn't misjudged. Despite what Rick had said about our staying out nice and late and having a good time, with the music reduced to a muffled pulse behind the heavy closed doors of the ballroom, I was gripped with a guilty sense of having called Rick's bluff. I grasped Keller's arm and, ignoring how sore my feet were in their trampled peep-toe heels, I pushed us both along to where the car was parked, Rick on both our minds, although we didn't say so. We didn't have to.

I knew that something was wrong the moment we pulled up in front of the house. Pax was barking, his deep and alarming bark, the one Keller said he'd used when cornering an enemy. The tone of it rose into a wolfish descant. Keller was out of the car and in the house before I could even open my car door.

"I'm okay. I'm okay." Rick was flat on his back, his head half in the open cupboard, his useless legs at an awkward angle, and yet he kept insisting that he was fine. It took a couple of tries, but between us, Keller and I got him up and into his bed. His nose was bleeding and a fresh bruise was ripening on his cheek.

Keller dashed into the kitchen for ice.

"What happened?" I was gathering the shards of the broken water glass. Shards once again. My life seemed as though it was forever breaking into bits.

"Did either of you realize that I can't shut the goddamned radio off?"

Rick was all right I mean, as much all right as he could be. I knew that the humiliation of being on the floor when we got home was injury enough. Keller got him ready for bed and I went in to say good night. It was our anniversary, and the best I got from my husband was a dry kiss. He pulled back when I cupped his head in my hand and pressed my lips on his. "I'm tired. Good-night," he said.

I tamped down a little flare of anger. It had been *his* idea for us to leave him. His insistence that we have some fun. His assurance that he could be left alone without harm. And the first thing he did was blame us for his stupid action. The anger was snuffed almost before I had a chance to recognize it. We'd left the radio on for him, thinking that in some way it meant he could be a part of our evening. The evening that should have been his and mine, not mine and Keller's. It struck me then that all the time we'd been dancing to the ballroom orchestra, he'd been listening. I blushed a little, a guilty blush that somehow he might have seen how close I let Keller hold me. And how nice it had felt. Maybe that's why he'd been so determined to shut the radio off, so that the image of his wife happy in the arms of another man would shut off.

"Happy anniversary." I swung the sick-room door half-closed. Rick didn't answer.

Keller waited for me in the kitchen. Even though we'd had most of two martinis that evening, he held out a bottle of lager to me and popped the cap off another. Pax was conspicuously absent. I think he was upset about what had happened, too, and maybe thought in his doggy way that he needed to stay close to Rick that night. It was more likely that Rick wasn't asleep, and Pax never left his side until he was. So we didn't stay in the kitchen, afraid, I suppose, that some-

318

how Rick would overhear us. And even worrying about what we might say that would
upset him, upset me. Nonetheless, we
drifted into the garage. Keller offered me
his rescued easy chair and leaned back
against the workbench. We didn't speak, just
took mouthfuls of the beer, studied the
labels, our fingers, the ceiling. My
adrenaline-charged heart rate slowed with
each sip and, along with it, the conflicting
emotions of anger and self-inflicted guilt. I
rested the bottle against my forehead and
sighed. I didn't feel teary, just done in.

"He's fine. It wasn't our fault." Keller
squatted in front of me.

"Is that what you think?"

"I'll fix it so he can control the radio."

"You think you can fix everything, don't
you?"

Keller didn't say anything, just swallowed
the last of his beer and stood up. He'd
shucked the jacket and tie and stood there
in his white shirt, the cuffs folded back,
revealing surprisingly fine-boned wrists. It
was late, almost eleven-thirty. My beer had
gone warm and flat, and I really didn't want
the rest of it. But I wasn't ready to call it a
night. To get up and go now would leave
the last thing I'd said to Keller hanging in
the air. "I'm sorry. I don't mean it like it

came out. You're a godsend."

"It's all right, Francesca. Everything is all right."

That's what Keller said, but it wasn't true. Nothing was all right, and I couldn't believe that it ever would be. I think that that evening was when I finally came to terms with what the rest of my life was going to look like. Rick wasn't going to improve beyond where he was. It was always going to be a delicate balance of helping him without humiliating him.

Rick wasn't alone in the extent of his injuries. Hundreds upon thousands of other soldiers had returned as damaged as he had — or even more so. But Rick's soul had been injured along with his limbs, and that was something no amount of physical therapy or a state-of-the-art prosthetic device could improve on.

"We should call it a night." Keller took my unfinished bottle of beer and offered his other hand to help me out of the chair. "Things always look better in the morning."

The warm touch of his hand made me realize how chilly I was there in the garage. "It's cold in here. You should think about moving into the house."

"Not yet."

CHAPTER FORTY-SIX

The letter from Miss Jacobs is waiting for him when he gets home from class. Keller sees it propped up on the hall table, resting benignly against the empty china vase, which is the sole object on the table other than the car keys and, occasionally, a random dog toy. Pax comes out of Rick's room to greet Keller, ready for a break from his duties. Keller can hear Francesca's voice coming from the room and the sound of a spoon against china, so he knows he has a moment to take the dog out. The postmark suggests that the letter has been some time in reaching him, having followed him from the retraining center to here, and he thinks that he should have thought to write her to let her know that he's working and in college. She's going to be pleased with him.

Keller slides the letter into his pocket and snaps his fingers at Pax. "Let's go." They head out into a blustery November afternoon. Leaves skitter in front of them as they walk down the sidewalk. Pax becomes puppyish and chases them as if they're little animals scurrying away. A stepped layer of cloud bank hovers in the northeast, reminding Keller of when his days were forecast by the sky. These are merely clouds.

Keller doesn't think of the letter again until he takes his supper into his garage room. Even before he gets a first mouthful of ham, his dinner is cold. He should have started the space heater earlier, but he hates leaving it untended. It may be time to swallow his reluctance to move into the house. Keller sets the cold plate aside and pulls out the letter.

My dear Keller,
I know your uncle Clayton hasn't heard from you, so I am compelled to put my oar in. Your uncle is not well. In fact, I think you could say that he is failing. He's suffered from a cough for months now, and, typically, is refusing to see a doctor. I'm no physician, but I'd guess he has pneumonia. He's still working, but Stan at the fish market says that he brings in only a half bushel of quahogs or a penny's worth of bottom fish. What I'm trying to say here is that he needs

you, Keller. I know things weren't good between you, but you're all he has.

Keller carefully folds the letter without reading the rest.

"Keller, come into the kitchen and let me give you a new plate." Francesca leans into his doorway, wraps her arms around herself against the chill, and shakes her head. "Don't be stubborn. We're finished and I'll be doing up the dishes. Come in where it's warm."

Keller nods, picks up his unfinished plate, leaving the folded letter on the ammo box. The breezeway is cold, too, so that the warmth from the kitchen touches his skin like a blanket as he comes into the house. Francesca takes his cold plate and hands him a new one. Macaroni and cheese, ham and canned peas. There is a pat of butter melting on the peas. He unbuttons the heavy woolen army-surplus sweater he wears in his room.

"Keller, you need to move into the house. I can't have you freezing to death out there."

Discomfort has overcome any reluctance, and Keller nods. "I guess maybe it's time."

"We'll have to move your stuff up there, because I don't have a bedroom set for that room. I've just dumped a lot of stuff in it that I haven't had time to put away properly. You wouldn't believe that we've been in this house for so long and I still haven't really moved in. I just don't know what fills my hours."

Keller catches the glint in her eye, and laughs, pleased to see her good humor return after a long absence — since the night Rick fell out of his chair. Sometimes it seems to him that no matter what Francesca does, Rick has no true appreciation. She goes into that room all smiles and comes out looking upset, looking like she's trying hard not to let him know that she is. It makes him crazy. Rick should be kissing the ground she walks on for the way she's always there for him, and he treats her like . . . Keller reins in his thoughts. It's none of his business. Married couples aren't always lovey-dovey. He sure knows that from observing his aunts and their spouses and how they snapped and snarled at each other and called it marriage. Rick snaps, but he has every right to. Not at Francesca, but at his situation. Keller has to keep reminding himself of that. Over and over.

He has to remind himself that he has no idea what a marriage really looks like.

He's been upstairs now for more than a

week. Empty, the bureau wasn't heavy, and Keller and Francesca managed to get it up the stairs with only one misstep. His army cot was easy enough for him to wrangle by himself. Francesca carried up one armload of clothing; he carried up another. The room is too small to afford him a sitting area, but he has commandeered a small table to use as a desk.

That first night, he lay awake, listening to the sounds of the house, listening to the creak of the floorboards as Francesca walked to her closet, to the click of her lamp being shut off. The pipes banged a little as the furnace kicked on. He'd left his door ajar, just enough that Pax could push his way into the small bedroom and climb in with him. Because the door stays open, he can hear it when Francesca leaves her bed to go downstairs to the bathroom in the middle of the night, and he lies there, half-dozing until he hears her return. Within a few nights, he's gotten used to being up here, accustomed to the sound of another warm, breathing person within calling distance.

CHAPTER FORTY-SEVEN

Pax approves of Keller's new sleeping situation. It is so much easier to keep track of all the inhabitants of the house when two of them are nearly side by side and the third just below them. He can sit at the top of the stairs and hear everything that is going on in the house. So Pax hears Keller's restless shifting on the army cot. He hears the sleepless sighs of Francesca and his acute ears pick up the barely audible sound of Rick's dry eyes blinking. Outside, the late-fall wind scurries the leaves against the rough surface of the sidewalk and moans through the naked branches of the oak tree in the front yard. Sometimes his hackles rise at these sounds, a purely involuntary response to the domestic unrest.

Eventually, they all sleep and he is free to climb in with Keller. But first Pax checks in with Rick, testing the air for any distress. Then Pax stands for a moment just outside of Francesca's firmly shut bedroom door. He never scratches for admittance, simply makes sure that the noises from within are those of a sleeping human. Satisfied, Pax pushes the other bedroom door open and noses Keller into moving over. Keller reaches for the dog in his sleep, spooning him like they once did in bombed-out cellars and foxholes. The dog heaves a sigh. Things are not quite as they had been. The routines are the same, his duties the same. But there is an undercurrent that the dog feels deep in his bones; like the scent of winter in the air, the season in this house is changing.

CHAPTER FORTY-EIGHT

They're going to make him leave his room for dinner. Rick is trying hard to not make a big fuss about it. After all, it is Thanksgiving, and the smells coming from the kitchen are a visceral reminder of much happier days. Francesca's cousin Sid and his rather snooty wife, Clarissa, are coming. Keller will make it an odd number at the table. Rick has sussed him out on whether the man *wants* to spend a national holiday "on the job," but Keller assured Rick that he'll be there to help. It was a bit awkward, but it had to be asked. "You'll eat with them, of course, won't you?" Rick knew that Keller usually ate by himself in his garage room. Now that he's moved upstairs to sleep, Rick really doesn't know where Keller is eating, just that he still keeps out of this room at dinnertime, leaving Francesca and him alone. As if they have something important to say to one another. As if they needed marital privacy.

"I'll eat with you." And then, as if what he just said might be misunderstood as giving Rick a free pass to stay in his room, Keller added, "In the dining room."

Keller is a good carpenter and the widening of the door into the dining room looks like it has always been a wheelchair-wide archway. The landlord will have no complaints that their tenancy ruined his property.

Sid Crawford comments on the changes as soon as he and his heavily pregnant wife come in the front door. "You know, you ought to see if the landlord would be interested in selling the place to you. I mean, with the GI Bill and all, you can get a low-cost mortgage and do whatever you want to the place."

"I don't think we've ever considered making this a permanent home," Francesca calls from the kitchen, showing off her powers of carrying on two conversations at the same time. "I think we want something bigger, don't you, Rick?" She's clearly thrilled to have him out of his room; with every sentence she speaks, she bounces her thoughts over to him, as if he is some guest needing inclusion in the conversation, not a man fully capable of putting in his two cents.

"We've really never talked about it. We're fine as we are." Rick sips from the glass of eggnog in his left hand. Francesca has been liberal with the rum.

"For now, maybe. But you have to admit it's a bit tight." Francesca is like a jack-in-the-box, popping her head out from the kitchen and then ducking back in. Or a turtle. Clarissa is in there with her, stirring or peeling something. She greeted Rick with a quick hello and shrugged off her mink into Keller's hands, as if he were a butler, then disappeared into the kitchen. Rick thinks the sight of him bothers her. Frankly, the sight of her bothers him, but he can't quite admit to himself that it's because she's expecting. If things had been different, that might have been Francesca, twice over. Unfair, uncalled for, and stupid, but that's the thought that teases in the back of his mind. How can Francesca stand to be around her?

It is a bit tight with four upright adults and a man in a wheelchair, plus a big dog hovering around, hoping that someone will forget that he's not allowed to be fed from the table. Already he's vacuumed up the spillage inevitable in the preparation of enough food for a platoon. Rick suddenly feels a strange wistfulness about the Thanksgivings he and his platoon endured. A can of C rations and a round of personal memories of Thanksgiving coming from the war-weary company. Not close enough to a USO station to get the better meal; and yet, those little stories of mom's fiasco with a pumpkin pie or dad's mishap with a carving knife, of the world's best stuffing and the biggest turkey in the land were as much a true Thanksgiving as any he'd ever had.

Keller is quiet; maybe he's thinking of his Thanksgivings past.

They've given Rick the head of the table. Tradition, or is it because that's the best place for his chair? Keller asked him earlier if he thought he might want to sit in a regular chair. The dining room chair with the arms is the one they call the "captain's" chair, and, presumably, he might not fall out of that one, but the shift from wheelchair to dining room chair would be ugly, so Rick shook his head no. If Clarissa is discomforted by the sight of a man like him in a wheelchair, she'd be more uncomfortable watching the process of moving him from one place to another.

Francesca sits at the opposite end, the kitchen end. Keller, useful, to his right; Clarissa to his left, and Sid beside Clarissa, next to Francesca. Pax is remanded to a corner, but that doesn't stop him from watching everyone with the avidity of a hungry wolf. Francesca has outdone herself. The table looks wonderful, all their wedding china trotted out for the occasion, pieces he's never actually seen in use. New tablecloth, new napkins. Candles. In the bright sunlight of a pristine November day, they flicker pale and unnecessary but cheerful. The turkey is delivered ceremoniously and they fold their hands as they were taught to do in Sunday school for grace. Rick simply fists his existing hand and stares at it. No one says anything for a moment, and Rick suddenly realizes that they are waiting for him, as host, to intone the prayer. "For what we are about to receive may we be grateful." The gathering choruses a ready amen and the serving bowls begin to fly.

Like the master of the house, Keller removes the blessed bird and takes it back into the kitchen to carve it. Rick tries not to let the bitter reminder of his disability spoil this day. It would have been worse to have Sid do the honors. At least Keller doesn't act out of pity, but utility. Keller returns with two platters. One has whole slices of white and dark. One has small pieces of cut-up turkey. This one, he puts next to Rick's left hand.

The conversation wends its way around the topics of their Iowa family and friends, the rate of inflation, and the latest headlines. Keller is politely asked about his college class; Clarissa talks at length about her layette for the baby due next month, oblivious to Francesca's sudden disappearance into the kitchen on some trumped-up desire for more cranberry sauce.

Sid wants to buy a new car and is thinking of getting a Studebaker. What does Rick think of them?

"I always liked their line of personnel carriers." Rick has a dainty arrangement of meat and mashed potato firmly on the tines of his fork. Somehow he's managed to do it without thinking about it.

"Well, I'm thinking of something a little more, um, family-size."

"The Starlight?" Keller hasn't offered much until the subject of cars came up.

"I think so. I like the styling of the trunk. Lots of room for luggage."

"Sid thinks that we should drive out to Iowa for Christmas, but I think that it'll be too hard with a new baby." Clarissa rests her hand demonstratively on her belly.

"Babies are good travelers; after all, don't they sleep all the time."

"Sid, my darling cousin, I don't think you

have any idea what babies do." Francesca gets up from the table to replenish the squash bowl. Keller follows her, empty platter in hand.

Rick gathers another forkful, but not quite as neatly, and the clump falls back to his plate.

"So, Rick, giving any thought to getting a new hand?"

"I'm sorry, what?"

"You know, a hook. A guy in my building has one. Uses it like a tool."

"Sid, we haven't thought about such things." Francesca is in the room, half-full squash bowl in her hand. "We're not ready."

"It's okay, Fran. No, Sid, no one has suggested that a *replacement* is an option." Rick sets his fork down carefully.

"I'm sorry. I shouldn't have said anything. I was just asking." Sid reaches for another dinner roll. "Just thought you might be thinking about it, that it might help to get you back on your feet."

"If you haven't noticed, a hook won't do that for me. Or, do you mean getting back into the ball game? I don't think a hook will help me do that, either." He's gobsmacked, more shocked than furious. Sid speaks of things he knows nothing about. If he thinks that Rick's life will ever go back to *normal* just because he's got a hook attached to the stump of his pitching arm, he's nuts.

"Mr. Stanton's wound isn't properly healed. A prosthesis isn't possible right now." Keller sets the turkey platter down in front of Sid. "When it is, I'm sure he'll be open to the idea."

"Keller, that's not your business, either." Rick pushes himself away from the table with his good hand. "I'm feeling a little tired. Would you please take me back to my room."

"Actually, I won't. There's a mince pie coming in here with your name on it." Keller's smile is supposed to make the whole exchange look like a comedy routine. Rick is left pushed away from the table, and he has to get himself back close enough to enjoy that pie.

Sid and Clarissa hung on long enough to finish their dessert before Clarissa claimed weariness and they left. Sid clapped Rick on the shoulder on the way out. "It will get better." In the interest of family harmony, Rick allowed that as a clichéd and weak apology for Sid's ignorance. "I know. Time."

"Well, that went well." Francesca leans against the closed front door and rolls her eyes heavenward.

Rick reaches out with his good hand and takes hers. "Yes, it did. It was terrific."

She smiles down on him, squeezes his fingers, and then heads into the dining room to repair the damage.

Rick digs deep in the little pouch they keep attached to his wheelchair for his pens and pencils and crossword puzzle books. Amazingly, he's adapted to left-handed writing fairly well. His fingers find the twenty little white pills in his collection, hidden in that handy little pouch.

CHAPTER FORTY-NINE

Sid's incredibly insensitive remark about the "hook" really fried me. Sid was always one of those guys who speaks first and thinks second. For such a smart guy, he could really put his foot in it. At the same time, he was right. We were taking Rick's recovery at his pace. Why wouldn't Sid think that Rick was ready for the next phase of his recovery? I hadn't confided in Sid that Rick wasn't making much progress, partly because I think that I really didn't see it that way. Nowadays, they call it "enabling." Back then, we were just trying our best. I was trying hard to focus on small improvements, and getting Rick into the dining room for Thanksgiving was a big one. And into the parlor for Christmas was the best present I got that year.

Our house was so tiny that Pax very nearly took the tree down with his tail twice. Rick's parents had come for the Christmas holiday, and because I couldn't offer them a bed, they ended up driving from Connecticut and back in the same day. Maybe we did need to think about a bigger place, a place of our own. This was a stopgap measure, and even with Keller's improvements, it was inadequate for the long term. What was scary was that I had no idea how we would pay for it, GI Bill or no. Even with Rick's benefits, we were just scraping by. I needed to go to work, or Rick needed to get better enough so that he could. It might not be baseball, but he had a degree in accounting, and you didn't need two arms and functioning legs for that. But you did need to leave your bedroom. You did need to feel good. The other alternative: go back to Iowa.

The suggestion had come from my father during his Christmas phone call. "We miss you; I wish that you could be here. Why don't you think about coming home?"

"We need the VA here, Dad."

"We have hospitals. We could set you two up on the first floor of the house."

I promised to think about it and hung up. Rick was already back in his room; Keller was doing the dishes. Pax came out of Rick's room and nuzzled me until I got up from the little chair beside the telephone. "What do you want, Paxy?"

He pushed his big head against my waist. I swear he had overheard my conversation and was offering me a hug. "What do you think? Want to go to Mount Joy?" I rested my cheek against his skull.

I leaned against the doorjamb and looked into the kitchen, where Keller was busy scrubbing the roasting pan. His back was to me, but I knew he could see my reflection in the window over the sink, because he raised one sudsy hand and waved. What would Keller do if we moved to Iowa? Would Keller even consider such a move? It would put back on the table the thing that we had, with our arrangement, taken off: whom Pax most belonged to.

"Need some help?" I asked.

"You've done the brunt of it today. Why don't you go relax?" He flipped a dish towel over his shoulder and reached for the next pan. "Or take Pax out for a walk around the block. He's been in most of the day."

"I'll wait for you to be done. We can both take him." Rick wouldn't miss us, not for the fifteen minutes it would take to speed around the block in the cold. I went in and checked before we bundled up. My husband was sitting up in bed, a novel propped against the table over his bed, but his eyes were closed. I lifted the book, carefully sliding in the bookmark, and rolled the table aside. How could I ever have thought that he might one day be able to hold down a job when a day sitting up in his wheelchair knocked him out?

With the winter solstice past, there was a discernible light left in the sky as we walked out of the house. Pax was off leash, and he led us down the deserted street. Christmas tree lights sparkled in the front windows of every house we passed. Above our heads, a single star appeared, and Keller pointed it out.

"Star light, star bright . . ." I began the childhood rhyme, expecting Keller to join in. He didn't, and it was another reminder of the hard life he'd had as a kid. He didn't know about wishing on a star till I told him about it.

"Looks like I've been missing a lot of wishing opportunities."

"Guess you'd better make up for it now, before another star appears."

I was a little ahead of him, a footstep or so. The end of the block was a stone's throw away. I felt his hand in its thick glove touch my shoulder, and I paused. Pax, always aware of us, also paused, sniffed, decided all was well, and forged on ahead.

"Are you supposed to say your wish out loud?" Keller asked.

I was facing him now; the lingering light had gone and it was full dark, but the streetlight cast our shadows behind us. "No. Never. A wish spoken out loud will never come true."

"I see. Well then, I won't say it." It was the strangest thing, how he closed his eyes and held his breath as if he wasn't wishing, but praying. Then he opened his eyes and laughed out loud. "Okay. How long does it take? For a wish to come true?"

"Keller, it's just a silly tradition. I swear you're falling for it." I gave him a playful shove with both hands on his chest.

"I am. Falling." As if to neutralize his oddly plaintive remark, Keller grabbed me, playfully wrapping his arms around me and rocking me from side to side, as if he was going to toss me in a snowbank. I laughed and struggled to get loose. My younger brother, Kenny, might have finished the job, landing me in a snowbank and then rubbing my face in it for good measure. Keller just suddenly let me go and called Pax back to his side.

We walked back to the house, laughing like little kids, with Pax romping up and

down the snow heaped along the edge of
the sidewalk.

CHAPTER FIFTY

Another letter from Miss Jacobs, and Keller knows that it won't bear good news. Good news will keep and bad news won't go away, so he leaves the unopened envelope in his back pocket, until he forgets that it's there. There is so much else to think about. Rick is running a low temperature. Just low enough that they decide to wait and see if he comes down with a cold, or if it will eventually rise high enough that the question of a new infection will come into play. There has been so much activity, so many people in the house, that Keller is fairly comfortable with the idea that Rick is just run down a little and open to the common cold — given his rather isolated existence, he has no resistance — and not something more sinister like a bladder infection.

"Just under one hundred. Let's see if we can knock it back with an aspirin." Keller tips a couple of Bayer into his hand and hands them to Rick.

"Where's Francesca?" Rick has that bleary look of someone who has just awakened from an unscheduled nap.

"You remember. She's off to Sid and Clarissa's to see the baby. They got back last night from their trip to Iowa."

"Right. What did they call it?"

"I don't know. I think it's a girl."

"Sid's probably a little disappointed."

"Why?" Keller hands Rick a glass of water freshly poured from the pitcher on his table.

"Not a boy. Doesn't every man want a boy?"

"I guess so. Never thought about it. Is that what you would want?"

Rick hands the glass back to Keller. "No. It wouldn't have mattered to me. Although I suppose I did imagine having a son. Someone I could teach to play ball."

Wouldn't have. Keller hears the past tense. "I played some in school. We had one teacher there who was a pretty good coach. Of course, they collected all the bats and counted them before we left the diamond."

"Were you any good?"

Keller straightens the sheet over Rick. "I could hit if the ball was thrown right at me. But we had one kid, big ugly guy, he could hit. Couldn't run worth a damn, but man

he'd pound those balls right over the fence."
Ralph Patterson. He hasn't thought of the
man-size boy in a long time. School bully.
Far and away too old to still be in reform
school.

Keller is finished in Rick's room, but he
wants to keep the subject of baseball going,
to press on and see how long it takes Rick
to close down. "The Little League team
here in town had a pretty good season. Bet
they'd love some attention from a former
pro. You know that their field is at the end
of the street."

At first, Rick doesn't say anything, and
Keller figures he's pushed a little too far. "I
don't think so. You don't learn anything
from a fool."

"What?"

"A fool. A man who believes that he can
strike out the enemy with a live grenade."

"You do remember, don't you?"

"Oh, I remember. Francesca doesn't think
I do, but I do. Not everything, of course,
but I have a very clear recollection of my
colossal error. Hubris. Do you know that
word?"

"Yes."

"We didn't have the advantage of a dog
like Pax. So my squad was surprised by a
machine-gun nest. Pinned us down on the

edge of a cliff. They were above us, and we were sitting ducks, as they say. From our angle, we couldn't get a bead on them." Rick's fingers are flexing, catching the blanket, releasing it in an unconscious gesture.

Keller keeps still, as if he's afraid he'll spook Rick out of telling his story.

"I got the bright idea I could pitch a grenade up high enough that it would land in the middle of the nest. Absolutely confident in my right arm. High and fast. Really high. Almost ninety degrees high. Like standing at the pitcher's mound and hoping to hit the moon straight up." Rick pauses, gathers his words, and Keller understands that this is the first time Rick has ever told this story. It's like he's tasting it, feeling the words for how painful they might be. In a moment, he continues. "They told me I couldn't. I'd have to expose myself, and there was no way I could do that without standing straight up. I had a grenade in my hand. I remember juggling it in my fingertips, as if I were looking for the seam, like you do with a baseball. I figured I could find the right position, that sucker would sail. Knuckleball? Sidearm? I wasn't top at either of those, but I had a killer curve, and that's what I was going to throw. Literally pitching for our lives."

Pax utters a soft whine. He's left his basket and is standing between Keller and Rick. Pax has his eyes on Rick and he drops a big paw on Rick's blanket-covered leg. Keller reaches out to touch the dog but pulls back.

"I juggled that grenade, adjusted my grip. What I failed to realize, or take into account, was the fact that a true pitch requires the whole body. I was betting our lives on my arm. An arm is only as strong and accurate as the kick. Up against the rock wall, on that narrow ledge, I didn't have room to kick. I pulled the pin and threw the grenade as hard as I could. Gravity is a bitch. Fucking thing came right back down and I stood there like an outfielder, ready to catch it."

"Holy shit. You caught it?"

"I did."

Keller slips his hand into his pants pocket and feels the edge of the envelope and, not for the first time, he wonders if, had that first letter from Miss Jacobs reached him at the retraining center, would it have changed things? Despite his adamant promise to himself that he would never return to Clayton Britt's house, would he have gone if he'd known about Clayton's illness? Was there in him, postwar and undirected, a vestigial decency? After all, he'd had no other place to go at the time. No. It wouldn't have been an act of compassion for Clayton. If Keller had thought for a moment about it, it would have seemed like an answer to his desire to keep Pax. He might have left the retraining center with Pax in his car and disappeared north, not doing the right thing in bringing Pax here, never meeting Rick. Never knowing Francesca. Keller simply can't imagine not being here. It's as if his whole life has condensed down to this small house. Far from feeling trapped, he revels in the freedom. For the first time in his life, he is safe, well fed, and as close as he's ever come to living with a family. A real family.

Miss Jacobs was right: She was sticking her oar in. What does she know about it, about the way Clayton used him? What does he owe Clayton anyway? Why should he owe him anything? Didn't he pay for Clayton's guardianship in hard work? Clayton was a stage in his life, that's all. Something he's overcome. If Clayton hadn't claimed him, he might have ended up like Ralph. Unwanted, a man in a reform school.

The people he owes allegiance to are right here. This man needs him, and so does she. And he needs them. Keller never felt connected to Clayton, not like he does with these folks. It sends a little shock wave down his spine, this realization that he has never been happy before.

"Do you want me to find the latest *Life*? I think I left it upstairs," he says to Rick now.

"No. I'm just going to take a little nap."

"Again?"

"I'm just so tired." Rick does look tired, more gray than pale, dark circles beneath his eyes, and his skin looks rough and aged. He looks like an old man. This story has been hard to tell, and hard to hear. So many men died because of mistakes. Blown off the edge of the cliff, Rick may have lost his pitching arm and broken his spine, but he also lost his entire squad. Keller gets it now, Rick's despondency. His darkness.

Pax noses Rick's hand, which is draped over the side of the bed. Keller watches Rick's fingers find the dog's comfort spot, just the inside of his ear. Pax closes his eyes in ecstasy as Rick rubs the little whorl. Pax reaches with one paw and draws Rick's hand to his mouth and licks it with a gentle tongue.

"Hey, Keller?"

"Yeah?"

"Don't say anything to Francesca. Please."

"I won't."

■ ■ ■ ■

Miss Jacobs's second letter can contain no good news, and Keller is pretty certain he knows what's in it. He hasn't written her back after her first letter, where she told him about Clayton's illness. He doesn't know how to say that he cannot, will not, go back to Hawke's Cove and take care of the old man. He just can't. Especially now. He has two other people to care for.

Dear Keller,
I wish that I had heard from you before I had to send this letter, but I haven't, so I don't know if you will be shocked to hear that your uncle passed away last night. He was stubborn to the end and wouldn't go to the hospital. But he wasn't alone. I was with him. You probably don't know that Clayton and I go back a long way. Or maybe you just never imagined that the schoolmarm and the fisherman might once have been young.
    The funeral is Saturday. I hope that you'll attend. You were his only living family, Keller. He wasn't an easy man, God forgive me for speaking ill of the dead, but I am certain that he loved you.

Saturday. Tomorrow.

Out of the question. Rick isn't well, and there is no way Keller is going to leave him to Francesca. It's a four- or five-hour drive or a long train ride. He can't be gone all day. Anything might happen.

I am certain that he loved you.

CHAPTER FIFTY-ONE

Pax didn't like it, not one little bit. Keller had gone away. It was different from the usual gone away, which generally meant that he was to keep guard over Rick until Keller came back. This time, Keller carried things that belonged to him out of the house. This was not good. Pax whined and paced from sickroom to front door, literally putting himself between Keller and the outside, as if Keller was about to step off a cliff.

"It's okay boy. I'll be back later." Keller ruffled up the dog's fur and thumped him on the ribs, but that didn't make Pax feel any more secure about this strange turn of events. Francesca patted Keller on the shoulder like she sometimes did him, but Pax didn't see praise in the touch, more like the way a mother dog pushes a pup away from the teat.

"We'll be fine, Kel. Don't worry about us. You need to be there."

Pax didn't understand Francesca's words, only that she was exuding a fear scent even as she was making those sounds that the humans communicated with. His comprehension of their vocabulary was much better than their understanding of his vocabulary, but he still didn't quite get what was going on.

"I'll be back in the door by nine tomorrow morning at the latest. Anything happens, you call Sid. Okay, promise me?"

The pair stared at each other, standing so close, Pax couldn't hope to fit between them. Francesca made that gesture of placing her lips against Keller's cheek. It wasn't quite like the submissive gesture of a supplicant to a pack leader, chop licking; and not quite charged enough to be a sexual overture, but there was a radiant warmth that exuded instantly from both of them that made him study their faces for a clue as to what it meant.

Keller squatted in front of him, stared Pax in the eye like the leader he was. "Watch out for them." These words, the dog understood.

From Rick's room came the nearly inaudible sound of a man's fingers brushing against the bedsheet. Pax knew even before the humans could detect it that Rick was warm. Not the warm of comfort, but the warm of illness. He could smell it on him, this illness. A faint but growing trace of infection deep within his body. Keller shut the front door and Pax trotted to his post, but he didn't curl up in his basket. He placed himself beside the bed, where Rick remained despite the sunrise. He rested his long muzzle on the bed and closed his eyes as Rick's agitated fingers found his ears.

Keller had left and taken his belongings.

CHAPTER FIFTY-TWO

Rick and I had both sworn to Keller that I could get Rick up, but when I went in to him, he was asleep again. The dog, who had made such a fuss about Keller's leaving, was sitting there in his usual place beside the bed, and there was something in his posture — his attention — that chilled me. I put a hand on Rick's forehead. His eyes opened and he smiled at me, then waved me away. "Just let me sleep at little more. I'll call you when I'm ready to get up." I knew that getting up was a process for him, and for anyone helping him it was strenuous and a struggle against indignity for both parties. I'd done it alone for so long before Keller's arrival. Now, having had help for these past few months, I dreaded it, so I was just as happy to let him stay there.

I sat in the kitchen and drank a second cup of coffee. Keller's breakfast plate was still on the table, a film of egg yolk clashing with the white. He had been so torn about this funeral. I really didn't know why he told me about it; he could have just kept it to himself and not gone if it was that difficult a thing to do, but he'd told me that he'd received word his uncle — great-uncle — had died and he should do the proper thing and go up to Hawke's Cove to the funeral. He wanted me to ask him not to. He gave me every opportunity. "I don't have to go, Francesca. I really wasn't close to him."

"Keller, he was your family. It will look odd if you don't go."

"To whom?"

I smiled at the grammar. Keller was excelling in his English class. "To the lady who wrote to you. Miss Jacobs? The one who gave you the book, right?"

"So you're saying I have to take a day off so that I don't disappoint Miss Jacobs?"

"Or yourself. He might not have been easy, but . . ." There it was, my tendency to speak before thinking, and I stopped myself.

"He took me in. Ergo, I should be grateful?"

"I suppose." Standing over him, I poured him a little more coffee. He smelled of his shaving soap, of the castile shampoo that he used. His hair wasn't slicked back yet and I noticed a little whorl at the crown, like a

356

little kid's. I resisted the urge to comb down the unruly cowlick with my fingers.

I'd seen the letter. Keller had shown it to me the night before, handing it to me at the top of the landing before we headed into our rooms. It made me a little sad, wistful in an odd way. The schoolmarm and the fisherman. Was there a romantic story of unrequited love in between the lines?

I set the percolator back on the stove. "We'll be fine. Go pay your respects." After all, what else could I have said? Don't leave me alone with my husband?

So he'd gone, and here I was, sitting at my kitchen table, wishing he hadn't. I had lost a buffer I hadn't known he'd been providing. A buffer between me and the hard reminders of my husband's condition. When Rick hadn't called me before noon, I went in to wake him up, thinking that he simply shouldn't be sleeping all this time. Pax was still frozen in that alert pose. When I went in, he turned his head and looked at me, and if a dog could ask for help, this one was.

Rick was burning up. I ran water into a bowl and placed the wet, cold cloth on his head. This woke him up, and he stared at me as if he didn't know me. I stripped off his blanket and examined his catheter, then called the doctor.

We had been so careful, but in those days, we had only those clumsy rubber gloves that required boiling. There was no hope we could simulate sterile conditions in a made-over den. I can't remember the doctor's name. Isn't that odd? He must have visited us forty times, and to this day, I can't recall anything except the fact that he always smelled like clove. Like maybe he was chewing it to mask the odors his profession subjected him to. At any rate, this doc, whatever his name was, shook his head when he came out of the room. "I'll call the ambulance."

It wasn't the first time this had happened, so the sense of the bottom falling out from under me was only mild. I knew what to do, what to pack, how long it would take, and I projected myself ahead to the happy moment when Rick would suddenly be better, alert and sorry that he'd caused so much trouble. I wanted to get to that part right away. Keller had said to call Sid, but there was nothing Sid could do, and, besides, he was needed at home. Clarissa was a needy mother. Besides, I didn't want Sid. I wanted Keller. I needed him to tell me it was going to be all right, that things were under control.

Pax seemed to know exactly what was going on. He didn't get in the way; he didn't whine. He watched from out of the way, sitting on the staircase as the ambulance crew came in with the stretcher. Maybe he'd seen this before, on the battlefield, the medics transporting the wounded to ambulances. I knew that Keller had been wounded. Had this dog witnessed him being lifted away?

I buttoned my coat and searched for my gloves. All that time, the dog sat still, patient and calm. All of a sudden, I realized that I was, too. That things *were* under control. I stroked his head from black nose to ears and kissed him. "Such a good boy."

CHAPTER FIFTY-THREE

Keller has inadvertently taken the local, so his journey to Great Harbor is painfully slow, interrupted every few minutes with pauses at outlying stations along the route. The slowness of the journey is actually not a bad thing. He's in no rush to get there, to go through the motions of the funeral and the pretense of caring, but he'd make darn sure to get the express on the return trip. He'd called Miss Jacobs to let her know he'd be there but hadn't prolonged the conversation much beyond telling her which train he'd be on and that he'd get Great Harbor's only taxi to take him to the funeral home. No religion for Clayton Britt, not at this late date.

He's got a paper cup of coffee cooling in his hands and a cruller in a bag on his lap. Every now and again, he reaches into the bag and breaks off a piece of the cruller. He's being careful not to get crumbs on his suit. Rick's suit. He's wearing the striped tie of fashionable width that the Stantons gave him for Christmas. He runs his hand down it every now and again to make sure that it's still in place. Keller has his reading assignment beside him on the seat, but he can't make himself pick it up. He just watches out the window as the urban landscape begins to give way to country, but he isn't really paying attention to the scenery.

A funny thing happened a week ago and Keller is still thinking about it. He was out shoveling the walk when one of the neighbors ventured over. This was a guy he'd waved to a couple of times, a businessman who kept long hours, coming home after five and leaving just as Keller was taking Pax out for his morning walk at sunrise. Early train into town, late train home.

"Hey neighbor." It was a Saturday, and the guy was dressed like Keller, ready for chores. "Bob Tuthill. Insurance."

"Keller, Keller Nicholson." Keller jabbed the shovel into the snow, put out his hand. He didn't have a ready job title to toss back.

"Nice to have you folks in the neighborhood. Sorry I haven't been by before this, but you know how it is," Tuthill said.

"I believe that Francesca and Mrs. Tuthill know each other." Bob's wife was one of the few neighborhood ladies who occasionally dropped by for midmorning coffee with Francesca. "Lady time," he and Rick called it, and Keller would break out the chessboard and keep clear of the kitchen.

"Yeah, wives are good about those things. Always borrowing sugar. Right?"

"Right." Keller knew that he had a foolish grin on his face and that he should enlighten Tuthill, but for some reason he didn't, and he was relieved when Pax came bounding over, curious about the newcomer.

"Nice dog. Always like a big dog." Tuthill reached out to pat Pax, but one look at the dog's face and he pulled his hand away. "Say, that her dad or yours I see you wheeling around?"

Before Keller could answer, Tuthill jumped topics and asked if Keller had a second shovel. The handle of his, it seemed, had snapped off.

There was something so lovely about Tuthill's mistake. He'd validated a barely concocted fantasy, that Keller and Francesca were a couple. A fantasy that Keller was ashamed of but nonetheless let rise out of empty moments; a fantasy he could never wish into reality. To do so would be to lose Rick. Despite the bumpy nature of their acquaintance, he and Rick had become

362

friends of a sort.

Somewhere along the way, Keller has fallen asleep, the crumpled bag of cruller crumbs still gripped in his hand. The conductor shakes him awake. He can see the railway sign: GREAT HARBOR. Despite all his intentions never to come back, here he is. It seems like a hundred years since he boarded this train at this station and headed to war. He left here a boy, and now he's a grown man, a veteran of war, and, against all predictions, a college student. Despite the slow train, he's an hour early for the funeral, so he decides to walk. He's over the causeway bridge from Great Harbor in fifteen minutes and on the main street of Hawke's Cove in twenty.

Nothing has changed. He may have been gone for years, but Hawke's Cove has sat, like Brigadoon, in a time warp. The storefronts haven't changed, their businesses existing in some kind of stasis of moderate success, the hardware store, the grocery store, Linda's Restaurant. The only suggestion that it isn't still 1942 or 1938 or 1893 is the late-model Oldsmobile parked along the curb, all fins and chrome. There's Joe Green from the dairy, and the Sunderland boys — even in their sixties, the bachelor brothers have always been called the Sunderland boys. Neither of them looks a day older than the last time he saw them. Keller waves from across the street and they wave back without a moment's hesitation in figuring out who he is. Maybe he hasn't changed all that much. The feeling that he's returned to Hawke's Cove a grown man dissipates, until Keller thinks that maybe he's dreamed it all. Maybe he's still that ruddy-faced adolescent hauling lobster pots out of the cove with his great-uncle, who's heaping abuse on him because he's dropped a marlin spike overboard. Maybe it's all been a fever dream filled with the energy of war and the contentment of living in a small Cape-style house with his dog and the people who seem to care about him. And he's about to waken. Even dead, Clayton Britt has a power over him, the power to make him feel worthless.

The funeral home is an unimpressive square building that once held the livery stable. A white clapboard facade dresses it up, and a canvas canopy suggests that those who enter here should be humbled. Keller removes his fedora and hangs it on the hat rack by the door. He can hear voices, and he walks toward them. A small group is gathered in one of the viewing rooms. At the far end is a casket, and for the first time Keller realizes that he's going to have to look at his uncle. Somehow, he had overlooked that part of the American ritual. The last look. Keller had hoped that he'd had his last look at Clayton Britt that day at the Great Harbor railroad station. *You can come back, you know.*

"Keller, how nice to see you." Miss Jacobs has come up beside him as he stands flummoxed in the doorway of the viewing room. She takes his face in her hands and draws him down to her for a kiss on the cheek. "You look well."

"So do you." Miss Jacobs, like everything else in this town, hasn't changed. "You're still the most beautiful girl at the dance."

"Keller, when did you learn to flirt?" But she's not displeased; she blushes girlishly and takes him by the arm.

He wants to resist, but he knows that he must carry out this awkward task, so Keller lets Miss Jacobs lead him to the head of the short line of those paying their respects to a hard, cold, solitary fisherman.

It's as if the undertaker has played a joke on Clayton. If the man never smiled in life, the mortician has him smiling in death. Keller feels a little sick. This waxy smiling effigy of Clayton Britt is just plain ghoulish.

Even the undertaker hasn't been able to disguise the work-worn hands serenely folded over Clayton's breast, the gnarly grayish knuckles, the blackened thumbnail, the cut alongside one finger from his last haul. Keller stares at those hands, recalling the only time he ever touched them, one of them — the handshake Clayton offered the day he left for war. No. Keller remembers that Clayton used both hands that day, covering Keller's right with his left, as close to an affectionate gesture as the man had ever made. *You can come back, you know.*

Keller finds himself staring blindly at those hands until Miss Jacobs nods toward the kneeler. He sinks down to offer an unpracticed prayer. He has no idea what thought to loft to a God he's never been introduced to, so he just closes his eyes and thinks, Go where you belong, old man. May God have mercy on your soul. He tries to think of Clayton, but Rick and Francesca come to mind instead, and he finds himself praying for them. All of them.

Hawke's Cove's cemetery occupies a rise and is filled with the bad-teeth remnants of ancient slate headstones cheek by jowl with more modern and durable granite ones. Even though the temperature hovers just above freezing, the sandy soil is no obstacle in Hawke's Cove for a winter funeral and the gravesite is ready to accept Clayton. Keller shoulders the casket along with three others, two of whom are employees of the funeral home. The other pallbearer is the fish market owner, Stan Long. He keeps patting Keller on the shoulder and muttering, "A shame. A real shame." Keller isn't quite sure what shame there is in an old man's dying. It wasn't as if Stan was a friend. Or at least Keller had never thought of him as Clayton's friend, but he supposes that, living in such a small place and having daily contact, qualifies a person as a friend, even if that friend was never once invited to darken the doors of Clayton's French's Cove Road house.

Keller is surprised at the number of folks who have turned out on a blustery January day for the funeral of a near hermit. They don't hang around long after the final words are said, climbing back into cars and trucks or walking down the hill to the collation Miss Jacobs has arranged at the new VFW hall. Free lunch. No one has sniffed into a handkerchief. Released from the solemnity inherent in a graveside service, the attendees quickly fall back into the normal pitches of chat and laughter. They've shaken his hand

and patted his shoulder, done their duty, and are now happy to have an excuse to stay away another hour from work or household.

Two headstones away is a granite slab engraved with the name of a kid Keller went to school with. KILLED IN ACTION. Not far from where Keller had been in the war. There but for the Grace of God . . . He'd noticed a couple of other casualties of war, but this was a kid he'd played a little basketball with on those rare occasions when Clayton gave him a little off time after school. Days when, like today, it was too windy to go out on the water. Keller bets that the mourners surrounding those graves didn't so quickly cast off their grief.

The view from this hillside cemetery is astounding. Keller looks at it with a new appreciation, as if by Clayton's death, the scales have fallen from his eyes and he can see the beauty of his surroundings. His memories of this place are cast in black and gray, but today he sees Hawke's Cove in brilliant Technicolor.

Keller thinks that he'll just skip the collation and wander around the cemetery a little, see if there is anyone else he should be paying his respects to. Then, because it's early enough, he won't have to stay the night, but can head back to the station and catch the late train to Boston. Keller sucks in a deep breath; the salt air carries a hint of tomorrow's weather. Yeah, head back tonight. Don't take chances. It was hard enough leaving Francesca alone to care for Rick, but this low-grade temperature of his is worrisome. He'll get back late, well after midnight, but he won't wake anyone when he gets home. He has a key. Pax will greet him and they can have a little walk around the neighborhood. Pax was so distressed at his leaving, as if the dog thought he wasn't coming back.

A lift in the breeze licks his cheek, and Keller thinks of Francesca's lips against it just this morning. The soft breath as she kissed him. What discipline he'd shown in not turning that cheek to catch those lips against his. The breeze also speaks of the feel of her fingers on his other cheek, grazing it lightly.

Keller sets his hat on his head, tilts it just so. The grave diggers are patiently waiting at a remove to get to the second half of their job, closing the grave.

"Walk me down the hill, Keller." Miss Jacobs is standing beside him, and she takes his arm but doesn't let him turn away from the grave, the lowered coffin still glinting warmly in the thin January light. It is then that Keller realizes that Clayton's grave already has a headstone. That seems odd. How can a gravestone arrive before the tenant?

FLORENCE BRITT 1893–1919. BELOVED WIFE.

"Is that his mother? No, it can't be. The dates are wrong."

"No, Keller. Florence was my sister." Miss Jacobs leans over and dusts the top of the stone with her gloved hand. "I wanted the headstone to reflect that she was Florence Jacobs first. But he didn't seem to remember that fact."

"He was married?" Keller is incredulous. How could he not have known this?

"You didn't know?" Miss Jacobs doesn't sound surprised.

"He never said. You'd think he might have mentioned it."

"It near killed him, losing her." Miss Jacobs links her arm through Keller's. "Influenza."

"I simply cannot imagine him in love." Keller shakes his head.

"Oh, he was. Head over heels. Keller, you have to understand that Clayton was a much different man then. He had everything going for him. He was a confirmed bachelor, had inherited his family's property, was making a decent living for the times, dragging. Happy living life as it came to him. Then we came to town, two spinsters ready to teach school. Flo was my baby sister, and I always believed that she was too beautiful, too vivacious to resist, that spinsterhood for her was just a temporary state. Well, Clayton took one look and fell under her spell. He was everything my excitable sister needed, rock steady, loving, and kind."

Keller shakes his head again. This is a story about someone else, not his uncle.

"It was like, having discovered real happiness, then losing it, Clayton turned against all happiness. Like so many then, she got sick, and there was nothing that could be done. It was over in forty hours. Clayton just never regained his spirit. It wasn't that he grieved; it was that the grief poisoned him."

"She was my age."

"And he was twenty years older. I didn't like it, but he was as good a husband to her as I could have wanted. Maybe I was jealous of her. I've often wondered if I was. I didn't think so at the time; I was just being a cautious old bat. The problem was that he didn't have her for very long, six months, maybe. Seven. He went from being a honeymooner to a widower. They hadn't had enough life together for him to have anything but happy memories. And they haunted him, so he stopped."

"Stopped?"

"Thinking, feeling, living."

Why does that sound like Rick Stanton?

Keller doesn't know what to say. He closes his elbow against Miss Jacobs's arm and takes her back down the slope to the VFW. Keller tests the idea of losing someone you love and can only imagine Francesca, whom he does not truly have. Nonetheless, by that wholly imaginary circumstance can Keller understand the depth of feeling that Clayton had had once in his life, and how its loss turned him. He needs to get back. They need him.

"I'm going to keep going, Miss Jacobs. It was wonderful to see you."

"You'll get everything, you know. He died intestate, but the law will figure you for the heir."

Keller gently squeezes the old woman's fingers, which are encased in fine black lambskin gloves. "You have my address. Give it to the lawyers."

"Keller. You remind me of him."

"Don't say that." It frightens him, this idea that someday he could become that angry old man. That disappointment in love has that much power.

CHAPTER FIFTY-FOUR

I never heard him come in that night. I was in such a deep and dreamless sleep that even the sound of the front door opening in the night didn't waken me. I couldn't remember the last time I'd slept so well. Having Pax in the house assured me of my personal safety. Having no one else in the house to worry about lowered me into oblivion.

Rick was responding well to the penicillin and they said he would be home in a day or two. He'd sent me home from his bedside, with the help of a stern nurse. "Get some rest," he said. "I've got all the help here I need." The stern nurse handed me my coat.

I got home to a dark house, having left at midmorning and come home late into winter dusk. Thank God Pax was there, that there was another mouth to feed and a beating heart to hear. He kept me company during those hours when he would have been in with Rick. He didn't seem to be asking any questions, and I marveled that he seemed to be taking this odd turn of events — no men — in his stride. It was so cold that I cheated him out of the good walk Keller normally would have given him, going only as far as the end of the street before heading back into my empty house.

When I went up to bed that night, I stood in the doorway of the nursery-cum-storage-cum-bedroom that Keller occupied. His cot was made up, with the blankets pulled military tight, and not an object was out of plumb. Hairbrushes aligned side by side, toiletries that I hadn't convinced him to leave in the bathroom erect in their basket. I never trespassed in there. It wasn't like his garage space, with the sitting area and the open invitation to come and sit and talk out of earshot of Rick when we needed to. Or maybe just talk about his reading or the weather. An oasis. This room, tiny and spare, gave me back almost nothing of Keller. I crossed the sill and went to his bureau, picked up those brushes with the boar's bristles dyed by the oils of his Brylcreem. How he fought to keep that lock of hair disciplined, and how I longed to touch it.

I was alone in the house for the first time in a very long time. Neither man was there and so I had only myself to hide from. When Keller had come out of the bath the night before, I'd caught sight of him dashing, towel-wrapped, up the stairs, his clothes bundled under one arm, his bathrobe left upstairs by accident. Bare legs, bare shoulders still glistening from dampness. Slender waist and long back, his spine a darker concavity against the polished muscle of his back. I'd turned away before he saw me staring. Before I embarrassed him with the flicker of want that I felt in a place that had been dormant for so long.

I set his brushes down, caught sight of myself in his mirror, the reflection of his cot behind me. I walked out of the room, leaving his bedroom door wide open, leaving mine wide open, too. Every other night, the click of my latch had proclaimed our respectability. Pax didn't come upstairs right away; I could hear him moving through every room of the downstairs, checking things, making sure that we were safe. As I fell asleep, I heard him come upstairs, satisfied all was well. For the first time ever, he came into my room and I invited him up on my bed. He curled up on the end, not lying next to me as he did with Rick during the day and Keller at night.

It was the sound of running water that

finally woke me that next morning. A comforting sound, until I remembered that I was supposed to be alone. Pax, whose weight had held me down all night, was gone. Still, I didn't jump out of bed. The fact that Pax hadn't made any fuss was enough to settle my startled nerves and push me back into the pillow. It was obvious; Keller had come home. I stretched, yawned, and went right back to sleep.

"Hey, sleepyhead." Keller tapped lightly on my open bedroom door. "I've got coffee, if you're interested." He stood there in profile, as if trying not to look in.

"I'd love some." Before he moved away from the door, I threw off my covers and swung my feet over the side. I pulled my housecoat on over my nightdress and followed him downstairs. The house was chilly — I'd turned the heat down a little too far — but the kitchen was warm in the mid-morning sun coming through the window. Pax lay in a patch of it, as if sunbathing. The sunlight burnished his silver-gray coast, making it look like mink.

"So, it wasn't a cold, then?"

"Bladder infection. Catheter was a little clogged or something. The doc admitted him."

"I wish I'd known, I never would have left."

"We managed. We've done it before." I didn't mean it to sound like it did, a little mean or cavalier. "I mean, it wasn't the first time this has happened, so I knew what to expect." I didn't confide in him how frightening it was, no matter how often it happened. I didn't tell him that every time one of these infections occurred, it could mean months back in the VA hospital. This time, we'd caught it early. I thought of Pax sitting there, his steely posture and the look of alert concern he'd given me.

"The problem is that we have to wait for the visiting nurse to do the catheter. If we knew how, we could change it more often." Keller set a cup down in front of me.

"You don't want to get into that level of nursing. It's not meant for amateurs." That was Keller, always thinking he could fix things. One more task, one more challenge. "Some things are just best left to the professionals. Tell me about the funeral."

"Not much to tell. It was all right. More people showed up than I would have expected."

"Not unusual in a small town. In Mount Joy, everyone shows up at most funerals because it's considered a civic duty."

"I found out he was married."

I could tell that this bit of ancient history stuck in Keller's throat. He didn't say it like it was interesting or puzzling, but as if it somehow *bothered* him. Like Clayton had been holding back on him. So I asked the next logical questions. "Did he have kids?"

"No. She died in the influenza outbreak, just at the end of it. She was twenty years younger than he was. She was my age when she died." For a man who had seen the youth of the country dead on the battlefield, he sounded surprised that a young woman might perish from disease.

"That's so sad." So my intuition of unrequited love had been a little correct. Just a different lover and a different cause.

"I keep thinking how miserable an old codfish he was, and wondering how different it would have been had she lived. Miss Jacobs said that he loved her." Keller lifted his face and looked at me as he said this. *He loved her.* "I keep thinking how powerful love is. That losing it can change a person so deeply."

"Having it changes a person, too."

With Rick out of the room, we decided to give it a good cleaning. Armed to the teeth with the tools necessary, we dragged or wheeled out all of the furniture, stripped the books off the shelf, and took down the venetian blinds, which I soaked in the bathtub in ammonia water. Pax curled his lips up in a hilarious mask of distaste and retreated to the breezeway. We each took two walls and washed them down until the pale blue brightened like an old master's glory revealed. Keller scrubbed down the bed, removing the mattress and running a sponge all over the mechanism that raised and lowered it.

By four o'clock, all that was left untouched in the room was the wheelchair, and Keller decided that would best be handled out in the garage, where he could give it a good going-over without getting the mopped floor wet again. "I'll tighten up the bolts while I'm at it."

While he was occupied with the chair, I rooted around in the cellar for a couple of pictures we'd had hanging in our first apartment. I would put them up on the unadorned but sparkly clean walls. One was a landscape painted by a local Iowa amateur that my aunt and uncle had given us for our wedding and the other a view of the Public Garden we'd bought ourselves from a street vendor at Downtown Crossing. They were cheerful in an uncheerful space. The hospital bed was made up like a normal bed, with the spread tucked neatly under the single pillow. The books had been moved to the higher shelf and the radio was where it should have been all along; the table over the bed had been scrubbed clean and pushed out of the way for the moment; the bedside table had been neatened up, and I put a new lamp on it, swapping out the rather institutional one with a bedroom lamp abandoned in the basement. The sickroom looked almost, but not quite, like a real bedroom. But it didn't look right. I stood in the doorway, my rubber gloves still on, the bucket of dirty water at my feet, and I couldn't help but think that, without the wheelchair, it looked like we had expunged Rick. As if we didn't expect him back.

Chapter Fifty-Five

Keller and I went to the hospital together for evening visiting hours. Except for the fact that Rick had a roommate, an old gent with a prostate — or "prostrate," as he kept calling it — problem, it could have been any evening with the three of us sitting around a small space filled with medical equipment. Rick was so much better, although they'd found another decubitus starting on his left flank. We tried so hard, and still we weren't able to keep his skin completely healthy.

When we arrived, Keller grasped the trapeze dangling over Rick's bed. "We should get one of these. Think how much it would help."

Rick ignored the suggestion. "How's my Pax?"

"Pax will come with us when we come spring you out of this place." Keller let go of the trapeze and it swung gently over Rick.

"He's missed you."

"I miss him. You be sure to bring him."

I shouldn't have, but I couldn't help feeling like Rick missed that dog more than he missed me. I thought it was true. I wasn't jealous, not in any serious sense. I remembered so distinctly then the first time Rick had taken me to his place, Pax sitting there waiting for him, suspicious of me, and Rick's absolute confidence that I would love his dog as much as he did. Now all I wanted was for him to love me as much as he did the dog. That sounds petty and dramatic. I don't mean that he didn't love me as much, but the quality of the love he had for that dog was so much purer, less troubled. The dog had gone to war and come home unchanged. Neither of us could say that about ourselves.

Keller and I were exhausted from our day's labors, so weren't very talkative, and Rick noticed. "What's wrong?"

"Nothing, just really tired." I told him what we'd been doing.

"So, you cleaned everything, even the chair?"

Keller nodded. "Yeah. Even the wheelchair." He was sitting to my left, and out of the corner of my eye I saw him lean back and cross his arms. I don't know why Rick sounded like he was talking about something else, like the word *wheelchair* was a euphemism. Maybe I was just so tired, I was hearing things.

The man next to Rick was trying to get out of bed and that didn't look like a good idea to me, but before I could say anything, Keller got up to look for a nurse.

Rick watched him leave the room. "Good time for me to get out of the way, then, I guess. Early spring cleaning." I thought the topic had pretty much run out and I didn't understand Rick's combative tone. That wasn't my imagination.

"More like late fall. I never did give that room a proper going-over when we moved in."

"I'll try to plan my hospitalizations to be more convenient."

I was too tired to rise to his bait. "Actually, I could only do it because Keller was there to help me."

"As always."

"Just being useful, Rick." Keller was back in the room. "It's what you pay me for."

"Right. Just doing your job."

That was enough for me. "I think it's time to go. You're getting tired."

"And cranky?" Rick looked away, and he did look cranky, like a little boy kept inside while his friends go outside to play.

"Yeah. A little." I bent and kissed his forehead, just like you would with a cranky little boy. "I love you anyway."

He took my hand and held it tightly, almost too tight, pulling me a little closer. "Good." This time, we kissed like proper lovers, but I couldn't help but get the feeling that it was for Keller's benefit.

Chapter Fifty-Six

Pax has inspected every room in the house. He's listened, sniffed, looked in every dark corner, taken a lick at a missed drip on the side of the stove, lapped at his water bowl, and stood over the heat register to enjoy the blast of heat. Like a good sentry at his post, Pax feels confident that this house is safe. Safe and empty. It is the first time in recent memory that the dog has been left all alone.

Pax eyes the living room sofa, leans against it a little, rubs his chops against the nubby fabric. One paw, then another, and suddenly he's aboard. From the height of the sofa, he can sit and look out the window unobstructed. The neighbor's cat pauses at the curb cut, stretches, and sits to wash her face, as if she knows he's looking at her and she is taunting him. He has no quarrel with cats, but he doesn't much like this feline's attitude of entitlement. He barks. One full-bodied *roof* and the cat stops her washing and blinks. Moves on, question-mark tail in the air. Insouciant, but warned.

The people in this house aren't where they belong, and the routine has been disrupted. But Pax has long since learned to cope with disruption, to be flexible and to be alert to what he needs to do. Right now, he needs to sit on this couch and wait for the sound of the car to return. Once he detects the singular sound of *their* car, he'll jump down from the couch. Not because he knows he isn't supposed to be on the couch, which he does, but because he always needs to greet them at the door; that's part of his job. And, if a dog can hope, he's hoping that all three of his people will be in that car.

But only Francesca and Keller got out of the car this day, and Pax knows better than to look behind them to see if somehow Rick has been left outside. He greets them with the same enthusiasm as he would have his missing Rick. They talk to him as if he's supposed to understand all their language. The only words he understands are *Rick* and *tomorrow*. Not *tomorrow* as a concept, but the word always means "later on, not now." Ergo, *Rick, not now.*

CHAPTER FIFTY-SEVEN

We had worked hard on that room together, enjoying an easy companionship over buckets of Spic and Span. The radio was on and we sang along with some of the popular songs. Keller had a serviceable voice and I wasn't too bad. We muffed the lyrics and laughed. A little water might have splashed, a sponge thrown playfully. We were like two kids on a snow day, released, however temporarily, from the burden of our daily routine. All right, I'll say it, released from the burden of my husband. We both loved him; I know that. And that's what made it all right for us to acknowledge that we were enjoying one day, maybe two, without his presence. His very paternal presence. His dark presence over the lightness in ourselves that we were holding down. We were still young. I sometimes forget that. Keller and I were still in our twenties.

We'd come back from visiting Rick in the

hospital less cheery than when we had gone. Rick's grumpiness had put a damper on our spirits. We hadn't said much on the way home, Keller driving my car. *Our* car, I should say, even though Rick would never drive it. I sat in the passenger seat and stared out the window until I felt his hand in its thick winter glove touch mine. "It's all right, Francesca. He's all right." He gave my hand a little tug. How like Keller to read my thoughts. I'm not sure if I was grateful or a little afraid.

Back at the house, we sprang Pax from his solitary confinement and walked to the beach. Keller threw sticks for him and Pax bounded and raced, splashed in the freezing water and barked at us as if he were a puppy without manners. The Harbor islands looked like great dark humps in the dusk and the Boston skyline glittered in the cold air, jewel-like and competing with the stars just emerging. As we walked back, the brightness of postwar illumination paved our way home.

We'd left the lights on, so our house was as brightly lit as any we'd passed. Warm and welcoming. We stamped old snow and beach sand off our boots and left them in the breezeway. In unshod feet, we scampered over cold tiles into the warm kitchen. Keller fed Pax and I rummaged through the Frigidaire for something to cobble together for dinner. We sat at the same table and ate scrambled eggs and toast. Face-to-face, close enough that Keller reached across and tipped a flake of egg off my face. I spooned my leftovers onto his plate.

The three of us flopped on the living room couch to listen to the radio — a little railroad train of hips and shoulders, mine next to Keller's and Pax's next to his in an unprecedented lapse of training — Pax especially enjoyed Jack Paar's show. We stayed up well past our usual fall-into-bed hour. It was as if we didn't want to let the day end. As if neither of us could figure out the best way to say good night without calling attention to the fact that we were, for all intents and purposes, unchaperoned.

Pax jumped down and stretched fore and aft, then went to the front door for last call. Keller put on his jacket and out they went. I shut off the radio and the house was suddenly too silent. Without thinking, I headed into Rick's room, as I did every night. The sight of the empty bed jolted me back into the moment. My husband was in the hospital and I was alone with Keller.

CHAPTER FIFTY-EIGHT

It's an accident, this meeting on the stairs. She's heading down to use the bathroom; he's going up after taking Pax out for his late night walk. He should turn this way and she should turn that. Instead, as she is one step above him, they find themselves face-to-face, body-to-body. He can smell the faint mint of her favorite Lifesaver. She can, no doubt, breathe in the taste of his last cigarette. He touches the inside of her elbow. She touches his cheek. The moment lingers, as if, having made these experimental gestures, neither one has a way of making sense of them. Here is a question being asked, for which there is no answer. He traces his thumb against the soft surface of her skin. She fans her fingers against his stubbled cheek, holds it as if she is puzzled at the contours of his bones. He's surprised to see that her eyes aren't simply green, as he thought, but flecked with shards of amber.

At the foot of the stairs, the dog sits, his gaze upon them, but he is silent.

They need to invoke Rick.

"I'm going to make cocoa. Come down." Her hand is still on his cheek as she says this.

"I will." His hand is still on her tender skin.

The moment passes and they continue on their separate ways: She goes downstairs, pauses, looks back at him, doesn't smile. He goes to his room, where he shuts the door and sits on his cot. Is it possible that his fingers burn with the heat of her skin? Keller touches his lips with the hand that touched her so tenderly. He then touches the cheek where her hand had held it, holding him still so that their gazes matched. He doesn't go downstairs to sit across a kitchen table from her, an unwanted mug of hot chocolate held in a hand already heated by a want that transcends mere lust. By the time she finally comes upstairs, he is asleep.

Pax remains as he is, at the foot of the stairs, alert and panting gently.

His cheek was so different from Rick's — his day-old beard darker, the angles sharper. His deep brown eyes softened the longer he looked into mine. The brush of his thumb against my most sensitive skin had sent a radiating pulse down into my deepest parts. For months — no, years — I had been untouched. Rather, touched only in dim affection by my husband, who had lost the ability to want me. Touched by Keller only within the confines of this platonic ideal we were living by out of respect and common decency and the love we both held for Rick.

I heated the milk and got out two mugs, but I knew that he wouldn't come down. I was relieved, to tell the truth. It was as if there was a thin membrane between us, a membrane that separated us from each other and temptation. On those stairs, we had pushed against that membrane. And so it was fragile right now and there was a grave danger that it would burst at the merest provocation.

CHAPTER FIFTY-NINE

It is almost time for his afternoon walk when instead Pax is asked to get in Keller's car, something he loves to do, although this time he's made to sit in the back, not next to Keller as he most often does. Francesca sits there and he supposes that that's all right. Pax puts his head over the back of the front seat, in between Francesca and Keller. They are unusually quiet, but also unusually close, so he has to push a little to get his head in between them. She keeps adjusting her gloves; he keeps pulling on his earlobe, as if he's about to issue a thought, but then keeps silent. They are making him nervous.

Pax's canine eyes are inadequate for detail, but he recognizes that they are traveling along familiar roads for a time. Then they turn, heading in a direction he's never been before. When they park the car, Pax expects the command to stay, guard the vehicle against thieves. Instead, Keller asks him to get out and fall in. Francesca is on Keller's right side and Pax is at heel at his left. They march to the front door in almost military precision. Left, right, left.

Pax is aware of people standing on both sides of the walkway leading to the entrance of this building that harbors odors that remind the dog of his new purpose. At the entrance, a man speaks to Keller, but Keller clearly doesn't see him as an obstacle, more like a subordinate, and keeps a firm touch on the leash. The door opens to them and Francesca and Keller, with Pax at his side, go in. Pax isn't certain about the tiny windowless room that moves, but he betrays no concern, although he sits in order to feel more secure. The door opens again and everything has changed. He takes one deep investigative breath and doesn't need any further guidance at this point. He knows where they're going and whom they are going to collect. He can hardly make himself stay at heel as they walk down the long corridor to where Rick waits.

Roo, roo. Pax forgets himself as he fairly leaps into Rick's lap. He wriggles like a puppy and has no shame.

"Good boy. Good boy."

All three of them say it: "Good boy, Pax."

It's as if he's done something of a heroic nature, although Pax doesn't have any idea what it is. Still, it's good to be the object of praise, even for a dog that has never lacked for praise.

CHAPTER SIXTY

Keller wheels Rick to the car, where the awkward business of getting from wheelchair to front seat will be enacted. Pax is close by to lend moral support and Francesca is bringing up the rear with a bagful of his belongings. There is always something noxious about personal items brought home from the hospital, and she'll be tossing everything into the washer as soon as they get home.

The little pouch that holds his crossword puzzle books and pencils, and the precious trove of little white pills, isn't attached to the wheelchair, and Rick scans Keller's face to see if there is any suspicion; if, in giving his chair a good cleaning, Keller has found the twenty-one little pills safely resting at the bottom of that cloth pouch, hiding like fish beneath the reef of a crossword puzzle book. Keller betrays no hint that he's found out Rick's secret. But there is a tension in his jaw, something that makes him look like a man with something on his mind.

Keller wedges him into the front seat and Francesca leans in to kiss him, as if she's staying behind, not climbing into the backseat with the dog. Her lips are warm despite the frigid air, as if she's held on to some of the warmth of the indoors. But she doesn't look at him.

It's on his bed, the little pouch. The crossword puzzle book is there, and a newly sharpened pencil. He can't help himself: He grabs it almost as soon as Keller wheels him into his room. He dips his fingertips in the pouch and closes his eyes. They're there. He'll count them later, just to make sure, but it feels right. He doesn't even care if Keller is watching, curious.

"Missed your crosswords so much?"

"It's pretty boring in there."

"I'd have brought them. Why didn't you ask?"

"Hey, no problem. I just thought of an answer I missed; I can complete one of the hard ones."

Keller still has that tense look.

"What's on your mind, Nicholson?" Get it out in the open, deal with the consequences.

"I need a little time."

"You're entitled. You never take a day off. I mean, for things other than funerals."

"No, just the afternoon. I have some stuff I have to do."

"Go. We're fine." Relief blunts any curiosity. If any man needs some downtime, surely Keller does.

"Okay. Thanks."

"Don't thank me. It's not like I'm not going to dock your paycheck." Rick smiles, broad and real. But Keller doesn't and that tense look migrates across his face.

"Tell Francesca I'll be back by dinnertime."

"Fine."

Keller stands in the widened doorway. "She's a good wife. Don't you ever forget it."

Rick nods, perplexed and a tiny bit annoyed. Keller has stepped a little over the line. Pushed himself a tiny bit too much. Of course Francesca is a good wife. What's his point? Rick slides his hand into the pouch and begins to count his pills. What if Keller found the morphine? Would he have told Francesca? Or would he just have put them back in the vial, which he'll keep out of both Rick's and Pax's reach? Honor among thieves? Honor between veterans of the same killing fields? *She's a good wife.* Are they teammates or are they rivals?

CHAPTER SIXTY-ONE

"Don't make lunch for me. I'm going to go get gas in my car." It's the best excuse he can come up with, but there's no way he can stay in this house, smile over grilled cheese sandwiches, and pretend that everything is all right. He just isn't that good an actor.

"Eat first. It's all ready." Francesca is holding a plate with four sandwiches stacked on it.

Keller grabs half a grilled cheese sandwich, bites into it, then calls the dog. "Pax will go with me."

"He just had a ride."

Keller doesn't answer and he doesn't care if Francesca is puzzled by him. He just needs to get out of this house. He swallows the rest of the half sandwich, calls the dog, and pulls his jacket out of the coat closet. "I won't be long. You and Rick enjoy a quiet lunch. Have some time together."

"What's going on, Kel?"

"Nothing." He takes a shallow breath. "Nothing's wrong. I just need some air." He won't look her in the eye. He doesn't want to see if she believes him, or if the boat of their friendship is taking on water. *Nothing happened.*

Keller drives aimlessly, following Quincy Shore Drive for a mile or so, circling around Hough's Neck to get another view of the Harbor islands. The water is choppy today; cream-topped waves leave foam on the gritty shore. Pax sits beside him, as close as a girlfriend on the bench seat of the second-hand Ford. He stops for gas, throwing fifty cents' worth into the tank. He could just keep going. There's nothing at the house that he can't live without. No memorabilia, no souvenirs. Nothing he owns has senti-mental value. Keller ruffles Pax's fur around his neck. "What do you say? Where would you like to go?"

Pax huffs, sneezes, but has little other comment.

"Someplace they couldn't find us. Someplace far enough away they couldn't come looking for you."

Keller checks his wallet. Every Friday, Francesca leaves an envelope on his bureau, as if handing him a paycheck would somehow remind him that he isn't a member of the family but what he really is, a paid employee. Slightly better than a boarder, not quite a friend. *Not anymore.* Thirty bucks. Enough to keep moving for a while. A little tremor of excitement tickles him under his rib cage. A bit like that tremble of anticipation as he left Hawke's Cove for the service. Then he'd had a destination, a plan, a destiny. Right now, he's rootless and as free as he's ever been in his life; he can point this car in any direction and just go. No wrought-iron fences keeping him in. No authority, whether Clayton's or the army's, telling him where to go and what to do. A break from this tension-wrought situation.

The idea of that freedom is enough to make Keller go a little too fast through these city streets, his right foot empowered by his thinking, until he slams on the brakes at a stoplight.

Pax is unseated by the sudden halt, and he bangs his muzzle on the dashboard.

"Sorry, fella, so sorry." Keller pats the dog and takes a deep breath. Something catches his eye; the handle of Francesca's purse peeks out from under the front seat, where she'd stashed it out of the way for the trip home from the hospital. The sight of that singularly Francesca-associated object puts paid to any notion of flight. He can't leave her, even if it would be the best thing. Oh, he could return the purse and gather his few possessions, give notice in a proper and professional way, and then leave. Nothing stopping him from doing that. And they would find another aide. Now that they know they can adjust to having the help, a properly trained aide would be better for them anyway. Someone who comes in without any strings attached. Without any strings growing stronger every day. Pax would stay in the car; they'd never realize he was gone until Keller was long gone.

In his life, Keller has had most everything stripped from him by circumstance. But he's not sure that he can strip Pax from Rick with the same harsh entitlement that his aunts had in stripping him of his freedom; or that Clayton had in using him as slave labor. *For your own good.* And unless he stays with Rick and Francesca, Pax will be stripped from him. And every day he'll be forced to tamp down this unforeseen and unwelcome desire for another man's wife. Which is the harder choice? Lose Pax or lose Francesca? Keller realizes that there is no choice. Leaving, he will lose both. In fact, the truth is, he has neither.

When the light turns green, Keller turns

left, heading back to where Rick, in his perpetual gloom, sits in that room. And where Francesca waits, maybe a little worried about him instead of Rick for a change.

CHAPTER SIXTY-TWO

Francesca has come in with lunch, but Rick can see that she's preoccupied. Three and a half sandwiches. For once, she doesn't come in smiling and full of chat for the sake of filling up the silence in that room. She talks, but her heart isn't in it. "Do you want another half? Do you want tea or coffee?" She doesn't realize just how well he knows her. Keller's absence is the gorilla in the room. Rick wonders if maybe they had a fight.

She'll just keep pretending that everything is hunky-dory. It is so wearing. Sometimes he thinks that Francesca is holding up his world on her back, and it plagues him that she won't admit that she's tired. On her most aggressively cheerful days, he thinks that he'd give his other arm for her to be honest with him, to rage against the shitty end of the stick she's holding. He's survived another bladder infection, but that only serves to pump up her shortsighted optimism that he's going to improve, that these things are just temporary setbacks. Get back in the game! She's like a fan who never gives up hope. A real fan overlooks bad games and cheers for the team no matter what. Francesca really needs to accept defeat.

But this time, Rick can see that Francesca's preoccupation isn't about him, and it's like he's being cheated. Why should she be so concerned about their *aide's* wanting a little break? So what if Keller didn't want to eat his lunch. Why should she even be thinking about it? He goes back to thinking that Keller and Francesca have had a disagreement. But when a man and a woman have a fight, there has to be a certain kind of intimacy to fuel it.

Rick bites a chunk out of his sandwich; doesn't answer Francesca's benign question about beverage. He hears only the high note of tension in her voice, as if she's being garroted with an unspoken question.

"He took Pax with him?" The grease from the sandwich coats his fingers.

"I guess so. Yes." Francesca hands him a napkin. "That's all right, isn't it?"

"He shouldn't be taking Pax if he's going out for any length of time. I need him."

"So does he." Francesca drops her unfinished sandwich on the plate. "Did he seem upset to you?"

"No. Just a man needing an afternoon off to clear his head." Really, why is she so concerned? Like a teenage girl worrying about the disposition of her crush. Rick shoves the rest of his sandwich into his mouth to stop it up before he says something he will regret.

"Are you done?"

It takes a second for Rick to realize she means done with lunch. "Yeah."

She removes the plate with the uneaten halves and leaves him as he is, sitting in that chair, facing the door, through which he seldom goes, the grease from his sandwich still on his fingers. Pax should be here to lick them off. Rick manages to turn his chair around so that he is facing the interior of his room. What sky he can see through the open blinds is opaque in the thin daylight, and the first sting of wet snow hits the pane.

It seems like hours pass before Rick finally hears the front door open. He closes his eyes with relief. Pax is back. Keller has brought him back. The big dog bounds into the room, his fur cold and sprinkled with hard balls of sleet. He shakes and sprays Rick with moisture, then commences licking Rick's fingers one by one, like a mother dog licks the ins and outs of her puppy. Careful, considered, and devoted. Done, the dog's tongue unfurls to lick his dewlaps and he settles his head in Rick's lap for an ear rub. Rick strokes deep into the ear, sliding his fingers up the length of it, moving the cilia. In the pearly winter light, a darker skin emerges within Pax's ear — his tattoo. The mark that designates him as a war dog, a dog who saw service. Who, like him, was wounded in action. Keller's loyal partner on the battlefield.

Not one of the men with whom he served in that doomed squad survived. Removed from the battlefield, Rick was also removed from his platoon. Languishing for months in the hospital, first in England and then here, Rick lost contact with anyone he served with. Some guys, he knows, cling to those associations, reluctant to give up the camaraderie, the mythical brotherhood of battle, but he doesn't. Nor is he willing to seek out any connection. Not after what happened, and the fact that he survived. "Survivor's guilt." — that's what the shrink called it the one time he met with one. *Don't beat yourself up. You tried. Wasn't your fault.* Oh my, how many platitudes have been lobbed at him by all and sundry. Doctors, nurses, the shrink, Francesca. But not Keller. Keller listened to his story, but he didn't attempt to absolve him.

Rick can't read the numbers written on the inside of his dog's ear. The thick cilia obscure four of the digits; he'd have to shave the inside of the ear to read them. Pax whines a little; Rick is holding that ear too tightly. He lets go, pushes the dog off his lap.

The sound of sleet hitting the window. The room is a little cold and Rick shrugs more blanket up over his shoulder. As he does most every night, he has awakened suddenly and without a known disturbance. He hears the click of the dog's toenails coming down the stairs, Pax alert, as always, for his awakening. Usually, the dog is there before his eyes open, sensitive to Rick's coming awake even from a distance. But lately, Rick has awakened alone in this room, comforted only by the quick sound of those nails on hardwood.

The dog comes in and touches him with a cold nose, as if he's been outside. He wags his tail and does the doggy equivalent of tucking Rick in, resting his head in the crook between Rick's shoulder and chin. Rick knows that as soon as he drifts off, the dog will go away. Go back up to the bedroom Keller uses now that he's been invited into the house, a narrow landing width away from Francesca and the room she occupies alone, sleeping in their marriage bed, a room he's never seen but pictures exactly as the one they had in their first apartment.

Sometimes in the quiet of the deep night, when the street traffic is done and the furnace is satisfied with the temperature and shuts off, Rick thinks he can hear them. The creak of a floorboard. The sound of a bedspring complaining. Like someone has gotten up and moved to another bed. It's just house noises, he tells himself. But tonight he hears murmuring. In the middle of the night, they are close enough to whisper to each other.

Last night they were alone in this house.

Rick presses his ear against his pillow, covers his other ear with the stump of his pitching arm. But he still hears them. Whispers carry farther than the natural voice. He uncovers his ears and strains to listen for distinct words. There is only the rising and falling of tone, and a slight crescendo/decrescendo, as if the conversation were scored with musical notation.

Is it the wind singing through the naked pear tree in the backyard, or the water gurgling in the radiators? It must be the sound of windshield wipers on a lone car on the next block. The train whistle, a foghorn. The sound of his own blood squeezed through his heart? But no. It's voices above him. Whispering to each other. He's sure of it.

Chapter Sixty-Three

Pax circles and paces, utterly aware of Rick's agitation. He won't go back upstairs again tonight because he knows that Rick will not fall back into deep sleep again. There is a peppery scent emanating from him, and the remnant sharp scent of the hospital, where they found him and brought him back here. Rubber and alcohol wipes, baby lotion and iodine. Pax wrinkles his nose at the odors but keeps his chin on Rick's bed so that Rick can touch him. Through those fingertips, the dog judges that Rick's racing heart is slowing, but the agitation has not diminished and the clutch of those fingers occasionally becomes painful.

It's like when Keller and he were on night patrol, both of them listening for the sounds of the enemy. Sounds weren't enough, and everything depended upon Pax's being able to distinguish the difference between the scent of German sweat and that of his people. As different as black and white to the dog. Sounds weren't always as distinctive. A German bullet dropped from a cold and clumsy hand sounded the same as an American bullet hitting the bare earth. In the fog, sounds from the east could sound like they were coming from the west. All muffled, blurred. But scent told the story, and the dog ensured his comrades their safe passage through tight boundaries. Rick's scent is as different from Keller's and Francesca's household scent as that of the Germans was from the Allies'.

Rick is listening, and so Pax listens. Outside are only the normal sounds of night creatures moving and cold drizzle pinging off the gutters. Inside, he hears the breathing of sleeping people, the tick of the kitchen clock. Because Rick is, Pax is also on alert, but he cannot fathom what he's supposed to be listening for. It makes him anxious, and he pants a little, paces, returns to Rick's side. They are both awake until a heralding bird announces the momentary arrival of dawn. It has stopped sleeting and the nocturnal creatures have slipped away. Between that early bird's reveille and the laggards' the moment of predawn is more silent than the entire night.

Overhead, a bedspring protests the shift of a body. A floorboard creaks. Very softly, Pax murmurs. Rick is finally asleep.

CHAPTER SIXTY-FOUR

I waited that whole afternoon, listening for Keller's return, half-expecting that he wouldn't come back, maybe more than half-hoping that he wouldn't. It was all too complicated. I loved my husband as much as I ever had, but the spiky passion that had pushed us into a quick marriage and then had elevated to grand heights during our failed baby-making attempts was withered and in danger of dying out entirely. Which was all right. Unnecessary, only a vestige left. Love between us was different now.

Keller's touch had reminded me of passion, that's all. I would not act on it. I didn't need it.

When he came home late that afternoon, the sun long down, the headlights of his car beaming briefly against the white wall of the living room as he pulled into the driveway, I kept out of the way. I heard Pax's nails skittering down the hall to Rick. I could smell the winter air seeping into the house through the breezeway as Keller passed from garage to kitchen. I stayed where I was, turning on the lamps, pulling the drapes. I felt him approach more than heard it. I threw my shoulders back and pasted a smile on my face. There is no avoiding someone who lives in your house. The membrane between us had to be retained. We hadn't broken it; neither could we try testing it again.

"I'm glad you're back. How about hot dogs for dinner tonight?"

Keller slid his jacket off his shoulders and reached into the hall closet for a hanger. For a tense moment, I thought he wouldn't speak to me, that he didn't understand that we had to move ahead, to maintain our alliance as Rick's cobbled-together family. "Sure. Beans, too?"

Such a funny topic for reconciliation. Hot dogs and beans.

"Oh, and I found this." Keller held out my purse. "It was under the front seat."

I took it from him. "How careless of me."

He headed in to check on Rick, leaving me in the hallway, my purse in my hand. I had to wonder, had my purse not been in his car, would he have come back?

CHAPTER SIXTY-FIVE

Francesca had given him new shoes for Christmas, a nice pair of cordovan oxfords like he used to wear on travel days. Rick had smiled and thanked her, then watched as she put them away in his closet to be forgotten. It was so Francesca, to have given him something that suggested he might someday be seen in public again. For his birthday, she'd given him new pants, a pair of everyday khakis like he used to wear on weekends. Something presumably to replace the stained and thin-in-the seat pants he's maneuvered into every morning by Keller. Rick wonders if these pants will even fit him. She'd bought his usual size, thirty-four, out of habit, not allowing for the fact he no longer has muscle on those thighs. He's shrunk. The only muscle he seems to still have is the one in his left arm, pumped up from playing tug-of-war with the dog. It's the only muscle he's using, although the therapists keep after him to use as much as he can of his back and shoulders. Rick has used the weather as a good excuse not to bother going to physical therapy. Too cold. Too snowy. Too icy. Too windy. Too lazy. It's too much. Too much to keep asking Keller to wrangle him in and out of the car, in and out of chairs, in and out of buildings. Keller doesn't complain. They should give him a damned raise.

Now, along with the resurrected paintings, there is a new calendar on his wall, a Christmas gift from the hardware store that Keller patronizes, featuring an old-fashioned tractor on the top above the months. He doesn't know why Keller stuck that in here. Rick's not the Iowan. What does he care about tractors? What does he care about dates? The worst part is, no matter what month it is that, red riderless tractor sits in that same cornfield. They're up to March and still that cheerful tractor doesn't make any progress. The calendar is supposed to chart his progress. But that isn't moving forward, either.

Since his last hospital stay, Francesca and Keller have become determined that he not spend all day, every day, in this room. Francesca says, "It's time, Rick. It's just no good to be sitting here mostly alone for so much of the time."

"You need to get moving, bud," Keller adds.

They cite the bedsores and the chance of succumbing to pneumonia as reason enough to get moving.

It's like leaving the safety of a cave for the uncertainty of an open plain — darkness to light. The afternoon light in the west-facing living room bothers his eyes. The overhead light in the kitchen glares down. It exhausts him. On good days, Keller and Francesca pile him, all bundled up in wool coat, hat, and gloves, into the car and she drives him down Route 3 to "see the sights" while Keller goes to school. They pass through Hingham and Duxbury, admire the scenery and make wrong turns here and there, giving the outing the aura of an adventure. But they don't talk about much of anything. She repeatedly makes sure his numb legs are covered with the plaid picnic rug, as if he could feel the cold on them.

At night, he feels like a little kid made to sit at the grown-up table. Keller and Francesca sit on opposite sides and carry on conversations based primarily on gossip about the few neighbors Francesca has come to know and people Keller meets at college. Rick has nothing to contribute until they touch on current events, and then he can trot out opinions gleaned from the newspaper and the radio. He's become quite an expert on the rise of communism, but he knows nothing about his neighbors.

"Spring training starts next week." Keller helps himself to more mashed potatoes, as if he's oblivious to the challenge in that remark. Is he kidding? Bringing up a subject like that, as if Rick *cares*.

"Doesn't seem possible another year has flown by." Francesca is a party to this. She hands Keller the butter dish.

"Or at least another season. I've only got six weeks left in the semester." Keller slices off a pat of chilled butter. "I'll be out by early May." This semester, Keller has taken on a full course load, and he spends every minute that he's not tending Rick's needs with his head in a book.

Rick gestures for the butter. "Have you declared a major yet?" He's going to give the spring training remark a pass. Keller is a man, and men do pay attention to such things.

Keller leans over and cuts the butter for Rick, dropping the pat on his potato. "That's kind of like deciding what I want to be when I grow up." He laughs a little, then shrugs. "Believe it or not, and Francesca thinks this is a good idea, I'm thinking of education."

"A teacher." Rick presses his fork onto the solid bit of butter, squashing it into the mound of mashed potatoes. *Francesca thinks it's a good idea.* It's like he's the third wheel in this ménage. Keller and his wife are always having these little casual exchanges, just as if they were the married couple and he was the goddamned tenant. Catch up if you can with their private jokes and the showy finishing of each other's sentences. Try filling the holes in the dialogue that, for them, need no explanation. Keller hands her the butter *before* she asks. "Good for you to have a goal. A real career."

"Speaking of which . . ." Francesca sets her utensils down, folds her hands.

He remembers when she would cast her eyes down like this, when they were alone and he knew that the moment she raised her eyes to his, he'd be incapable of denying her anything.

"Rick, we think that maybe it's time for you to start thinking about what you might want to do." Francesca looks him in the eye.

" 'We'?" He lays his fork down on the side of his half-full plate. "Do? Do what?"

The little moue of annoyance is a new

expression for her. "For a living."

"Well, as you say, spring training has started already, so I guess I'm too late for baseball."

"Good one, Rick." Does Keller actually believe he's joking? Does he think this conversation is going to end in guffaws?

"Sweetheart, there are things that you can do." It's like she's a lion tamer and *sweetheart* is her three-legged chair. She cracks the whip. "We need you to at least think about it." Again the *we.*

"How can I —"

"You have an accounting degree, right?" Keller's perfect right hand holds a fork suspended in mid-flight. His perfect left hand is clutched in a gentle fist and rests on the table.

"Yes." They're ganging up on him. He can't believe this. "And how am I supposed to go to an office? Are you going to chauffeur me every day? And hang around so I can be helped to the bathroom? You know, to empty my bag?"

Rick feels Pax's nose bumping the sleeve-wrapped stump of his arm, lifting it as if he expects Rick to pet him with that invisible hand. He ignores it. A paw goes onto his leg and he's aware of that only because he can see what the dog is doing. The dog is breaking the house rules against approaching the table and no one says anything until the dog speaks: *Roof.* He might be asking Rick to settle down, calm down. He is asking and, in pushing himself against Rick, pushes Rick away from the table.

How easy it is for people who don't have disabilities to imagine that it's mind over matter to overcome them. How dare these two conspire against him; how could Francesca be consulting with Keller about things that should be only their concern, between husband and wife? It's none of Keller's business. Francesca's disloyalty brings a hot flush to Rick's face, but his anger is turned at Keller. Keller is overstepping himself. "Take me to my room. Now."

"Rick, we're just saying that you're in much better condition than you were even a month ago. It's time. Time for you to —"

"Keller, maybe it's time for you to shut up."

CHAPTER SIXTY-SIX

Pax put himself in between them, his front end in Rick's lap, his tail end backed up to Keller's chair. He whined a little, an oddly plaintive sound in the silence that followed Rick's hard-sounding words, like a human growl warning off a challenger. His tail wagged slowly, like a dog that expects a beating and hopes a show of submission will prevent it. Ears back, nose down. This discord was agonizing. They had finally begun acting like a proper pack and Pax was sorely afraid that now the pack, his pack, was disintegrating. Only one male can be leader; the other must either submit, or leave.

He followed as Keller pushed Rick back to his room. Instead of settling Rick in, Keller turned and walked out, leaving Pax to decide where he should be. A soft snapping of fingers and Pax went to Rick, sitting down in front of him, ears still in the supplicant position, hoping that Rick's heart-beat would slow to normal and the blast of heated anxiety would lessen as he found Pax's ears.

"What do they want of me?" Soft whisper into an ear, a susurration that tickles him a bit. *"What does she want of me? I'm not the man she married. Is that what this means? Because I'm no longer a provider?"* A ragged breath. *"They don't understand that I'm scared. Scared that I've lost everything."*

Rick's fingers dug deep into the nape of the dog's neck. Pax closed his eyes, infused with the primitive recollection of being safe in his mother's jaws. When she'd gripped him thus, she'd been moving him out of danger. Rick's grip suggested that there was some danger Pax could not glean through his usual senses. Some danger emanating from within Rick.

Pax could hear the tiny *tick-tick* of the pills bumping into one another as Rick groped into that bitter-smelling pouch at his side.

CHAPTER SIXTY-SEVEN

An official-looking envelope arrives, a string of lawyers' names emblazoned on the upper left-hand corner. Clayton's estate has been probated and Keller Nicholson is the sole heir. He now officially owns the house, the boats, the moorings, the pier, the acre of unkempt pasture, and the half-acre wood-lot. Keller has never owned anything in his life but that secondhand Ford, so the idea of this, even something as shrouded in unpleasant memory as that house, is a novelty. Becoming the default owner of Clayton's holdings has had the unexpected effect of coloring Keller's worldview. He may be a boarder here, but elsewhere he's a man of property.

Mooring rental will pay the taxes. Clayton had redone the roof a couple of years ago, so the house is in pretty good shape. He doesn't have to see it, or even pick up the key from the lawyer. The foursquare two-story fisherman's house can sit and wait for him, for when he's ready. For when he knows what he should do.

Francesca bends over her tangled yarn and Rick yawns over a magazine. Keller has his textbook open to the chapter on the Romantic poets and is making notes. Pax is in the fetal position in his basket, twitching in some rabbit dream. Or maybe a night-patrol dream. Keller still has those. But now his nightmares are informed by Rick's story. Of explosions and falling through space. He dreams all too often of losing Pax, of not being able to find him. Or finding him in pieces. He wakes in a cold sweat from those nightmares, relieved beyond words to always find the dog still there, in one piece, hogging the narrow cot.

Keller closes his textbook and excuses himself from the domestic scene. The dog is instantly awake, ready to do whatever Keller asks. He waves Pax back. The dog belongs in this room with them. As if to underscore that, Rick speaks to the dog. "Pax, stay here."

Keller suppresses a flash of annoyance; it's as if some other handler has ordered his dog. As if his command needs seconding. But this isn't some other handler; this is

Rick. Rick, who has every right to command Pax. Keller has successfully turned the scout dog into a useful tool; retraining not only has reverted the war dog to a safe family pet but has also turned Keller's canine partner into a lifeline for his once and future master. For Rick. Francesca is focused on her yarn; her mouth twitches as she struggles to untangle the rat's nest of blue worsted.

Rick has everything, Keller thinks. He leaves the room before he can blush at the selfish and unbelievably juvenile thought. He's jealous of a cripple.

He's got an army reserve weekend coming up and he's actually looking forward to it. He definitely needs a break from this stultifying atmosphere of domesticity. He's deeply tired. A couple of days outside, obeying clear and emotionless orders, forgetting the quotidian tasks of caring for an inert and angry man, will go a long way in refreshing his own spirit. Since the abortive suggestion that Rick start thinking about what work he might take on, they've kept their silence on the subject, waiting, hoping, that Rick will come around. But the black thing that inhabits him hasn't lifted enough to make that possible. They have begun color-coding his days: Today he's a little blue — a gray day. Very black today. Pax has become their bellwether. When he gets Rick to throw a toy, engage in a persistent game of fetch, then they know it's a good day. It's mid-May, and the semester is a week from done. Warmer weather has meant that on the days that playing with the dog brightens Rick's mood to pink, Keller wheels him outside. But when the dog comes out of Rick's room with a squeaky toy hanging out of his mouth and teases Keller or Francesca into playing, they know that it's a bad day for Rick. He won't emerge from what Keller has dubbed his "Cave of Gloom," and everyone else will tiptoe around, as if afraid to disturb the black thing that draws him into himself.

Francesca has released the yarn from its Gordian knot. She smiles and begins to cast on. She is relentless in her knitting. Socks and scarves, sweaters and vests. Keller's bureau drawer is filled with her largess. They all itch. He itches to touch her. Their chaste adherence to a dual loyalty and honor doesn't mean he doesn't *think* about breaking this unspoken and mutually enforced prohibition. There are days when Rick is so intolerant of her, days when Keller wants nothing more than to take her away, show her how it is to be loved properly. And then he watches her eyes as she deflects Rick's antagonism, wholly absent of hurt. Keller can't overlook the other days, the ones when Rick's equilibrium is level and the two, husband and wife, share a joke or a smile fraught with the secret code of marriage, which Keller can't begin to understand.

But then there are the other moments, when the three of them — and Pax — become something like a family. Keller doesn't imagine that he is their child or some hybrid husband and brother, but a valued member of a small family that has built a retaining wall out of necessity. And those are the days that most break his heart. If he desires Francesca, it is as a man desires the unattainable, with bittersweet longing. If he feels like a part of a cobbled-together family, that fulfills a greater and more gentle longing.

Keller heads through the breezeway into the garage, checks the hardware store thermometer on the wall. Fifty-eight degrees. Warm enough. Tomorrow he'll bring his stuff back down here, where he can get away from feeling like he's skating on thin ice; no relief from proximity. Pax pads in, sniffs the corners, and sits beside him. "Ready to move back down here?"

Roof.

"Me, too."

The envelope informing him that he's an heir takes up space on his workbench. He's left it there with Miss Jacobs's letters, as if they were tools or scrap wood. Keller rips a sheet of paper from his notebook.

Dear Miss Jacobs,
You were absolutely correct. I have the dubious distinction of being Clayton Britt's sole heir, with the attendant inheritance taxes. So, without looking for it, I have it all. Nonetheless, I won't be back anytime soon. I've got a good thing here, and my studies are going very well. You'd be impressed with my vastly improved vocabulary.

He asks her to keep an eye out for potential tenants. He could bank the income. Add to the little nest egg built on his mainly unspent pay from his active service. A little more money would help to keep things afloat here. The occupational therapist and the physical therapist agree with them that Rick is perfectly capable of working at an office job, but until he accepts that he's as healed as he's likely ever to be, a little silent contribution to the household expenses from Keller will help keep them on an even keel. Francesca never needs to know that he's paying for groceries or home improvements out of his own pocket.

I've got a good thing going here. That's an enigmatic statement for sure. There are days when he's perfectly happy, and others when he questions his sanity. What is really keeping him here? Pax nudges his writing hand as if to hurry him along. "Please think kindly of me and let me know how you are."

Maybe he should think about selling the house, but Keller balks at the idea. No, the house in Hawke's Cove will wait for him. For when he finally has had enough.

CHAPTER SIXTY-EIGHT

Lately he feels a stiffness in his hindquarters that he's never had before, not even in those few days after he'd been wounded and strangers had handled him until Keller came back from his own wounds. It's just a little harder to get up, and the basket is so much more comfortable than the floor, even if the square of light warms it up. Better yet is the couch, and he's been deliberately disobedient every chance he gets, having been encouraged into misbehavior by the couple of times Francesca and Keller have invited him up to sit between them as they listen to the noises coming from the box in the living room.

Nothing else is diminished. His hearing is just as acute, his eyesight what it has always been. And his nose, superior instrument that it is, still carries the stories to him on the air — the air in the house and the air outside. In the house, the air is thick with the story of his people. How they use their voices but say nothing. How they emit the olfactory aura of discontent. He sighs and yawns and settles his head or paws on each of them in turn. But they don't take as much comfort from him as they did. Keller disappears. Rick dismisses him. Francesca orders him out of the kitchen. Even those painful times when Rick clutches at his nape, sucking the stillness and comfort out of him, have changed. Less frequent, less successful. Almost as if Rick has chosen to suffer his fear and distress alone. Like a mother hiding her nest from other dogs, even perhaps her mate. A hidden den is easier to defend.

A walk to the beach with Keller usually gets the kinks out. Pax hears the breezeway door open and he looks to Rick to see if he can go greet Keller. Rick's eyes are down, as they often are, and his fingers are playing within that little pouch he has attached to his chair. The bag holds those tiny white pills that the dog can smell even through the thick duck cloth. They clatter together as Rick fingers them, audible enough to the dog, if not to anyone else.

CHAPTER SIXTY-NINE

Pax materializes at Rick's bedside. Rick has gotten himself into a sitting position, the undisturbed blankets still neatly across his lower half. His pillow is folded in half, propping him against the headboard of the hospital bed. He holds a glass in his remaining hand. On the canyon formed by his motionless legs is his collection of twenty-two little white pills. The twenty-second spheroid is today's victory. He's been counting them. The number never changes, never improves, never becomes a sure thing.

"I'm all right, Paxy. You can go back to bed." Rick sets the water glass down on the bedside table. "Just counting."

Pax sits, his amber eyes on the man. He yawns, releasing a tension he's picking up from Rick.

"You're just like him, you know. Always watching me." Rick makes a little pile out of his collection. He's a miser hoarding gold coins. "Are you wondering what I'm waiting for? Is that it? Should I be dramatic, or just efficient? Will they figure out my reason?"

Pax sets one paw on the edge of the bed, noses Rick's dead leg as if trying to push him into getting up. It was what the dog once did, a hundred years ago, when they were both young and vigorous and had a wide-open future. When Rick would flop down on the sofa of his bachelor apartment to catch a few z's after practice, the puppy would poke at him with his nose, up and down his arm, into the back of his knee. *Get up! Play with me!* Rick mildly wonders if the dog really understands what is wrong with him, if he thinks that Rick is just being lazy. "I wish I could take you out, run you on the beach, race you home. I wish that almost more than anything else."

Francesca left the window open a little when she came in to bid him good night. A light breeze stirs the curtains, a spring zephyr reminding Rick of those taken-for-granted days of spring training. That very first practice, when the morning air was still cold but the sun promised an afternoon warmth that would have them stripping off their shirts by lunchtime. There was a taste to the air, as if excitement had a flavor. Now all he can taste is the metallic flavor of medication.

"You want something, don't you, Pax? You want me to jump up and play with you like Keller does?" Rick hates it that the dog's head cocks in an ever-so-cute fashion at the sound of Keller's name. "You like him better than me?"

In answer, Pax stands and shakes, as if Rick is asking him unanswerable questions. He sits again to stare at Rick. It's as if the dog will keep his eye on Rick all night long, making sure that the man doesn't do anything rash. He's a guardian and defender, a preventer of final acts. Rick points to the basket. "Go to bed, Pax. Now."

With an almost human reluctance, the dog peels himself away from Rick's bedside and goes to sit in his basket. But his eyes never leave Rick's face. He's looking at him with human eyes — Keller's eyes — that portray a deep concern. A trick of the bedside lamp, and the dog's eyes become Francesca's, filled with an ancient love. She still loves him; she does. Despite Rick's night terrors, his middle-of-the-night paranoia about Keller and Francesca, deep down he knows that whatever is growing between his wife and his caretaker, she still loves him. This tripartite living has cast them all into mutable roles. Husband, patient, wife, friend, sister, brother, stranger, caregiver, war veteran, war hero, fool. The only immutable quality is their love of Pax.

Rick digs deeper into the empty cloth pouch, his fingers searching for another morphine pill. Maybe he's missed one. He is so tired. His wife and his friend might blame him for leaving them behind, but he is more cursed than blamed for having survived when his buddies had not. The one irreconcilable, the one factor that transcends all the other reasons for ending this struggle, the one he might scrawl on a piece of notepaper laden with his awkward left-handed writing, is his colossal and unforgiveable screwup. Keller idly remarks about coaching Little League, as if Rick could ever again lead a group of boys. Boys just a little younger than the ones in his squad, slaughtered because he thought he could pitch his way out of the situation. Killed by his own grenade, or finished off by the laughing Germans. How can he ever confess the shame of that? Yet without that confession, how can he ever make Francesca understand the magnitude of his despair? He allows her to think it's his wounds that grieve him, and she allows that partial truth to be enough to account for his gloom. But maybe not enough for the desperate act he intends.

Keller will get it, the truth of why Rick has done this thing, and maybe he can leave Keller to tell Francesca the story of the grenade and Rick's hubris. If he hasn't already. Is there a code between them as there is between husband and wife — no outside secrets? Some code. Rick has hung on to his shameful secret, keeping it from Francesca and letting the sharp edges of guilt chisel away at his self-esteem. He doesn't know if he's more afraid that she'll forgive him for putting his squad in danger, and try and make him forget that it happened, or hate him for it, for not being the man she thought he was.

Pax is back at his bedside. His eyes are no longer asking questions; they are zeroed in on what his hand is doing, the gathering together of his delivery from the constant pain of failure. He lifts his eyes to Rick's, makes a tiny vocalization that sounds almost like the word *no*. Rick puts the pills, one by one, into the handy cloth bag, counting them yet again. There are still twenty-two.

CHAPTER SEVENTY

Pax dreams a running dream and his feet twitch and his chest compresses with silent barks. He's chasing a man through trees and grass, across streets and into the deepest woods imaginable. The dream scent is as potent an aggression aphrodisiac as any he encountered while performing his duties as a member of the K-9 Corps. This threat is only six feet in front of him; he just needs to put on more speed to catch his man. But something holds him back; some weight prevents him from that final burst of speed and energy. Frustrated, he yelps like a kicked puppy. And then he wakes up.

Keller's arm is what's holding him down; in sleep, he's flung it over the dog's body. A thin gray light is visible in the bedroom window, filling the frame with a new day being sung in by the first bird. Pax raises his head, listens, sniffs the air. *Something.*

Pax extricates himself from Keller's embrace and slips to the floor. His ears move back and forth, judging the outside sounds against the inside sounds. Birdsong. The milkman two streets over. Breathing. Keller's. He walks through the breezeway passage, stands still. Francesca's soft breathing. Two are sleeping deeply. One is not. Rick.

The fur between his shoulders rises and Pax lowers his head, centers his weight over his strong forelimbs. As did his hunting forebears, Pax moves in a slow, liquid motion through the house on noiseless pads, as alert to danger as he had ever been on patrol. *Something.*

CHAPTER SEVENTY-ONE

Rick has decided that twenty-two is enough. One makes him feel good. Two make him drowsy. Surely, now that he's half the man he used to be, twenty-two should be more than enough. The trick isn't to swallow them all at once, but parcel them out over fifteen minutes, not long enough to fall asleep before the deed is done, but long enough between pills that he won't throw them up. Oh yes. He's thought a lot about this.

The pills are lined up on his tray table like a row of ammunition. His bedside lamp is on, casting a cheery yellow warmth to the white tablets. He's said good night to everyone. Francesca didn't understand that his kiss good night was the final farewell; the lingering sweetness of her surprised response to his kiss is almost enough in itself to make him step back from this ledge. And when Keller popped his head in to say good night on his way to the garage, Rick smiled and maybe confused him a little when he said, "Good night. And thanks. For everything." Keller just said "Sleep well" and left. Rick heard the kitchen light snap off and the sound of the connecting door being opened.

The prompt to this being the night was so simple. Johnny Antonelli, at age eighteen, had become a starting pitcher for the Boston Braves. Eighteen. The age of cannon fodder not long ago. Kid would have been a schoolboy during the war. The age when your body seems invulnerable. At twenty-eight, Rick was already ten years older than Antonelli when he got what should have been his big break. And even then he was already icing a sore pitching arm after every practice. This kid can probably pitch a whole game and then go play tennis. Even if he had come back whole and been put back on the Braves roster, a kid like this would have shown up sooner or later and shoved Rick out. Traded probably, or rarely played. It seems so unfair. Rick knows that this is crazy thinking, but it's been enough to get him to empty out the pouch and line up the pills. Rick has assiduously avoided the sports page, refuses to listen to games, but even he heard about this player, this paragon. This upstart wearing his number.

The pills are lined up on the tray table. Pretty little things.

He just can't go on this way. The darkness always there, the weight of his sin; the sharp point of his professional disappointment. His utter failure as a husband, unable to give his wife a child.

Keller will take care of Francesca, take care of Pax. He, too, is wearing Rick's number.

Rick swallows the first pill. Pax is suddenly there, his eyes fixed on him with a stare that is a thin degree from hostile. He should have known the dog would be in as soon as he stirred from the sleep he'd been feigning. Rick has spent the night tallying up his grievances, weighing out his justification, letting the pain in his phantom limb keep him awake. He's not sure if he wants the dog to be there for this final sleep, to be a silent witness to his cowardice, because, yes, Rick knows that he's taking the coward's way out, but that's okay. Rather a dead coward than a live fool.

"Go to bed."

Instead of going to his basket, the dog stands beside Rick, chucks his nose under Rick's hand to get a pat. That first pill has relaxed him, the pain in his phantom limb throbbing with less intensity. Rick spends a long time stroking the dog, whispering things into his tattooed ear that he'll never say again. Telling him that he needs to be a good dog. "You're a lucky dog, Pax. You have good people to keep loving you."

Pax doesn't wriggle with pleasure; he stiffens instead, the same kind of immobility he displays when a squirrel comes along. The same kind of immobility that Keller speaks of when talking about Pax's years as an army scout dog. A dog for defense. The silent alert to danger. It's almost enough to make Rick look up to see if there is an intruder. The dog's body is rock solid with tension. His eyes aren't on some distant mark, but looking right at Rick. As if he is the intruder. He backs away and lowers his head, eyes fixed on Rick's. He growls, a soft inquiring sound.

"It's all right. Go to bed." The last thing Rick wants is for the dog to alert Keller.

Pax remains where he is.

"So be it." Rick reaches for a pill, picks up the glass, washes it down. Sets the glass down, reaches for another pill. The dog's nostrils twitch, as if he can smell it and is repulsed by the odor of the morphine. Rick takes another. And another. Ten go down. He's got to be careful; he's swallowed nearly half the glass of water that Keller has left for him should he get thirsty in the night. He's not sure he could manage to chew his way through the remaining collection of pills.

Rick sets the glass down to gather up the rest of the pills for one last swallow. As he does, Pax suddenly leaps up onto the bed, knocking the tray table over, scattering the remaining morphine pills to all four corners of the room. And he commences barking an alert, a warning as vital as any alarm he made during the war.

Rick doesn't hear the dog or feel the weight of him standing on his chest. Rick gives in to the weight of the morphine as it pulls him down and down.

CHAPTER SEVENTY-TWO

The dog's first bark puts Keller on his feet.
A purposed bark, a warning and a threat.
Pax barks and barks, and barks until Keller,
barefoot and shivering in his boxers and
T-shirt, is in Rick's room. Not for an instant
does he interpret the barking as a sign that
there's an intruder or a squirrel. The dog's
meaning is as clear to him as if the animal
is speaking to him in English. *Danger, danger.* The moment Keller steps into the
room, the dog ceases his alert, jumps down
from the bed.

Rick is sleeping peacefully. Impossible.
Not with all this noise. Not with the eighty-
five-pound dog on him, barking in his face.
Keller feels as if he's stepped on a land
mine; his gut twists and he can't remember
to breathe. In seconds, Francesca will be
down, grasping her tattered housecoat
around herself, looking to him to solve this
problem. He touches Rick's face with shak-

ing fingers. Still warm. He feels for a wrist pulse, but his own pulse is beating so hard, he can't distinguish the difference.

"Rick, wake up!" Keller manhandles Rick's pajama front, lifting him and slapping his cheeks. "Wake up!" Where is Francesca? Why isn't she here? Surely the noise has awakened her, too. He just can't figure out what's wrong. Rick was fine when they went to bed. *And thanks. For everything.* Rick's words now seem sinister. And then he sees it, a single white pill caught in the folds of the blanket. Morphine. "Oh shit."

Keller tries for a pulse in Rick's neck. Maybe there's something. Please let there be something. Rick can't do this to them.

It's what he wants, Keller thinks. He lowers Rick back to the pillow. Leave him. From some deep, impulsive place, an unspeakable thought snakes into his brain: Just let him go. Everyone will be better off. The thought is outrageous enough to freeze him into a moment of hesitation that might be seen as his not knowing what to do, not as if he's impaled on the sharp point of treason. He has to get to the phone, the new extension he had installed is on the other side of the bed, but he can't move. She would be free, he thinks.

"Rick!" Francesca appears exactly as he

imagined, the threadbare housecoat sloppily tied with the frayed belt. What he hadn't seen in his mind's eye is the frantic reach of her hands, pushing him aside, as if she has a greater influence on this outcome. Keller grabs the telephone, vastly relieved to be shoved out of the way.

They are sitting in a small windowless room, more closet than something meant for anxious family members. The emergency room's waiting area had been overcrowded with people, as if there was a white sale going on in this cheerless place. Two for one! Stock up! A nurse, capped and starched into authority, had taken them out of the general waiting room to leave them here in this closet with its two hard chairs and tainted scent of used linen. Keller wonders if it's a room designated for the bereaved, for people who need to be out of the general population because of the weight of their particular emergency. Not a room for those bringing in vomiting drinking buddies or kids with broken bones or babies with a rash, a fever. This is a special room for those whose lives are about to be changed.

Francesca sits quietly, her gaze upon her clasped hands, a handkerchief woven between her fingers. He paces, a useless exercise in this ten-by-ten room — really more dramatic than meaningful. Around and around he goes, a prisoner in his cell. He's pacing out of habit; this place is so like the isolation room at Meadowbrook. Sentenced for crimes as varied as insolence or instigating a food fight, Keller spent his incarcerations in that room, walking a perfect square, north, south, east, and west. It was better than huddling on the bare floor and straining to hear the sound of someone coming to release him from his punishment.

"I just don't understand." Francesca is still keeping her eyes on her hands, as if by addressing her clenched fists she can say what's on her mind. "I don't understand."

Keller stops pacing; waits until she can articulate her thoughts.

"How could he do this to me?"

Keller tips the door to the tiny room closed, kneels beside Francesca, and gently holds her in his arms. "It's really complicated."

She leans her weight against him and he thinks that he can stay like that forever. She pulled on a simple housedress to come to the hospital, the one she had been wearing all day, his favorite, a pale yellow sprigged with tiny roses. He thinks she looks lovely, even with her curls uncombed in her haste to dress. Maybe especially. She looks young, vulnerable, and willing to let him contain her within the strength of his arms. Arms bulked up with the daily effort of lifting an inert man. These are the wrong thoughts to be having. His place is to comfort and console, not desire.

"Can I tell you something?"

He feels the vibration of her voice against his chest.

"Of course."

"Doesn't he know how much it would kill me if he died?" Francesca laughs a little. "How easily we use those words — *kill, die.* But it would. I would die if anything happened to him. Happens."

Suddenly, it's uncomfortable, this kneeling on the hard linoleum floor. Keller shifts, squats in front of her. His hands are on her arms, and he shakes her to make her look up, away from her hands, into his eyes. He can't help himself: He strokes away one of the more unruly curls, the one that lingers by the side of her mouth. He takes her face in his hands. "It's more than that, Francesca. I mean, his pain is more than his wounds." How hard it is to put into words the answer she needs. "Sometimes what happens on the battlefield is so awful that it's impossible to talk about, but it never leaves you."

She looks at him blankly, puzzled, but doesn't try to take her face away from his cupped hands. "What has he told you?" She unlinks her hands and places them on his, which cup her face. He can't tell if she means to pull his hands away or secure them there. She studies his eyes, desperate to understand what he means.

"It's what happened, the day he was wounded."

"They were attacked from above. It was only a miracle that he survived." She drops her hands.

"Rick thinks that it was his fault that everyone was killed." Keller wraps his arms around Francesca so that he doesn't have to look her in the eye when he tells her an abridged version of the story Rick told him. Keller feels like he's betraying a confidence, yet without this betrayal, Francesca will never understand the truth behind Rick's self-destructive act.

"He told *you* this?"

"Yes."

"And not me." Francesca's face is so close to his, he can feel the soft puffs of her agitated breathing on his cheek. "Why couldn't he tell me?" Abruptly, she sits back, pulling away from his touch.

A knock on the door stops Keller from saying anything more. The capped and starched nurse leans in. "You can go in now."

Keller stands up and offers his hand to Francesca.

Hers is warm, a little damp. "I can go in by myself."

Keller steps back, letting Francesca go.

CHAPTER SEVENTY-THREE

I was gutted. Hollowed out. I looked down on my husband, who would not look at me. Was this the same man who had kept glancing up at me from the bull pen as I stood in the grandstand, cheering on the opposing team? The man who had smiled at me and I'd felt the electric charge of connection pass between us? I'd thought that we were two halves of the same whole. This was the man to whom I had committed my youth and my life, eyes wide open. The lover who had made me believe we knew each other so profoundly that we experienced everything as one. But we hadn't. And my husband, my dearest, hadn't trusted me with his shame, his self-condemnation. It was as if I didn't know this man at all.

When he had arrived at Walter Reed, grievously wounded and so damaged, I was sent by the head nurse into a ward filled with other wounded soldiers. The massive room was cluttered with traction rigs, stainless-steel trolleys, and simple curtains on frames rolled between beds. The antiseptic stench was pervasive in that ward, I fought against putting my hand to my nose. Every bed contained a ghost wrapped with the dead white of gauzy bandages, hiding missing eyes and protecting burned faces. They all looked the same, the mummification rendering the wounded into grotesque Kewpie dolls.

But I'd unerringly walked directly to Rick's bed; the obscuring bandages unable to hide him from me. I'd known him out of all the disguised wounded. And now I looked at him, his scars so familiar that they no longer occurred to me, and I didn't know him at all.

They would transfer him to the VA hospital once he was stabilized, and Rick would have to remain there until the doctors were confident that he wouldn't try again.

They drive home in silence. What is there to say that isn't obscenely mundane or too useless? They will eat leftovers; they will not ask questions that begin with the word *why*. When they pull into the driveway, Keller shuts the engine off and doesn't move to get out.

Francesca pulls the door handle, swings open her door, but she stays seated. "You go in. I want to take a little walk by myself."

Keller nods, willing to let her clear her head, hoping that when she comes back, she'll let him know that she doesn't hold him in contempt for keeping Rick's confidence. He watches in the rearview mirror as Francesca starts down the sidewalk, the yellow of her sprigged dress too cheerful for the look of grief on her face. The warm day has turned gloomy; a heavy cloud lurks in the southeast.

Keller and Pax wait in the kitchen for Francesca to come home. He's pulled out the leftover pot roast and potatoes and is slowly reheating them on the stove. He stirs, listens, stirs some more. The first strike of rain hits the kitchen window. "Come on, Pax. Let's find her." He shuts off the gas beneath the pot.

Keller wishes that he still had the flat leather service collar that told Pax he was on duty, but his words are enough to get the dog's attention. "Seek."

The dog doesn't bolt; he casts slowly along the edge of the driveway, down to the sidewalk, turns left, then right, adjudging the depth of Francesca's most recent scent against the one she might have left earlier in the day. It's raining harder, and Keller wonders if the scent will be washed away before the dog can locate her. He unfurls the umbrella he snatched from the hall closet and repeats his command: "Seek."

Pax drops his nose to the sidewalk and strikes the scent. They march off toward the beach, then take a sharp right, as if she'd changed her mind. The blocks aren't perfectly shaped, and she's left a trail of indecision and confusion. A blind alley, a narrow sidewalk with crumbling cement lifted by old trees and a decade of frost heaves. Back toward the beach. Keller despairs that they are going around in circles, like children playing around a tree. Catch me if you can. They come to a playground, where Pax breathes in the scent of her footprints impressed in the new mud forming at the swing set. Did she sit for a moment on these swings? Maybe lifted herself up like a girl again, allowing herself to feel the freedom of leaving the ground? Or just rocked gently back and forth?

Pax doesn't mistake this "seek" for a game. The distress rising out of the fast-diluted scent powers him forward. She is in trouble. She is lost. Keller, the most rock steady of partners, is close to panic. Something has happened, and even a dog knows that it has something to do with what happened in Rick's room. Rick is gone again and maybe Francesca has tried to find him. Humans have such inadequate noses. Why didn't she call on him to help? Now she's missing and it is becoming more challenging to discern the scent molecules that she's left behind in her wake as they get closer to the shoreline and the rain beats down harder. Keller's scent of worry almost obscures the faint tracery of her scent in the air. Pax pauses at the footprints, gathers a fresh sample of Francesca, and raises his head. She's not far. He can hear her.

Pax nearly pulls Keller off his feet as he charges across the busy shore drive to the Squantum Yacht Club pier.

Francesca is drenched, but she leans against the wooden rail of the pier as if she's standing there on a summer day, oblivious to the way her dress clings to her body. Even before he reaches her, Keller sees how violently she is shaking and he pulls off his shirt to cover her shoulders. "Come home, Francesca. Come home."

She leans into him and he can see that the shaking is less from the chill of a late-spring rain than from the emotions that have driven her out here, staring down to the flat muddy shingle at low tide fifteen feet below the narrow pier.

Pax, quarry located, stands at her knees and pushes himself against her so that she moves away from the rail.

Francesca offers no resistance as Keller wraps his arm around her and the three walk the most direct way back home. The umbrella over their heads affords the illusion of intimacy as they walk through this neighborhood. A shelter for their shared distress. Keller is the one shivering now, but he isn't cold. His muscles twitch with unexpressed tension.

Keller carries her upstairs as if she's his bride. Francesca is impassive, but she closes her eyes as he towels her hair, her face, her neck; gives a little moan as he unbuttons her soaking dress and rubs her shoulders. He wraps the bath towel around her and makes her sit so that he can remove her shoes. He slides a hand underneath her slip to unlock the mystery of garters and carefully peels off her wet nylons. He holds her icy feet in his hands and, in a spontaneous and natural gesture, lowers his lips to kiss them.

She breathes in sharply, as if awakening

from a dream. Francesca takes his wet hair in both hands and forces his head up. And she kisses him.

Chapter Seventy-Four

At his insistence, Rick has been gotten out of bed and is sitting in the small hospital solarium. This wheelchair is hospital-issue and he feels as though he is higher up than usual. The orderly tucked an extra pillow behind him, so he's also more upright, as if one half of his body is at attention. He doesn't want Francesca to find him slumped and defeated. He wants her to believe that his attempt wasn't the act of a weak man, but of a decisive one. This is one failure for which he will take full responsibility, and for which he is sorry. Whether or not he is sorry for having tried or sorry for having failed will depend on the look on her face when she comes into this relentlessly sunny room.

The orderly has faced Rick toward the window, with its view of nothing more than the sky. There is no one else in the solarium with him, no obligation to make forced conversation, no contention for the better magazines. There is a clock on the wall, a pie-size Timex with an audible tick as the second hand moves in a persistent sweep around the face, counting off the minutes as Rick waits for Francesca. Official visiting hours don't start for an hour, but he expects her at any moment, although he can't say why he thinks Francesca will defy the rules.

Keller will bring her. He won't let her come alone. Keller, who has become so important to them — to him, to her. From a shy and nearly mute helper, Keller has been transformed into a friend. Nonetheless, Rick is hoping that for once Keller won't come along with Francesca. He really needs time alone with her, not like the hours they spend closeted in his room, but quality time. Time enough to say what he needs to say, tell her the truth about what happened in the Italian mountains; to beg her forgiveness. He can't do that with an audience. Keller may have a stake in this, but Rick has to rebuild his life with Francesca from the ground up.

Gradually, he'd been lifted out of his dreamless narcotic sleep into a dream-filled slumber in which he saw her fading away like a ghost, an ethereal revenant of the happy-go-lucky girl she was before his transformation from luckiest man on earth to this wreck of a man. As long as she's believed that he is a casualty of war, not of ego, she's been tied to him by a love that has been refined into admiration and devotion from the fire of passion. But if she knows the truth, how long will she want to be tied down to a vainglorious idiot? How strong is love when there is nothing more than marital duty framing it?

All too often lately he hears her laughing with Keller, hears that girlish trill that he no longer teases out of her. Keller makes Francesca happy. She deserves happiness.

Rick begins to cry. He doesn't want to lose Francesca; she is everything to him. His life. More important than any loss — limb, mobility, career, even Pax — losing her would kill him. But she has to know the truth. And that may drive her away.

My husband heard me come into the solarium, the click of my heels on the linoleum loud in that otherwise-silent room. His back was to me, but he sat up straighter and I watched him raise his hand to wipe his face, so I knew that he had been weeping. Those tears broke my heart. Then I was at his side, kneeling, touching his hand, and fumbling in my purse for my handkerchief. "It's all right, my darling, it's all right."

"I have to tell you something."

"No. You don't. I know and it's all right."

"Keller told you?"

"Yes."

"It's my story to tell."

"He needed to help me understand why you . . . why you did what you did."

"Where is he?"

And that was when I began to cry.

I awoke that morning to meet the pure light of a spring day and the certainty that Keller had to go. We had not succumbed. I kissed him and tasted his desire like thirst rising up to be quenched. Like mine had been in those early days of Rick's courtship, when we resolved it was best to get married rather than burn, when *burn* to me meant with unsatisfied desire, not the fires of hell. With his kiss, Keller instigated the memory of that old unrequited passion; his mouth and fingers ignited the fire of my physical desire, which had been tamped down for so long by circumstance of war and wounds. I wanted him. As I had wanted my husband from the first.

And it was the thought of Rick that stopped me.

"No. We can't."

464

"Francesca." His voice was deep with the words pressing to get out. "I love you."

"Keller. No. You can't."

"I do." Keller Nicholson was an honorable man. A good man. He gently released me and kissed my cheek. "But you love Rick."

"Yes. No matter what's happened, or what he did, he's my husband."

Keller picked up his forgotten shirt from the floor. "I love him, too, Francesca. I do."

Rick would be gone for weeks, or even months. Keller no longer had a purpose in our house. We would be dancing around each other, alone except for the dog. It wasn't concern for what the neighbors might say. Not at all. After all, he could rent a room somewhere else for the duration. It was that I wasn't sure I had the moral fortitude to have Keller so close. He'd poured his heart out in those three little words and I didn't know if I was strong enough to resist temptation — and afraid that someday I might take what comfort he offered. I could never forsake Rick, so all that Keller would ever have of me would be far less than what he wanted. Keller could never have my love.

So I said the words that effectively broke

everyone's heart. "Keller, it's time for you to go."

"Where's Keller? And Pax? What happened?" Rick hands Francesca back the handkerchief.

"I've asked him to leave. You're going to be away for a while and there's no reason for him to stick around."

Away. Rick appreciates Francesca's euphemism for being committed to the psychiatric ward of the VA hospital. He appreciates her sense of fair play for Keller. But there is something more at stake than Keller. "Fran, what about Pax?"

She bursts into tears again, this time gasping and inconsolable. "I don't know."

She is on her knees, her head in his lap, and he strokes her curls, not like he strokes Pax, for the comfort he gets from touching the dog, but in order to comfort his wife, who has effectively given the dog away.

Rick pulls Francesca into his lap, wraps his arms around her, and kisses her with all the passion of a capable man. There is something that she isn't telling him, and that's all right. In the end, he will never speak to her of his grievous mistake in the mountains in Italy and she will never speak of the real reason she has sent Keller away.

Rick holds his wife and is amazed at how good it feels.

CHAPTER SEVENTY-FIVE

It doesn't take long to stuff his duffel bag. Fold up the cot. Find his textbooks, his *Morte d'Arthur*. Packed up in minutes, Keller tosses everything into the backseat of his car, leaving the lamp and the chair. Into the ammo box he shoves a few of the tools he's bought — a hand drill, a screwdriver, a hammer. He can't find his winter coat, then remembers hanging it in the hall closet. All the time Keller packs, Pax is at his side, worried, making little grumbling sounds in his throat.

He's made a grave mistake, a life-changing mistake, in touching her last night and now she wants him to leave. They no longer need him. With Rick away for an undetermined period, Keller is free to go. Free to go. That's what she said. Free. He's never felt less free in his life.

"I'm sorry for what happened. I won't let it happen again," he told her, ashamed at the pleading in his voice.

Francesca looked at him with weary eyes. "Keller, it's time."

"What will you tell Rick?"

"That it was time." She didn't offer him breakfast; she was leaving to see Rick. It was too early for visiting hours, but she needed to go. Unspoken but implied: Be gone when I get back.

Hurt has evolved into anger. Fine, he'll go, but he's goddamned going to take Pax with him. He's going to do what he should have done in the beginning, packed the dog into his car and kept moving. Avoided all this unhappiness. If this is love, who needs it? If this is what loving friends does for you, screw it.

Going through to the kitchen, Keller spots Pax's bowls. His leash is hanging on the breezeway doorknob. He snatches them up, puts the bowls in the ammo box and hangs the leash like a bandolier around his torso. In the hallway, his winter coat reclaimed, Keller sees Pax's squeaky mouse on the top of the hallway table. He shoves it in his pants pocket. Then he notices that the drawer in the hallway table is pulled out slightly askew. The June humidity is oppressive and the drawer in the hall table is stuck cockeyed and half-open. For some reason, this enrages him and he pounds it with the heel of his hand to set it straight. Nothing moves, so Keller gives it a good yank to pull it open. The whole drawer flies out of the table and everything in it falls to the floor. Sheets of ecru writing paper scatter, along with a fountain pen, pencils, and a boxful of paper clips. A date book embossed with 1942 falls open, facedown. Keller gathers the objects, and when he picks up the forgotten date book, three photographs fall out.

Francesca and Rick at the Totem Pole Ballroom, grinning into the camera. They both look so young, so happy. The second photograph is of Pax sitting on the top step of a porch, his long forelegs on the next step down. Even in this black-and-white photograph, his color is brighter, sharper than it is now.

Keller looks at the last photograph. Someone, maybe Sid, has taken a family portrait. Francesca and Rick stand side by side on the porch steps. It is winter and they are wearing dress coats, perhaps on their way out to some party. It is so strange to see Rick standing up. Keller is a little surprised to see how tall he is beside Francesca, as if she's shrunk. She's looking up at him, instead of him looking, as he does now, up at her. The look on her face is worried love. Pax stands between them, his eyes, too, on Rick.

Francesca and Rick and Pax. Keller flips the photograph over and reads the inscription: *On our way to the station. March 1942. Smiles fake.*

Out of the depths comes the memory of seeing that couple and their dog on the station platform. And then it hits him: Rick and Francesca were the couple he saw at South Station that cold winter afternoon when he, too, was on his way to war. He sees again the man embracing the dog before he does his wife, but now he is Rick and the woman is Francesca. He remembers the dog forcing the crowd away from her. Protective. Pax. The little family that would never include anyone else.

The truth isn't a mallet hitting Keller over the head. It is more insidious, a wraith of smoke burning up through his gut into his bloodstream. Whatever he and Pax have had, Pax was and always will be *their* dog.

He takes the black-and-white photograph of Pax and puts all the rest of it away in the drawer.

CHAPTER SEVENTY-SIX

Keller is gone and Pax knows deep in his heart that he won't be working with him again. There was something so different about this leave-taking. Not just the packing but the heavy aura of completion, too. Something was finished, over.

Pax waited for his praise: *good dog.* The scratch on the chest to indicate he had performed well. "Stay with them. They need you." Pax understood the *stay* as an order. The other words just brushed his ears, along with Keller's two hands, his forehead pressing against the dog's big skull. But it was an order and the dog will perform it to the best of his ability for the rest of his life. He has a purpose, a job. And two people who love him very much. A good life for a lucky dog.

Keller will fade, cast into Pax's dreams as the touch of a hand, the sound of a voice. The memory of war. A time of peace.

■ ■ ■ ■

PART THREE:
2008

■ ■ ■ ■

CHAPTER SEVENTY-SEVEN

It shouldn't surprise him, to be contacted like this. It's not like he hasn't left a trail over the past fifty-odd years. Keller Nicholson may not have won the Pulitzer, but his plays have been performed to acclaim and his novels have received decent reviews. As a well-regarded professor of history, he's even been a regular talking head on the local NPR station when the topic is war, the essential ingredient in all his work: the effect of war on the human soul.

Even so, when Lila Stanton contacts him via his university e-mail, he is stunned. She says she wants to talk to him about her parents. Parents? Despite being an octogenarian, Keller lives in the twenty-first century and is facile with technology, so he quickly Googles this Lila Stanton. It's true: Francesca and Rick had, against all expectations, become parents after all. Checking her out on Facebook, he sees that Lila is

475

distinctly Asian and middle-aged, so Keller assumes she was a Korean War orphan.

He served in that war, too. Not as a dog handler in combat, but as a dog trainer at Fort Riley, in Kansas, primarily training sentry dogs. Decent dogs. Good dogs. But none of them, like any of the dogs he's lived with since, as smart as Pax.

In her e-mail, this Lila is a little vague about her reasons for wanting to talk to him. Isn't he just a footnote in her family's life? A blip on their radar? Someone who lived with them for a short time, a full lifetime ago.

"I was hoping that it would be possible to visit you. I live in Boston and I thought that I might zip up to Hawke's Cove some afternoon and take you to lunch."

He wonders if she's just using this weak and ancient association to impose herself on him. She's probably got some manuscript she wants him to look at. Or wants to pick his brain about getting published. A memoir, that's what it is. *How I Went from Being a Korean War Orphan to an American Girl.*

He wishes she'd said something about Francesca.

Keller hits reply. "Fine. Give me a date. I'll make lunch."

Even before he can power down his laptop, a reply pops up. She wants to meet this Saturday, and she has something for him.

Keller drove away from the Stanton's North Quincy house that day, his belongings heaped up on the backseat, Pax's leash still bandolier-style around his body. Deeply sorry. Deeply hurt. Aching already for what he'd left behind. He drove past the hospital and thought about going in to say good-bye to Rick properly, but he kept going. He knew Francesca would be there, and he just couldn't do it. So he kept driving, blindly following a northerly route until the scenery began to look familiar and he realized that he'd done what he'd sworn he'd never do. He was back in Hawke's Cove.

He'd stood on the back steps, the key from the lawyer in his hand. The sun was just setting and the afterglow burnished the water beneath the bluff to a rosy glow. In the distance was the edge of the rest of the world. The place where he'd blown it. Ruined his own chance at happiness.

Inside, the house was damp and cold and smelled of dead mice. It was exactly as the old man had left it. No one had been in the house since his death; no one had cleared away the remnants of the man. The mice had consumed all the dried foods; all that was left of Clayton's last loaf of bread was the wrapper, chewed into fragments. A glass was upside down in the drainer and a single plate flanked it, sentinels to an old bachelor's life.

Upstairs, Keller pushed open the door to his uncle's bedroom. In all the time Keller had lived in this house with his great-uncle Clayton, he'd never set foot in the old man's room. On the otherwise-bare bureau, a photograph in a surprisingly ornate frame was propped against the fly-specked mirror. Keller picked it up. The old man himself, his arm linked with a pretty young woman in a diaphanous white dress, her wedding headpiece low on her brow in the fashion of a long-ago decade, a veil floating around her like a phantom. Keller studied the faces. If there was a resemblance in the doomed Florence to her older sister, Ruth Jacobs, he couldn't see it.

This Clayton is smiling, and his joy in the moment is projected beyond the flat dimensions of the foxed old photograph. A brief golden joy that will soon become the lead of grief. Keller sees himself in the streaky mirror and thinks that he looks like Clayton. The Clayton he knew, not this younger, better version of the man. He slipped the purloined snapshot of Pax out of his pocket and set it beside the wedding photo of Clayton and Florence.

Lila is due at any minute. He sent her the address and decided to let her find her way to him via GPS. He's nervous and hates that he is. He can't figure out why he should be nervous, but then he thinks, What if she asks me a question I can't answer? Worse, what if she tells me something I don't want to know? His chest feels tight with anxiety and he presses at it with his fingertips. He's lived a full life since then, a good-enough life. Resurrecting those buried memories of the happiest he'd ever been before meeting Margie and having the kids serves nothing. Remembering old grief, when the more recent loss of his wife is still painful, is just a useless exercise.

Suddenly, she's there knocking on his door, and Keller welcomes Francesca and Rick's only child into his house.

CHAPTER SEVENTY-EIGHT

I couldn't bring myself to tell Keller Nicholson via e-mail that my mother had died. I know that sounds a bit odd; after all, she was in her eighties and had heart disease, and people in their generation can't possibly be surprised to hear of one another's passing, but it just didn't feel right to let him know that way. However, I was there on her behalf. She'd spoken of him so fondly over the years, as someone who had come into their lives when things were bad, when Dad was suffering from what we now know as PTSD. And, of course, no story of Keller could be told without stories of Pax. As a kid, I had the two of them inextricably linked in my mind, even though I knew that Keller had left them and that Pax remained with them for several more years.

"Pax our wonder dog." — that's what Mom called him. I swear that there were a thousand pictures of the dog — as many as of me as a three-year-old refugee from Korea. But none of this Keller Nicholson.

It wasn't until I was in grad school that I connected the Keller Nicholson of *Dogs of War* fame, the novel that was required reading in some high schools, and the Keller Nicholson of Pax and the time my parents lived in Quincy. They'd moved to Norwood the first year Dad joined WEEI's sportscasting team, having built a fully handicapped-accessible house on a fenced-in quarter-acre lot in the booming suburb. Dad had passed in 1985, but I'd only recently lost my mother.

"I brought this." We'd been talking, weeping a little, because I was riling up long-dormant feelings in him and more recent loss in me. I handed him a clasp envelope. "It was tucked in her dresser drawer with your name on it, so I know that she wanted you to have it."

Keller pressed his fingers against his chest, a soft gesture he'd been making all through our tomato soup and grilled cheese lunch. He didn't open the envelope right away, sort of just studied the handwriting on it, as if he couldn't read it clearly. When he finally did open it, the little brass clasp was so old that it broke as he bent it up, freeing the flap and revealing what my mother had left to him.

The leather of the dog collar was cracked with age and had been tightly coiled in that brown kraft envelope for so long that it looked like the inside of a nautilus shell. A dog tag dangled from the metal loop, a 1954 Norwood dog license, the same year they adopted me. On the broad surface of the leather collar itself was a brass nameplate with three letters stamped in bold Gothic type: PAX.

Keller made a soft sound, as if the air had been pushed out of him, but he was smiling. He held the dog collar in both hands like a holy relic, something sanctified. "Thank you for bringing this." And then he reached out and took my hand.

CHAPTER SEVENTY-NINE

Lila has gone, leaving the dog collar there on his table. Keller keeps looking at it, even as he tidies up the remnants of lunch. He washes two glasses and two plates, wipes the cast-iron frying pan out. Funny how this middle-aged Korean woman reminded him of Francesca. Nurture will win out, he supposes. The grace of brushing away a hair from her cheek, the way she cocked her head to listen to him, all gestures reminiscent of her mother, absorbed by observation instead of born into her. A little of Rick, too. The way she pursed her lips before she smiled.

Lila could have sent the collar through the mail, and she certainly deserved better than the company of a weepy old man and a lunch of grilled cheese, but he was deeply grateful that she had been there, that she understood how important this artifact from a lifetime ago was to him. Not simply Pax's collar but also a message from Francesca. She had remembered him.

Keller takes the dog collar with him into the parlor, sets it in front of the latest family portrait in residence on the end table beside his La-Z-Boy. There's a new Ken Burns documentary on tonight, but he doesn't turn it on. The last light of day has faded, leaving the room in shadow, but he doesn't move to turn on the light. From beyond the open window comes the soft lap of cove water against a low-tide beach. A little wind is frisking the fading leaves of late summer. The faint aroma of skunk wafts on it; the little skunk family beneath the scallop shed must have been startled by something. Even with that, it's really quite perfect here. Clayton's ghost was long ago exorcised by a living and garrulous family.

Another ghost has been laid to rest, thanks to Lila. A ghost Keller has been carrying around with him since the day he left the Stantons' house. Not so much a ghost as a grain of sand buried in the oyster of his heart. Francesca had forgiven him. The grain of sand has become a pearl.

Keller Nicholson picks up the dog collar and holds it to his breast. Pax. He was a good dog, the best. Pax had never been

without love, the love of his people.
One lucky dog.

EPILOGUE

The winter wind shakes the house, screaming over the water and through the wind-
break of juniper trees. Over the roar of the
day-old northeaster, Keller hears scratching
at the back door. It is a delicate sound, like
the very tips of a sapling's branches brushing against a screen. It deepens. No longer
random, the scratching at the door is delib-
erate and purposeful. Insistent. Demanding.
Keller pulls himself out of his chair, finds
his slippers with his toes. The house is dark.
Either he's forgotten to turn on the lights
or the electricity is out. But Keller isn't
hampered by the darkness; indeed, he sees
his way clearly as he walks toward the
sound.

Keller opens the back door. Now there is
no wind, no cold air, no sleet, no sound at
all. Pax is there, his tail wagging like mad,
like it always does when Keller has been
absent for a while.

"Well, there, Pax. Where've you been?" Keller kneels and wraps his arms around the dog, who raises his muzzle so that he can lick Keller's face. "I've missed you."

Pax shakes himself free and sits in front of Keller. He's wearing his flat leather on-duty collar and his long canvas military lead is attached to it. He faces the empty distance beyond the open door, then swings his big head back to Keller, his eyes bright with expectation, his mouth open in a doggy grin. He barks once.

"Time to go?" Keller takes up the leash.

The dog stands and shakes himself again. Ready.

"Okay, Pax. Let's go."

ACKNOWLEDGMENTS

This book would not be the book it has become without Andrea Cirillo and Annelise Robey, who have been my stalwart girl guides throughout the process. Their combined expertise and enthusiasm has been unflagging, and for that I am truly grateful. To the rest of the family at JRA: Peggy Gordijn, Don Cleary, Christina Prestia, Julianne Tinari, Michael Conroy, Danielle Sickles, and, of course, Jane Rotrosen Berkey, thank you for all you do.

Thanks, as always, to the team at St. Martin's Press, especially Jeanne-Marie Hudson and Joan Higgins, who understand the vast and changing world of publicity and social media, and cover artist Ervin Serrano, who has illustrated my imagination so beautifully. Thanks, too, to Caitlin Dareff, Sara Goodman, Chris Holder, John Murphy, Kerry Nordling, Sally Richardson, Matthew Shear, Anne Marie Tallberg, and a special shout-out to Carol Edwards, my brilliant copy editor. Thanks, too, to the folks at Macmillan Audio: Brant Janeway, Samantha Beerman, Mary Beth Roche, and Robert Allen.

A special note of deepest gratitude to Jennifer Enderlin, my editor extraordinaire, who knew that this book could be so much better and worked really hard with me to make that happen. Thank you for never giving up on me or on this book.

Of course, none of this would be as much fun without the love and support of my husband, kids, extended family, and friends. Thank you all.

SOURCES

Books

Downey, Fairfax, *Dogs for Defense: American Dogs in the Second World War, 1941–45;* by Direction and Authorization of the Trustees Dogs for Defense, Inc. (New York: Daniel P. McDonald, 1955).

Erlanger, Arlene, *TM 10–396* — War Dogs (Washington, D.C.: GPO, 1943).

Rosenkrans, Robert, *U.S. Military War Dogs in World War II* (Atglen, PA: Schiffer, 2011).

Web Sites

www.thedailyjournal.com. "World War II History: Dogs for Defense."

www.militaryworkingdog.com. (The Military Working Dog" (Military Working Dog Foundation).

www.qmfound.com. "Quartermaster War

Dog Program" (U.S. Army Quartermaster Foundation).

Video

Return to Norumbega: A History of Norumbega Park and the Totem Pole Ballroom. Bob Pollock. Produced by Joe Hunter. 2005. Remember Productions.

Suggested Reading

Luis Carlos Montalván, *Until Tuesday* (New York: Hyperion, 2011).